RETURN OF CHRIST

By
Jack Snyder
Pamela Cosel
Syed Nadim Rizvi

Return of Christ: The Second Coming
By Jack Snyder with Syed Nadim Rizvi and Pamela Cosel

Citrine Trading, Inc.
9810 FM 1960 West #295
Humble, TX 77338

Published by:
Elite Online Publishing
63 East 11400 South Suite #230
Sandy, UT 84070
www.EliteOnlinePublishing.com

Cover design by Pamela Cosel & Cristian Rodriguez

Research by Saadia Nadim

Printed in the United States of America

ISBN: 978-1093657227

DEDICATION

For my wife Carol and my mom.

CONTENTS

CHAPTER ONE – A HISTORIC DAY

RACHEL WILLIAMS AGGRESSIVELY PUSHED HER way through the crowd of people from around the region who gathered on the roof of Herod's Palace in Jerusalem. The air was sticky with unusually high summer humidity, though just as likely from the many bodies jammed shoulder to shoulder, some wearing traditional Middle Eastern clothing, others in suit coats. She had a job to do and intended on doing it no matter who she annoyed, be it man or woman. She usually tried to avoid flat-out rudeness but sometimes it couldn't be helped. At least that's what she told herself. All the other news correspondents were there for the same reason, and there was plenty of pushing and shoving as each jockeyed for position. The noise was an intense garble of languages.

News World was one of the top cable news networks in the United States and Rachel their go-to foreign correspondent. She had graduated top of her class from journalism school; that's why they hired her – partially, anyway. Her long slender legs and beautiful, flowing silky blonde hair had certainly caught the attention of the network's management team, she knew. Good looks were a necessary but unwritten requirement for on-air news personalities in the competitive media industry. Tough luck for the not-so-attractive print people who wanted to make the jump to television.

We all work with the tools we're given. Right?

Rachel made it to the front of the group where a raised wooden platform was assembled. Not a person stood on it. It held only a table with a microphone and two chairs side by side, with a second row of chairs behind them. Beyond the staging, the historical eye-candy in view was something most news people only dream about. The Jerusalem landscape spread as far as one could see. At dead-center was the Dome of the Rock. Sunlight that glistened off the massive golden dome was so dazzling and surreal it almost looked like a painting.

It was close to showtime and excitement filled the air as murmuring from the reporters, camera staff and observers grew louder. Grinning ear-to-ear, Rachel glanced back to the row of video cameras placed beyond the huge group of reporters. Each camera was mounted on a tripod of varying heights. Camera operators stood either behind or peered through the eyepiece of their camera, each displaying individualized news stations' logos. Shoulder to shoulder, the taller ones seemed to have the advantage; space was a premium for them too.

Rachel waved to Rick, her camera man from the New York office. "Everything okay?" she mouthed to him. He flashed Rachel a toothy smile and a thumbs-up sign, nodding. Rachel responded the same as he, satisfied that they were both ready.

Rick was tall and lanky, and among those with cameras mounted a bit higher than the others. She was pleased with his perpetually optimistic outlook. Something she wished she'd shared in. Most journalists were cynical, and she was no different. It was a good trait for sniffing out a story. But it certainly affected other aspects of one's life.

Rachel sighed with deep satisfaction. She wasn't cynical today, not at all. She could hardly believe she was at this historic site on such a wonderful assignment. At ground zero of what would undoubtedly be one of the most historic events of the 21st century. She was in Israel, on the rooftop of Herod's Palace. A place with a lengthy and storied history, dating back to just before Jesus's time and well beyond. Today it was a museum and tourist attraction. Funny how a place of so much turmoil and bloodshed could become a destination location where families from around the world traveled to take photos and purchase logoed t-shirts and hats. The thought brought an ironic smile to her lips. *Humanity was certainly a strange species.*

Then the moment everyone was waiting for arrived. The doors leading to the roof swung open and Israeli soldiers filed in armed with machine guns. No one was alarmed; this was to be expected. They flanked the roof and kept a constant watch on the crowd. They were followed by United States Secret Service Agents, and then more security personnel from other countries joined them. All were there to protect the final group that next emerged through the doors.

The world leaders. So close, Rachel thought.

More than a dozen men and women, dressed professionally, in outfits that cost thousands were the focus of everyone's attention. Unlike the security people, they strolled with a more casual gait, chatting amongst themselves. Video cameras swiveled on tripods to record the leaders, as hundreds of digital flashes burst brightly from the news crews' section.

"Mr. President, over here!" "Mr. Wright, please look this way!" "Sir, can I get a smile?" All of the reporters vied for the leader's attention like dolphins jumping up to catch a bite of fish.

Rachel focused her attention on three of the men. *POTUS looks pretty good – seems to have a fresh haircut*, she thought to herself. *First time I've seen the other two up this close.* She checked her microphone to be sure it was turned on. "Rick, can you hear me?"

He assured her he could.

Greg Wright, President of the United States, stood tall, thin and proud. As he should be. He did, after all, facilitate this meeting. The other two men were Rubin Gellman, the Israeli Prime Minister, and Ahmed Rahal, President of the Palestinian Authority. Each looked sharp in their tailored suits, with Rahal wearing the traditional head scarf – the Keffiyeh – worn by many Muslim men.

Gellman and Rahal were the reasons this meeting was taking place. The two were about to change the world for the better. They took their seats at the table while the rest of the global leaders sat in the row at the back of the stage.

President Wright was the exception. He stood behind the Prime Minister and Palestinian Leader, clutching a thick, leather-bound document. He reached between them and meticulously placed it on the table, sure that it was equidistant from each man. *Can't play favorites, no sir*, he thought. He flashed his best presidential smile at the reporters, turning to the left and right, patiently waiting for the hundreds of cameras to capture the moment for posterity. Soon, the photo op died down and Wright changed focus. With one smooth, well-rehearsed movement, the POTUS produced two pens from inside his suit jacket and placed them atop the document.

Prime Minister Gellman and Palestinian President Rahal flashed inscrutable smiles and nodded at each other, then signed the documents, Gellman going first at Rahal's insistent but pleasant hand-motion.

"I will be happy to sign first," the jovial Gellman said, picking up his pen. He waved it above his head as the crowd cheered before he put it to the paper. "Thank you for the honor, President Rahal." His signature was a flourish, and Rahal mimicked Gellman's style. They tipped their heads in a quick bow to each other.

Just like that, it was over.

President Wright clapped, prompting the world leaders, seated behind him, to stand and join in. All of the ceremony recorded in digital still photography and videography.

The reporters joined in with enthusiasm, their claps blending with everyone else's, Rachel included. She couldn't help herself. Normally, those who record history are not supposed to partake in it. Rather, they are to be dispassionate observers making a record. There to ask the tough questions if need be to bring more of the story to the surface. But she was sucked into the moment like everyone present. And possibly as those who watched from every corner of the globe. Satellite links connected worldwide networks everywhere to this point in time.

"Rick, did you get all that on tape?" Rachel didn't doubt his abilities, though was compelled to ask. She cupped her hand to her earpiece.

"Is the Pope Catholic?" he laughed. "You know you can count on me. The lens was zoomed in, right on their signatures." He waved at her from where he stood.

"Now that raises another question...I wonder if indeed the Pope was watching?" She laughed and signaled for Rick to move to where she stood. He shook his head no, not ready to shut down the camera.

What a wonderful day. History in the making indeed. No one knew that history would be made twice, however, and the second time would be nothing to cheer about.

Nearly six thousand miles away, in New York City, Daniel Murray impatiently sat behind his news anchor desk waiting to go on the air. He was the star anchor of News World; something most people knew, and he happily reminded those who didn't.

On a large monitor near his desk, the world watched the booming applause of the reporters and world leaders atop Herod's Palace in Jerusalem. Daniel wasn't the center of attention at the moment, and it irked him. But he knew he just needed a few more seconds of patience. Once the applause quieted it would be all about him. He wanted everything to be about him.

"Mr. Murray?" It was the director speaking to him from his earpiece. The control room was just beyond the hot lights; he couldn't see it due to the brightness.

"Yeah," Murray said.

"You'll be on in a second."

Murray smiled and nodded. *Of course, I'll be on in a second, you idiot. I know that.*

"Three... two... one... you're on!"

A smile broadened across Daniel's chiseled face, his white and perfect teeth catching the studio lights as he stared right into the main camera.

"The Jerusalem Peace Accord has just been signed between Israeli Prime Minister, Rubin Gellman, and President of the Palestinian Authority, Ahmed Rahal," Murray said. "It's been a long road for President Wright, who brought the two sides to the table. The signing of the Accord also brings Palestine into the United Nations. This is truly a historic moment being viewed by millions around the world. We now return to the rooftop of Herod's Palace in Jerusalem, where our correspondent, Rachel Williams, is."

The red light on the camera faded along with Daniel's smile. "Rachel?"

"Yes, Dan?" Though she was thousands of miles away and her voice was small in her earpiece, he could hear the frustration in her tone. He didn't care. *When you're the boss you don't need to concern yourself with such things*, he thought to himself. And it was, more or less, a private conversation. Just him, her, and everyone in the control room with a headset.

"You be sure to get a question in. I don't care how you do it."

"Of course. Now let me do my job." Murray heard her agitation, though it was contained.

A wolfish smile filled his features. *It's good to be king.*

It was chaos on the roof of Herod's Palace amidst the waving hands and shouted questions. All vied for the attention of the assistant with the wireless microphone who mounted the stage a moment ago. *Like a bunch of children trying to get the teacher's attention*, Rachel thought. But she had another way. And today was her lucky day because the assistant was male and about her age. She raised her hand just as the assistant's gaze crossed her path. A quick arm movement and she got his attention. His eyes caught sight of her as she'd hoped. She tossed her blond hair and smiled. Her piercing blue eyes glistened. That's all it took. He was hers. All she wanted was the microphone. He strode over to the edge of the platform and handed it to her. The noise from the crowd of reporters died down in disappointment.

She raised the microphone to her lips and spoke with confidence, tossing her hair over her shoulder for effect. "What makes this peace accord more substantive than previous ones, which have all failed?"

Her voice boomed for all to hear, sounding from the speakers placed at each corner of the roof. The camera microphones carried her voice to the news production trucks which lined the street below. From there, the audio signal went to the orbiting satellites where they dispersed to millions of viewers worldwide. Earth truly was a global village these days – exactly what Rachel loved about technology.

Prime Minister Gellman looked like he wanted to field the question, and the Palestinian President nodded his approval. He went into his most polished politician mode.

"In the past, we negotiated around our differences. These peace talks began with us focusing on our similarities. Both of our respective peoples have shared this land for generations, and we will share this land for generations to come. It is in everyone's best interests that we dissolve our differences and live in harmony. We are ushering in an era of peace the Middle-East has, arguably, never seen before." Gellman's stance was regal, his voice, calm and steady.

The assistant stepped forward to take the microphone as hands beckoned toward it like a pack of dogs jumping for a piece of meat. But Rachel's grip was tight and she drew it closer. She wasn't finished. "Politics aside, Prime Minister, the conflicts that arise are fueled by the differing religious faiths. How can that ever be resolved?"

As Gellman gathered his thoughts, Daniel Murray, in New York, spoke into her ear. "Very good, Rachel, put him on the spot."

She tried to fight her grin. For sure, Murray was happy, because it was his show, and his ratings, but she also knew it was a question he would've loved to have asked. Score one for her. One of these days the station will reward her with her own show, she thought. That was her hope anyway.

Before Gellman could speak, Ahmed motioned that he'd like to take the question. The Prime Minister nodded, and Rachel saw he was clearly relieved to be let off the hook.

Ahmed subtly adjusted his head scarf and looked Rachel directly in the eyes. His piercing gaze unnerved her. The Palestinian President was known for his quiet demeanor overlaying his intense convictions.

"We all share a common ground being that our various beliefs are all Abrahamic faiths. With that as a starting point – and if we remain diligent – we can work through our differences."

Rachel spoke quickly as the assistant stepped in, "With all due respect, sir, the tensions between Israel and Syria continue to escalate. If they aren't resolved it could—"

Gellman firmly raised his hand for her to stop. Moot effort, however; the assistant pulled the microphone from her.

"One step at a time, Ms. Williams. Now, others have questions." The PM moved closer to other reporters and chose a man from another cable news network.

Shouts for the microphone were cacophonous. Rachel was done, but she didn't care. She was the first to go, and – statistically speaking – television viewership drops off after the first question. Let the others fight it out for second place. And third. And fourth. And so on. She was on cloud nine. Not just because she was first. No. It was much more than that.

Gellman knew my name! The Prime Minister of Israel knew my name! I should be able to leverage that into a raise at the very least! What an historic day. And I'm a part of it. She smiled wolfishly.

The day wasn't finished with making modern history yet, and unbeknownst to her, Rachel would soon be in the middle of more breaking news.

A keen observer standing on the roof of Herod's Palace would easily spot the two grey domes atop the Church of the Holy Sepulchre, if they knew where to look in the ocean of structures made of Jerusalem stone that filled the landscape. The distance between the palace and the church was only a kilometer or so away.

The church was built over two sites; Calvary, where Jesus was crucified, and the tomb of Jesus – two of the most holy sites for Christians. Its location made the church itself one of the most holy places on Earth for Christians. Constructed in the 4th century, it still proudly stood in the 21st century even after a history of fires, earthquakes, and invasions.

Today, the church serves as the headquarters of many Christian denominations. It's also a tourist draw.

A man wearing sunglasses, with hair held back in a ponytail beneath a black hat, wore the traditional white collar of a Catholic priest, as did the eleven whom he led through the stone courtyard. They were headed toward the entrance of the massive church not far away. Dressed in full Catholic priest garb, the long flowing cassocks and clerical collars made them indistinguishable from each other. All appeared young, in their thirties. And collectively, they were on a mission.

The leader, called David by the men who followed him – though they doubted it was his real name – was excited about what lay ahead. They had all trained for months, running drills through different scenarios, planning for any complications that might arise. They were ready to leave a mark on history.

Directly ahead was a stunningly attractive woman – a tour guide – who led a group of tourists. As with so many groups before, they were people excited to be on vacation.

"The Church of the Holy Sepulchre has long been a major pilgrimage center for Christians from around the world," she said in English, with a small trace of an Italian accent.

David thought her sultry voice and accent were sexy. *I hope she survives. If she does, maybe we could...*

He pushed the thought from his mind. He left the chance for a life like that – something normal – behind him a long time ago. No turning back now. He, and the men marching behind him, had a job to do, and they were determined to complete it.

He led his men into the church. Though it was well lit it still took a moment for his eyes to adjust from the brightness of the clear blue sky outside. David's breath caught in his throat. The stone and marble structure were beyond words. Its high, domed ceiling with pillars and archways were stunningly beautiful. He shook his head as he readied for the task ahead. What a shame, he thought. *Oh, well. Time to get to work.*

Knowing exactly where he needed to go, he led his men past various groups of tourists and worshippers in the Nave, bowed in prayer, and down a dark corridor away from the main area. A few staff members curiously glanced at them, but none questioned where they were going. They were a group of Catholic priests after all – or so they appeared.

Much closer to Herod's Palace was the Dome of the Rock, built on the Temple Mount. It was one of the holiest sites on Earth for Muslims and forbidden for non-Muslims to enter though there were other areas on the Temple Mount open to all visitors. Israeli soldiers patrolled the grounds and kept careful watch on the parade of people who walked about, taking pictures, enjoying the day.

A group of Muslim women, covered from head to foot in niqabs, quietly strolled the grounds, taking in the sights. Only their eyes were visible, but even then, they were hidden in the shadows of their clothing.

As the women neared the Dome of the Rock, they turned as if one and casually strolled toward the entrance. The soldier guarding the entrance let them pass without giving them a second glance. They were Muslims after all. He knew most Muslim women in Israel did not wear the niqab, but he shrugged it off. In the following minutes he would regret that decision.

Inside the massive and colorful dome, the niqab-wearing women silently strode past many Muslims, men, women, and children, who knelt in silent prayer. The group walked with purpose toward a side corridor, disappearing without so much as glancing at their fellow Muslims in prayer.

Not too far from the Dome of the Rock stood the Wailing Wall. Also called the Western Wall or Kotel, and known in Islam as the Buraq Wall, it was an ancient Jerusalem stone structure in the Old City of Jerusalem. This was yet another of the most holy sites on Earth. A place where many events of the Old Testament took place.

Today, it was the destination for many Jews to come and pray and place slips of paper containing written prayers into the crevices of the wall. Official records claim the wall collects more than a million notes a year.

Today that practice would end forever.

A dozen Orthodox Jewish men traditionally dressed in black suits, white shirts and ties, black overcoats and hats approached the wall. All of them were in their thirties and sported well-groomed beards. They walked through the crowd, past Israeli soldiers, and lined up alongside the wall, standing nearly shoulder and shoulder, and silently prayed. Or so it would appear to a casual observer.

Inside one of the dark, stone corridors of the Church of the Holy Sepulchre, David, the lead priest, threw off his black robe, leaving his clerical collar attached. Dressed as a tourist, beneath his clothing a pistol with a silencer on it was clipped to his waist. The other priests followed his lead and discarded their robes, revealing similar clothes and weapons. Some had packs of C4 explosives strapped to them. Others had blasting caps, wires, and detonators. They were not here to do God's work.

David affixed a headset to his head and spoke into it. "We're in position."

His men expertly leaped into action, wiring up several pillars with the explosives.

Inside a dead-end corridor of the Dome of The Rock, the Muslim women pulled off their niqabs, revealing they were instead Caucasian men, armed for deadly action. In total, they carried enough C4 to level the building. One of the men, wearing a headset, nodded to the others and they went to work setting the deadly plastic explosives.

"Placing ours now," the man said into his mouthpiece.

"Acknowledged. Doing the same," one of the Orthodox Jews said into the hidden microphone he wore. The other men in the prayer line discreetly slid thin sheets of plastic explosives into crevices of the Wailing Wall. Wires ran between them, like a strand of Christmas lights, daisy-chaining the explosives together. The rigging was done in plain sight, but expertly shielded by the men's bodies as they pretended to pray.

***

"Take the Dome of the Rock," Palestinian President Ahmed Rahal said as he waved his arm to indicate the golden dome a couple of blocks behind him. "Built on ground sacred to all of us in this region. It has stood for thirteen hundred years." He gave a warm smile and nodded to Prime Minister Gellman. "That is why the Prime Minister and I have chosen this location for the signing of the Peace Accord. We want the dome to represent the symbol of solidarity between our faiths. We want this peace to stand as solid as the 'rock' behind us."

The reporters lost their professional detachment and applauded and cheered. Rachel was the exception; the skepticism on her face was as obvious as a mask.

"Oh brother, it's getting pretty thick there," Daniel Murray said into her earpiece. She couldn't help but smile. Bubbles of gentle laughter overrode Murray's voice in her ear. It was Rick, her camera man, from the back of the roof. It was hard to tell if he agreed with Daniel or was just joining in for the camaraderie.

Another voice chimed in, this one stern and professional. It was the director. "Stay focused, people. Rick, give me a tighter shot of the dome."

"Yes, sir," Rick snapped back. He turned the camera lens in the direction of the dome.

Rachel was now just a passive observer. She'd gotten her questions in, so now she waited until the Q&A was over. She'd soon go live on-camera for some back-and-forth patter with Murray. But at the rate things were going, what with the PM and PLO leader happily answering questions, that could be a while.

As Rachel rolled all of this around in her mind, she ignored the technical chatter that babbled on over her earpiece. She was so used to hearing such things it oftentimes fell beneath her notice. This time was no different. She, nor Rick, nor even Daniel, had any idea how significant it would turn out to be.

"I'm picking up interference in our audio signal." It was one of the station technicians back in New York. Undoubtedly in the control room. Rachel thought she recognized the voice but wasn't sure.

"Inform the on-site broadcast engineer." It was the news director again.

"Abe?" asked the tech.

Rachel didn't follow the conversation after that. She turned her full attention back to the Palestinian President as he continued to speak.

Down on the street in front of Herod's Palace was a row of television production trucks. They were massive eighteen-wheelers, parked nearly bumper to bumper, taking up two full blocks of the street, a row of orange cones forcing traffic to give them a wide berth, much to the chagrin of the drivers.

One such truck had NEWS WORLD proudly and stylishly splayed on the side of it. Inside were cramped quarters packed with production crew and equipment. Dark, like a submarine, most of the lighting came from the equipment lamps and meters. Working in one was certainly not a job for someone suffering claustrophobia, at least not for long periods of time. Abiyda – Abe for short – small, trim, and olive-skinned, looked completely at home in this world. With an oversized headset propped on his head, he hunched at an equipment panel and studied the moving lines on a wave-form monitor.

"I see it," he said. "Strong signal. Don't know its origin, but I'll check it out."

The technician spoke into his headpiece, in stereo. "You're our resident genius. If anyone can figure this out, it's you!"

"Flattery will get you everywhere," Abe chuckled back at him.

"I'm counting on it," the tech laughed.

"No worries, I'm on it," Abe said as he went to work.

"Non-Muslims had limited access to the dome, but as of today, it will be open to the public," Prime Minister Rubin Gellman said. "To people of every faith. Thus, begins a new era."

Another round of applause followed. Rachel grew tired of the endless and embarrassing adulation from her fellow professionals. It all sounded too good to be true. She was thinking ahead to her on-air time with Dan and was already rehearsing her responses to these impromptu speeches. It couldn't come soon enough, she thought.

David passively watched his men finish securing the bricks of C4 against the base of a support column in the church. An Israeli soldier strolled around the corner, his rubber soled shoes kept his movements silent.

David locked eyes with him and the two men stared frozen at each other for a moment before they leaped into action, going for their guns. The soldier swung his machine gun around, but David was faster and better trained. His pistol came up so swiftly it was just a blur.

Thwap – thwap! Two slugs fired from the silenced weapon, and the soldier went down. He moaned. Thwap. One more in the head stopped his anguished sound.

David's team watched the event without emotion, then returned to work with the casualness of people with desk jobs.

"We're about to set the timer in the church," David said into his headset.

"Same here in the dome," came the response through his earpiece.

"Ditto at the wall."

"Okay, let's do it." He quickly pulled off his headset and discarded it to the floor.

All the men slid their priest robes back on. One of them set the timer for sixty seconds, then they all hurried away, out of sight of everyone who prayed. There was no longer a reason to clean up after themselves. In less than a minute the blast would take care of the mess they had made.

At the Dome, the men who set the explosives were once again hidden beneath their niqabs as they hurried from the entrance. The Israeli soldier who had watched them enter earlier, furrowed his brow as they quickly hustled away. He thought their behavior odd but shrugged it off – a huge mistake. It would be one of the last thoughts he ever had.

One of the tourists at the Wailing Wall couldn't help himself from laughing out loud at the group of Orthodox Jewish men running from the wall as if in a marathon. He thought their swishing robes looked silly and motioned for his companions to view the sight.

An Israeli soldier who also watched the men didn't think it was silly, but instead was suspicious enough to step before them with his hand out like a traffic cop. He made sure they saw his other hand tightly clutching his machine gun.

"May I see some ID, gentlemen?"

They all silently exchanged careful glances.

"The interference has disappeared," Abe heard the technician say over his headphones. "Good job, man."

But Abe was confused. "I didn't do anything."

"Oh, you're being too modest," the tech laughed.

"No, really, it just cleared up on its own."

"But that's a good thing, right?"

"I suppose." But Abe was troubled.

As dozens of Christians prayed in the church, an Israeli guard strolled past a group of priests who rushed from the building as if extremely late for an appointment. He shook his head and continued down the hallway they came from as he made his rounds. He had no idea that this was the last walk he'd ever take. He gasped when he came upon his dead colleague lying on the cold marble floor. The corpse's head was turned to the side. His unmoving, open eyes stared blankly at the C4 bricks strapped to one of the pillars, directing the guard's gaze to the same spot. He saw the explosives, then focused on the timer where less than ten seconds flashed on the face of the device. The guard stared, unable to move, as the seconds ticked off.

"President Rahal and I felt the whole Middle-East was headed for a cliff," Prime Minister Gellman continued, as the journalists listened, along with millions of viewers worldwide. "We thought it would end in disaster if we didn't do something. A tremendous amount of blood has been shed over many years. Hatred has crept into the world's societies and there remains no more room for destruction. We must make sincere efforts toward peace and unity."

The soldier in the Church of the Holy Sepulchre sighed deeply, his head down, as the timer on the bomb hit zero. The last thing he saw in his world was a blinding flash.

The explosion was deafening. The shock wave radiated out from the church, violently shaking everything for blocks. Everyone on the roof of Herod's Palace had to steady themselves to keep from falling. Rick gripped the tripod to keep the camera from tumbling over.

"What the – ?!?" It was Daniel Murray shouting in Rachel' and Rick's ears. Not intentionally. It was a normal – but uncharacteristic for Murray – shocked human reaction to what he had just witnessed on the in-studio monitors in New York.

The Israeli soldier who detained the Orthodox Jews was distracted by the church erupting into a ball of fire in the distance. He stared slack-jawed in shock. A Jewish man who stood before him casually removed a pistol with a silencer affixed to it. He shot a bullet into the center of the soldier's forehead, and the young man collapsed in a heap, stone-cold dead. None of the tourists who stood nearby took notice. They were horrified by the sight of the ball of flame and black smoke rising in the distance.

The Orthodox Jews continued in a flat-out run, knowing they were at ground zero of a scene that momentarily would be a repeat of what just happened at the church. The destruction wasn't over yet.

Everyone on the roof of Herod's Palace had a front-row seat when the Dome of the Rock exploded. Cracks ripped through the golden dome of the ancient structure. It was unbelievable and almost didn't look real to those who witnessed the destruction. The building caved in on itself. In seconds all that remained of it was a thick cloud of smoke that clung to the area. The Dome, a feature on the Jerusalem landscape for more than a thousand years, was no more.

Rachel stood awestruck and immobile at the spot where the earlier interview had taken place. She hoped Rick was still connected to her earpiece and would hear her. "Rick, what happened?!" Did you get that on film? I don't know what to do!"

It took a few seconds for him to respond. "Yes...uh, yes...I think so. I don't know – a terrible explosion, so unexpected." His voice shook though he tried to remain the calm observer.

Rachel wondered how many people had died inside the structure, never having the chance to flee. She shook with fear, unsure of whether to run or stay where she was.

And then in front of her, another explosion rocked Herod's Palace. It was at the Wailing Wall but no one on the roof knew that. To them, it was another violent blast of fire and smoke from the cityscape. Rachel's instinct told her to get out of there, off the roof, and try to get away from the epicenter. She ran toward the elevator, knowing Rick would also run for cover, but she stopped at its door, knowing the electricity likely had been knocked out.

The scene on the roof erupted into chaos. The crowd that had earlier gathered for the historic signing screamed in panic, crying to God for help, not knowing if they would all be killed. Panic gripped everyone as news teams and world leaders bolted for the exits. Security personnel attempted to maintain control, but it was an impossible task. The crowd was reduced to a mob of frightened human beings, running for their own safety, scurrying, sobbing, acting on pure instinct and pumping adrenaline.

Rachel and Rick spotted each other in the crowd just as an aftershock shook the building. Rachel heard a piercing shriek so close it rang her ears. It took her a moment to realize the sound was coming from her own throat.

CHAPTER TWO – AFTER THE BOMBINGS

RACHEL HUNG ONTO RICK'S ARM as they both gripped the roof's railing and watched the chaos down on the street below. He had just packed up his gear when the latest explosion rang out, and he ran over to where Rachel was.

"Hey, I should set up my camera," he said, unzipping the case and popping it onto the top of the tripod.

"Yes, of course, sure – we need to get this..." Rachel said, her reporter's mind kicking in, though her hands and neck were drenched in sweat from fear. She smoothed her hair but realized her appearance didn't really matter at a time like this.

Others crowded along the railing next to her and stared down at the nightmare. Most were fellow journalists, but plenty of camera operators muscled their way up to the railing, toting their cameras on tripods as Rick did. He looked over at Rachel and gave her a thumbs up. But his goofy grin was gone, replaced by a sternness so unlike Rick that it took Rachel a moment to recognize him. She nodded at him, acknowledging that he had a job to do, knowing he should proceed.

Rachel returned her attention to the terrorist attack, assuming it was one. She didn't really know; she was still trying to process what had just happened. Her mind grew jumbled with the thought and she felt as if she might plummet over the edge of the railing. The people below on the sidewalks and streets ran every which way, wanting to get as far from the collapse of the dome as possible. Rachel witnessed others attempting to get close to the destroyed building. To see it up close, to gawk at it, the way drivers slow down on a highway to view an accident. Voyeurs of the macabre. The scene sickened Rachel. She wondered if she was one of those people, as her reporter mindset tried to be the observer and not the participant. She watched people running from the destruction covered in blood, thankful that they survived. Others limped, crying, holding onto other survivors. It was a scene from a horror movie, or a nightmare.

Sirens echoed throughout the city followed by the arrival of the emergency vehicles. Police cars, ambulances, and fire trucks sped to the site nearest the blasts. The professionals went immediately to work. The police jumped into crowd-control mode, the paramedics tended to the injured, and hoses the firefighters held arched massive, powerful streams of water onto the burning building. All of what she watched below gave Rachel some comfort but didn't erase the terror.

A ringing sound accompanied by a vibration against her hip snapped her attention away from the scene before her. She fished her phone from her pocket and looked at the screen. She was getting a Facetime call from Daniel Murray. She slid her thumb across the screen and Murray's face appeared. She recognized the back of the studio behind him. He was sitting at his news anchor desk.

"Are you all right?" he asked. His voice was small and distant, hard to hear over the cacophony of voices on the roof. She increased the volume on her phone.

"As well as can be expected, Dan." She tried to keep her voice from shaking as much as her hands were.

"Are you safe?" His tone held genuine concern.

She smiled to herself and nodded. Rachel knew Dan could be very sweet when the situation called for it, though oftentimes he was simply a jerk. It seemed those were the only two modes he had.

"Yes, but I'm still shaking. I was practically looking right at the dome when it exploded."

"I know. Rick's camera was pointed that way and we all saw it too," Murray said. "It's coming through on the studio monitors, which means Rick's still recording the aftermath. Good. Make sure he keeps it up."

That's a jerky thing to say, she thought. *People lost their lives. In a horrible way. But ratings are king, right?* But what she said was, "Will do."

Rachel heard the director's voice through her earpiece. "Thirty seconds, Dan." He had to be ready to go live again, with the commercial break coming to an end.

"Got it," he replied, then returned his attention to Rachel. "We heard that besides the Dome of the Rock, that the Wailing Wall and the Church of The Holy Sepulchre were also hit."

"There were definitely other explosions," she said as she absently glanced over the landscape in the direction of the church and the wall. "Considering their proximity to the dome, it makes sense those were the other two sites. Any word on who could be behind it?"

"Way too early to tell, but if I had to venture a guess, I'd say Syria."

"Ten seconds, Dan." It was the director again.

"Find out what you can," Dan quickly said to Rachel as he looked at the in-studio camera.

"Always."

Murray's image swished away as he lowered the phone, then ended the call.

Rick appeared, lugging the camera bag over one shoulder, clutching his collapsed tripod in the opposite hand. She threw him a look which he immediately understood as – *Aren't you supposed to still be filming?*

"They're throwing us off the roof," he said with a wave of his arm. "Well...not literally. But security said everyone needs to leave. It's for our own safety."

Rachel looked around. Sure enough, the various security agencies were walking through the crowd of harried journalists and film crews, telling them they need to vacate the roof. She assumed they didn't announce it over the public address system so as not to start a panic. Or maybe they simply didn't have a working system, given the conditions.

"All right then. Let's go." Rachel took one last glance at the destruction from the high vantage point, then turned to follow the rest of those leaving the roof.

"Back to the hotel?" Rick asked.

"Of course not. We're still on the clock. Come on." Rachel hurried toward one of the elevators with Rick lumbering behind her. They joined the crowd that had formed at the elevator and was surprised to learn that it was working.

Rachel had a fleeting memory of the 9/11 attacks in the U.S. Fear rose in her as she thought of the stories of the people who clambered to get on the elevators in the World Trade Center buildings on that terrible September day in 2001. And then how they suffered horrible and unimaginable deaths when the skyscrapers collapsed. *Is that what's going to happen to us as we wait atop Herod's Palace for the elevator?* She realized she was letting her imagination think crazy thoughts.

Funny how memories had an unexpected way of creeping into the forefront of one's mind, she thought. She was just a ten-year-old girl when 9/11 happened, so her memories weren't exactly her own. They were really just pieced together images of her mother and father reacting to the endlessly repeating footage shown on television screens of a passenger jet slamming into the south tower of the World Trade Center. Over and over and over again. All day. Day after day for a week. Though to her young mind it seemed like a year. She was traumatized vicariously through her parents, and their fears about how the world changed that day. Each year on the event's anniversary, the same scenes would replay on TV screens so that she had to relive the fiery and death-filled scenes, if her parents happened to be watching such shows. She couldn't know at that time her professional path would be to work in news media as someone covering news just as the TV reporters did for 9/11.

It didn't help matters that her parents went on continuously about 9/11 being a sign of the End Times. Though Rachel's mother wasn't particularly religious, her father delved deeply into Christianity, but he kept a lot of his thoughts to himself. Rachel would sometimes hear her parents discussing them, but they would change the subject if she entered the room. Nonetheless, they all attended church and instilled Rachel with the value of belief and prayer in one's daily life.

But those beliefs faltered after her father passed away suddenly when she was thirteen years old. In time, her mother stopped taking Rachel to church. Not long after that, Rachel quit believing in God altogether.

Years later she would realize that her parents' emotional reaction to 9/11 was something cultivated and nurtured through the media's presentation and milking of the events. Something the media did regularly with all crises, real or imagined, to maximize those valuable commercial dollars – something she learned as she began her own professional career.

Nine-eleven, and how it was presented by the media was one of the reasons Rachel went to journalism school. But not to become a part of that machine. She wanted to change it, improve it, return it to its roots of being a source of valuable information for people. Something that could bring comfort through knowledge, not fan the flame of hysteria as it oftentimes seemed to do these days. But there were some days she felt she'd lost her way. She frowned at the thought as the elevator doors opened, breaking her thoughts of the past. She redoubled her resolve to not let today be one of those days.

Journalists crowded in through the elevator's open doors, all hoping to fit inside. Rachel and Rick missed the first one, along with a dozen more reporters, left to impatiently wait for the second elevator to arrive.

"I can't wait to get off this roof," Rick said nervously. He placed the heavy camera bag and tripod down and rubbed his left shoulder where the bag's strap had dug in.

Rachel gave him a warm smile and lightly touched his shoulder. "Don't worry, Rick, we'll be fine."

Rick looked her into the eyes and the calmness that he saw comforted him.

***

The crowd noises down on the street were deafening, far worse than what could be heard from the rooftop of the palace. Screams. Cries. Sirens. Rachel and Rick jogged down the sidewalk alongside the row of production trucks until they reached a traffic light with a crosswalk. Rick, loaded down with his equipment, was coated in sweat but didn't utter a single complaint. It was not his nature to; he always sucked it up and did what was expected from him for his job. In the past, whenever Rachel offered to help him, he politely refused. He felt she had her job to do and he had his. It was a matter of pride to him. In time, it became normal for him to be the workhorse and for her to be network royalty and not lift a finger for the production side of things.

But normalcy had flown out the window today. Possibly forever, replaced by God knows what.

"Here, give me that," she said as she grabbed the tripod. But he held it tightly, not giving it up. *He can be stubborn!*

They stood at the intersection in a tug-of-war over the tripod as the sirens of more arriving emergency vehicles whooped all around them. Onlookers would have laughed at the sight on any other day. But today it fell beneath their notice.

"No, really! Right now you look like you're about to collapse from exhaustion and I need you to function!" Rachel was insistent and didn't let go of the apparatus.

He laughed and finally relinquished the tripod to her. "Whatever you say, boss. Thanks. I appreciate it." He adjusted the rest of the load that he carried.

They smiled at each other, seeing how tired the other was. The momentary levity was good for them. Just for a second, it turned their attention from the horror of the carnage surrounding them. Now they could regroup and focus.

The traffic light turned red and the "Walk" sign came on for them. The pair flowed with the pace of the crowd crossing the street. Rachel was frustrated that they couldn't move any faster, but checked her impatience knowing everybody wanted to get home and away from the day's events. Once they were on the opposite sidewalk, Rachel and Rick hustled toward the rising cloud of black smoke that hovered above what was once the Dome of the Rock. The cloud was so big and billowy it didn't look real, but instead like a CGI image created back in the studio. If Rachel didn't know it was only a half block away, she'd certain she would have lost a contest where she'd had to guess its distance.

They were almost upon the area which the police and military had cordoned off with yellow tape when a long, sleek limousine passed them, escorted by four Israeli military jeeps, two up front, two behind.

The armed soldiers guarding the perimeter opened an area of the tape for the limo and jeeps to pass through. The limo and its entourage came to a stop about a hundred feet past the tape. Doors on the limo swung open and men in dark suits and sunglasses emerged and stoically scanned the area without expression.

Probably the Prime Minister's personal security, Rachel thought.

Prime Minister Gellman and Palestinian President Rahal stepped out of the limo, followed by their aides. They slowly trudged toward the scene of the disaster. Their clothing sagged and Rachel noticed they had both removed their ties and appeared older than they had this morning.

Gawkers clustered as close to the cordoned-off area as possible to watch the leaders. Rachel pushed her way to the front of the crowd just as she'd done on the top of Herod's Palace. Rick followed closely behind, staying in the wake she created as she maneuvered through the mass of people. People with arms outstretched holding camera phones aimed at the remains of the dome snapped pictures and recorded video as bodies pressed against the tape. Flustered soldiers and police shouted threats of arrest at the people, attempting to get them to stand back.

As Rachel looked for a way to get closer, a fight broke out between two groups of men hurling racial epithets at each other. Police descended on them to break it up. Everyone's attention was drawn to the loud commotion.

"This is our chance, c'mon!" Rachel said as she quickly ducked under the tape.

"Are you sure?" Rick stood wide-eyed and motionless. He kept watch on the police only for a moment.

"Yes, yes, hurry!" She raised the tape and helped him under it as he clutched his camera bag close to his body.

They jogged toward the PM and PLO leader. Rachel led the way while Rick skittered along behind her as if a huge, loyal pet. He expertly pulled the camera from the bag as he ran, like a martial artist executing a graceful, fluid move.

Once Rick got the camera set on his shoulder, Rachel leaped into journalist mode.

"Prime Minister! Mr. President! Could you tell us who you think was behind these attacks? And what will this do to the Peace Accord?" She ran after them, breathless.

An aide intervened. "The Prime Minister has no comment." The man grabbed Rick's camera by the lens, covering it completely with the palm of his hand. Rick quickly backed so as to avoid any damage to his gear.

Police officers were on Rick and Rachel in a flash and grabbed them by the arms.

"You both are under arrest for trespassing!" one of the officers shouted at them.

Rachel took it in stride, but Rick looked like he was about to pass out.

"This is not necessary, you can release them." It was Prime Minister Gellman. He spoke with the soft assurance of a person completely in charge. "I will vouch for them."

Rachel nodded to him, nearly bowing. "Thank you, sir."

He smiled warmly. "You and your camera man need to step back behind the line, please."

The police took that as their cue. They motioned to a couple of other uniformed men who were neither Israeli police or military. The men stepped up to lead Rachel and Rick away. As the PM turned toward the remains of the dome, Rachel caught a glimpse of sadness in his eyes that tugged at her heart.

It might not be the end of the world, but it could be the end of his world, she thought. The end of everything he's worked for. Rachel felt sympathy for him, along with pangs of guilt for the hardball questions she pummeled him with earlier.

As she and Rick were led away from the area, Rachel noticed the patch on the shoulder of the uniformed man that was escorting her. It read Sharp Eye Global Security with an insignia of the Earth with an eye – that looked somewhat like a camera lens – superimposed over it. *A private security firm?* she thought. She hadn't seen it before and shrugged it off. The U.S. military used subcontractors all the time. Even got in hot water for it on more than one occasion. So maybe most governments did the same thing. Still, something to maybe look into. She filed it in her reporter's brain, knowing when she had the time, she would research the firm.

***

"Syria denies responsibility and condemns these attacks," Daniel Murray said in his seasoned broadcaster's voice as he seemed to look out from television sets all over the U.S. and into the living rooms of millions of viewers. Or so Abe thought and hoped. More viewers for News World meant job security for Abe.

Abe was watching him from the cramped quarters of the News World production truck parked in front of Herod's Palace. All the news organization trucks were still parked dangerously close to the destruction of the Dome of the Rock and the Wailing Wall. Something that all the production personnel who worked in the trucks, Abe included, tried to put out of their minds. When the day had begun, the parking area had been conveniently close to get the best information, video, and be fully accessible to their individual reporters. None could possibly have known how the day would end.

Behind him stood Rachel and Rick. As cramped, dark, and uncomfortable as the truck was, it was almost completely soundproof. It provided great respite from the deafening ocean of sound that was sweeping through Jerusalem at the moment.

Rachel grew impatient. Though she took pride in seeing the celebrity anchor of the station that employed her – as annoying as he sometimes was – she was an investigative reporter and wanted to get on with an investigation into those responsible for turning the world upside down in the last few hours. She thought for a minute about what approach to take.

"What can you tell me about the audio signal you picked up earlier?" she asked Abe.

Abe muted Murray then turned his attention to another screen, one filled with lines of computer code. He shuttled back via the software to an earlier time-code and explained the technicalities to Rachel and Rick as he viewed it.

"The signal continued until just before the first explosion, here." He pointed to a line of code as though they could understand it. Rachel couldn't; it was not her area of expertise. Maybe Rick did. He and Abe were both tech nerds and proud of it.

"*Before* the explosion?" Rachel wasn't sure she heard Abe correctly.

Abe twisted in his chair to glance back at her. The chair could rotate but in these cramped quarters – forget about it.

"Yeah. Just a few seconds before."

"If it had happened after the explosion, then it could have just been audio equipment in the area that the bombs destroyed," Rick added. "But losing the signal before sounds like someone shut the radios off."

"Exactly," Abe said as he pointed to Rick, nodding.

Rachel absently glanced over at the monitor with Daniel Murray on it, yammering silently. "Was it communication between the people who did this?" Rachel was overly direct with her question; she asked it as a journalist might, not as a co-worker or friend.

"Possibly. Better equipment, such as that used by law enforcement or Secret Service, would be able to dice it down," Abe explained.

Rachel gingerly leaned against a bank of equipment. It was nearly impossible to get comfortable in this place and it agitated her.

"Remember those emails I got some time back from that guy who went by the initials – CT?" She pulled her hair back, swiping stray hairs from her eyes which stuck to the moisture on her face. She wanted a shower but knew it would have to wait. This was more important.

Rick chimed in. "I remember those, yeah. That was a few months ago I think. You didn't say too much about them, other than commenting you get lots of messages from crackpots."

Abe searched his memory, then chuckled. "Oh yeah. The conspiracy theorist religious nut."

The mention of the words "religious nut" seemed to hit a nerve with Rick but he remained silent.

"What about him?" Abe turned back to face his monitors, wondering if he had an email from Rachel that he could refer to.

"He predicted several terrorist attacks on religious sites. And I believe the Dome, the Wall, and the Church were on the list. Back to back."

Both men looked at her with wide-open eyes. Abe had to crane his neck around to get a clear view of Rachel's face. The inside of the truck was eerily silent just for a moment, as none of them spoke. The outside noises faded as each were deep in their own thoughts.

Abe broke the silence. "Really?"

"Yeah. Didn't take it seriously at the time."

"Why would you? Crazy talk." Abe stroked his short beard. "Wow, what if…" His voice trailed off.

Rick shifted uncomfortably, then slid his camera bag from his shoulder and set it on the floor. He was like a guy in a suit who never, ever loosened his tie, no matter what the circumstance. Still, he seemed out of sorts, like he was troubled with their conversation. Rachel noticed.

"You all right, Rick?" She leaned a bit forward toward him.

"Yeah," he said and absently waved it off. "I'm good. Just thinking, that's all."

Abe brought the conversation back in focus. "You kept his emails?"

"Of course. I usually keep everything. He did send them from different addresses, as I recall. Wrote he must 'stay on the run.'" She glanced over at Rick, who was absently staring at Daniel Murray's muted broadcast.

Abe smirked. "Ohhhh...I guess paranoia goes hand in hand with 'conspiracy theorist religious nut.'"

Rachel stared off as she rolled it around in her mind. "What would you think if someone made a far-fetched prediction and it came true?"

Abe shrugged. "That they caused it? Or knew the people who did."

"Exactly," she said. "When I can get to my computer files, I'll let you know what I find."

"You'd better. Okay, I've got work to do – Murray's waiting." Abe faced his equipment and returned to his duties.

It was a cue for Rachel and Rick to leave. She worked her way through the ridiculous tight corridor of the truck, toward the exit door. Rick hoisted his camera bag back onto this shoulder and shuffled after her.

CHAPTER THREE – OMINOUS EMAILS

AFTER THE DUST FROM THE BOMBINGS settled with the sunset, Israeli soldiers with bomb-sniffing dogs patrolled the neighborhoods throughout the night to ensure no other explosive devices lingered in the shadows, ready to be triggered. The bombed-out ancient buildings were cordoned off to keep the curious and looters away. Israeli and United States troops worked side-by-side to keep order and prevent additional chaos from erupting. There was another presence among them, working with them. It was Sharp Eye Global Security. Always there, always in the background.

Military jeeps patrolled the streets throughout the night, and military helicopters did continuous sweeps of Jerusalem with spotlights. Normally, the residents would find such an intrusion annoying. But tonight, the noisy choppers passing overhead brought comfort to those below. In fact, the military didn't expect to catch any mad bombers prowling the city; they were fairly certain that whoever orchestrated the attack was either long gone from Israel or laying low, at least for now. The patrols were really designed to calm the fears of the citizens.

Rachel sat comfortably on top of the blankets in a king-sized bed in a luxury suite of the Jerusalem Intercontinental Hotel. Once in her room, she had showered, changed into her sweatpants and a comfortable t-shirt, brewed a cup of tea, and was propped up against a stack of white, downy pillows. She had a corner room on the tenth floor with wrap-around windows looking out over the Jerusalem cityscape. It was late, after ten o'clock, and the view was speckled with the lights of the city. Along with the occasional Israeli military chopper passing by, sweeping the area with a white-hot spotlight. It was three o'clock in the afternoon back in New York, so she felt she could yet put in a few hours' work.

She sat cross-legged in the middle of the bed with her laptop open before her, the glowing screen shining up on her face.

She had a file, labeled "Messages from CT" open on the screen and browsed through them. These were emails she had copied and pasted onto document files for archiving. There were dozens of them, all with cryptic subject lines such as WARNINGS ABOUT THE END-TIMES AS FORETOLD IN THE BI-BLE, and THE BOOK OF REVELATION FORETOLD THIS, and PRE-DICTIONS THAT TERRORIST ATTACKS WILL INCREASE.

The body of each email contained vague quotes from the Bible along with at-tempts to tie them to current affairs. Rachel shook her head, thinking this was a dead-end. People have been searching for signs of the End Times for centuries. Within a few years after Jesus's death, in fact. In recent decades, hundreds of books were written about this very topic. Authors from one year to the next would claim that what was happening in the world, right then and there, were the signs of the Antichrist in the world and the return of Jesus. It didn't matter how many times the predictions failed, new books hit the market every year. Books that attempted to tie the same Biblical verses to whatever the new politi-cal crises had emerged in recent years. Year after year they came, with no end in sight. Wash, rinse, repeat.

Rachel was just about to give up when she reached the last email. The date indicated it arrived about three months ago. In the subject line: THREE UP-COMING ATTACKS IN JERUSALEM. *This is it*, she thought. *Or maybe not. Probably just more vague predictions that are open to as many interpretations as the last batch of predictions.*

She smirked and clicked on the document. It popped open and filled her screen. The look on her face changed to one of concern. The message was short and to the point.

"Bombs will level the Church of The Holy Sepulchre, the Dome of The Rock, and the Wailing Wall on June 21st of this year."

"That's today!" It came out so fast and loud her own voice startled her. She read it several times. Nothing vague about it. No possible way to interpret it any other way than how it was written.

A wave of dizziness and nausea swept over her. She pushed the laptop away and laid her head back on the pile of pillows behind her. Hundreds of people were dead. Well, she didn't really know how many, as there was no official count yet. But official reports estimated upwards of three hundred people were killed in the explosions. That number was repeated on every news network in the world. Including News World, her employer. Straight out of Daniel Murray's mouth to millions of people's ears.

And three months ago, she had received a news tip for it. The news tip of the century. And did nothing. Then forgot about it. It's as if she killed all three hundred people herself. It was unbelievable, impossible.

Rachel curled into a fetal position and cried.

Abe sat in a wheeled desk chair before a hodgepodge of computers and monitors spread out in a semi-circle on a table in his hotel room. It was his make-shift editing station and portable television studio. He was in the same hotel as Rachel. The room wasn't as nice – didn't have wraparound windows or a spectacular view, those always went to the on-air talent – but it was decent. Rick had a similar room down the hall. *He's probably exhausted and sawing logs by now,* Abe thought. *Jogging up and down the sidewalk with a professional camera slung around your neck will do that to you.*

On one monitor, Abe had News World displayed. It didn't broadcast here, halfway around the world, he had to stream it through the internet. On other monitors were newscasts from other countries with only a trace of their volume turned up. Not quite enough to hear what the anchors were saying but enough to know the monitor was on. Some people worked with soft background music, but not Abe, he liked visual stimuli, even if it was only in his peripheral vision. It made him feel like he was connected to the rest of the world. But with everything playing on the monitors around him, Abe's attention was squarely focused on the still image of the sharply dressed, middle-aged but trim man staring out at him from his main monitor. The man oozed so much confidence that even his photograph was intimidating. And hypnotic.

A knock at the door snapped Abe out of his almost-trance. He bounced to his feet and opened the door after looking through the small viewfinder. It was Rachel. She wore the loose-fitting t-shirt but had swapped out the sweatpants for jeans. Her left arm was raised, her elbow resting on the door jamb. Her hair was a mess and a less than half-full wine glass dangled from the fingers of her right hand. Her face was red and puffy from crying.

"I would ask if you're okay, but I can see that you're not," he said softly. "Come in."

He stepped back and out of her way as she meandered in, a little unsteady on her feet, and plopped down onto the couch, sloshing what little red wine she still had in her glass. Abe didn't know what to say to her, so he waited until she spoke. Nothing, at first. He waited.

Abe sat down in the desk chair and rolled a little closer to her, his elbows on the chair's arms and his fingers steepled. He leaned forward and studied her face.

"Are you playing psychiatrist now?" she chuckled. The words were a bit slurred.

That forced a smile from him. "No, but I am wondering what's wrong."

"I found them. The emails. I reread them all, cried, then poured some wine, and here I am," she said, trying not to cry. She drank the last of the wine from her glass.

She told him about the emails from CT, the last one in particular. Abe sat back in his chair and pondered this new information. He could see that Rachel wallowed in guilt over it.

"You couldn't know, Rachel. It's not your fault," he said, putting his hand on her arm. "It was a crazy prediction. Who would've believed it? I vaguely remember you telling me about those emails months ago. I didn't believe it and forgot about it. If you're guilty, then so am I. And what could you have done about it, anyway? If you'd have gone to the authorities, they would have labeled you a conspiracy theorist and ignored it. Then after the terrorist attacks happened, you'd be a prime suspect. No good would have come out of it."

Abe thought a moment before he continued. Anger showed in his eyes. "In fact, this CT guy, or gal, or whoever they are, should've gone to the authorities himself. If anything, he's responsible for what happened. Either by not acting or being the terrorist himself."

"I didn't think about it that way. Thanks." She gave him a weak smile and rubbed her eyes, puffy from crying.

"Don't mention it. And I'm glad you came down. There's something I need to tell you." He leaned back in his chair.

"What?" Her curiosity was piqued, though she was tired.

"I was monitoring the Israeli military radio bands and—"

"Is that legal?"

"Probably not," he said, annoyed at the interruption, "but anyway, I discovered there's a large private security firm that works with them. They're contracted to protect all the religious sites in Israel. Which includes the three that were blown-up today."

"Sharp Eye Global Security." It was not a question, it was a matter-of-fact statement. Abe blinked more than once. He thought he'd proudly spring new information on her, but she had turned the tables on him.

"Yes. How did you know that?"

"Those were the guys who escorted Rick and me away from the Dome of the Rock site. Who owns this firm?" She stood up and walked closer to his computer set-up.

He smiled arrogantly, as he knew something she didn't. Abe rolled over to his bank of monitors, faced his main computer screen and pressed a few keys. "This guy," he said as he pointed at the main monitor, the one with the photo of an intimidating-looking man on it.

Rachel placed the empty wine glass on a side table and peered over his shoulder at the man's image showing on the monitor.

"Lucius Voland? One of the richest guys around." She was impressed.

"Yep. And he was in the news today. On our network." Abe tapped on the keyboard on a laptop and Daniel Murray appeared on the screen, sitting behind his anchor's desk. "This is from earlier today."

Abe hit the space bar and Murray's recording played. "With the attacks in Jerusalem today putting a strain on the peace process, philanthropist Lucius Voland met with Prime Minister Gellman to offer help in negotiations."

Abe tabbed the space bar which paused the recording. He rotated in his chair and faced her, leaning forward, his elbows on his knees.

Rachel plopped back down on the couch and held her face in her hands. She ran her fingers through her hair and looked at Abe.

"What if this was an inside job?" she asked.

Abe furrowed his brow. He wasn't convinced of that.

"Think about it," she continued, "if you supply security personnel at sensitive politically charged sites, it might be easy to manufacture an incident."

"To what end?"

"War profiteering. Of course, you'd have to start a war then."

Abe was skeptical. "Voland is a world-renowned philanthropist. No way."

"Call me cynical. And maybe it's not even him – Lucius Voland – maybe it's someone who works for him." The wine had worn off and Rachel was again alert and attentive.

Abe thought about it and nodded. Yeah, it made sense, but, still, it was a bit of a stretch.

Rachel went on. "Maybe our mysterious CT works for him. Where can I find Lucius Voland?"

He grabbed one of his laptops and pulled up a link. "He has offices and residences all over the world, but he spends most of his time at a palace right here in Jerusalem."

Abe enlarged the image of the palace on the laptop's screen. It was large and impressive, sprawling across lush, green rolling hills. It boasted several towering spires and the architecture suggested it was built centuries ago, but with tasteful updates added over the years that meshed with and complemented the original design. He turned the laptop around for Rachel to see the screen.

"Wow!" She was more than impressed. "This man has money!"

"That's an understatement. And he's hosting a social event there this coming weekend."

"Great! I have an idea. I need to attend... but not as a journalist. I need to be undercover, to figure out if Lucius Voland is involved in the attacks. I need another identity." She knew she was going beyond her reporter duties, but if there was a story there, she wanted to be the one to find it.

"I can take care of that. I'll get you inside," Abe smiled, confident in his abilities.

"You can?" She seemed genuinely surprised, which disappointed him.

"Don't question the master hacker." He threw her a cocky smirk. She grinned back.

***

New York City was seven hours behind Jerusalem, so when Rachel's alarm went off at four in the morning, she knew she could catch Daniel arriving home after his long day, or possibly in his office at News World before leaving. She could tried to contact him after returning her to room at 11:30 p.m. but he probably would've been splitting his time between the anchor's desk, his office, and meetings, and she knew she'd be at the mercy of his schedule, waiting for him to return his call like a teenager waiting for their crush to phone. Best to just contact him as the circus was ending though it would wreck her sleep. The idea of sharing her thoughts about Lucius Voland made her nervous but excited her at the same time.

After she freshened up in the bathroom and rehearsed what she was going to say, she picked up her phone and made the Facetime call to Daniel.

He answered immediately. "Did something happen?" His face was taut with tension, she could clearly see, though they were thousands of miles away. Technology rocked.

She realized he knew it was the wee hours of the morning in Jerusalem and a call this earlier could signal trouble, such as a possible new terrorist attack.

"No, no, not at all," she said and saw him immediately relax. "I just wanted to tell you something I discovered before you called it a night."

"Okay," he nodded as he moved around his home. She couldn't help but notice his surroundings. Suits, ties, and shoes on display like he was at Macy's or Nordstrom's. But he was just in his closet. A closet half the size of her apartment, she mused. He put his suit jacket on a hangar and hung it up.

She took a deep breath and told him about Lucius Voland and his efforts to become a part of the peace talks, his company Sharp Eye Global Security, and her thoughts on the three attacks being an inside job. She added that Voland was hosting a social event right here in Jerusalem that she should attend. She didn't mention her emails from CT. Those could wait for another time, no reason to overwhelm him. She just wanted to know how he'd respond to Voland's possible involvement.

"Lucius Voland." He said the name really slowly. She got the distinct feeling he wondered why she was wasting his time with a nothing call.

"Just chasing a possible lead." She was making excuses to him now and hated herself for it. One of the problems she'd always had with Dan is he made all his field correspondents jump through hoops to justify their stories. And then when the story panned out, he took credit for it.

"Yeah... but... I don't think he's involved in this," he said condescendingly.

"Wouldn't hurt to check him out though. Especially since he might become a player in the peace talks," she said pensively.

"Okay. But Syria still tops the list of prime suspects, regardless of their denials."

She shrugged. "Sure. Worst-case scenario I might get a great interview out of it."

"True. Very good then. Go for it. Keep me posted." Murray seemed distracted.

"Always." She smiled as he swiped the call off.

She tossed her phone down and laid back on the bed, her hair fanned out, her arms splayed. It was quiet and dark outside. Even the military choppers had given up for the night. Probably too many citizen complaints.

Rachel thought the call went well, all things considered. Dan wasn't all that receptive, she thought, but he didn't completely shut her down. She decided to get a few more hours of sleep before starting her day. She was excited to get her crew together – Abe and Rick – and plan out how she was going to get into

Lucius Voland's social event. It was going to be like a spy movie, and the thought exhilarated her.

Her thoughts turned to CT, the "conspiracy theorist religious nut" as Abe referred to him. His prediction of the attacks on the three religious sites still unsettled her even after her talk with Abe. And CT tying it all back to the Book of Revelation in the New Testament, and the End Times took her thoughts further into the past, to her parents and their panicked response to the attacks on 9/11.

And again, more talk about the End Times, complete with the appearance of the Antichrist and the return of Jesus. But it's been two decades since the World Trade Center towers came down. The world slowly returned to normal after that. Well... there still existed a new normal of endless wars against terrorists, real and imagined.

Wars and rumors of wars. That thought just popped into her head. Even the non-religious had heard of that Biblical verse. *But what does it mean*, she thought?

She sat up and opened up the top drawer in the bedside table. What she looked for was in plain sight, the only thing in the drawer, in fact, as in many hotel rooms. A Bible. She picked it up and paged through it, then realized it would take forever to find the verse this way.

What am I doing? It's the 21st century. She put the book back in the drawer and grabbed her phone. A simple Google search instantly pulled up what she was looking for.

It was Matthew 24:6. *And you will hear of wars and rumors of wars. See that you are not troubled; for all these things must come to pass; but the end is not yet.*

"But the end is not yet," she said softly to herself. After 9/11 the U.S. went to war and has been in an overseas conflict ever since.

So, when does the end come, she thought? The World Trade Center buildings were not religious monuments. But the three sites in Israel were. And they represented all three Abrahamic religions. Rachel was not a religious person – had no faith in anything spiritual, really, not anymore, anyway – but these recent attacks felt different than previous attacks that have plagued the world over the past couple decades.

When would the end come? It felt like a basketball or football game that was down to the last couple minutes, and one side – humanity – hadn't put any points on the board yet. In fact, humanity seemed to be oblivious to the clock running out. Except for a small percent of humanity. Like CT, whoever he or she was.

Rachel didn't like the direction her thoughts were taking her. It was too much, and it was sounding ridiculous. She turned her mind to the coming day and what needed to be planned with her team. She set the alarm on her phone for 6:30 a.m. and climbed under the bed's comforter, hoping sleep would find her. It did, but it wasn't going to make it easy. Dreams of the Dome of the Rock collapsing on an endless loop echoed through her mind.

Jack Snyder, Pamela Cosel, Syed Nadim Rizvi

CHAPTER FOUR – KEEPING
THE FAITH

OVER THE NEXT SEVERAL DAYS, Rachel, Rick and Abe developed a plan for getting Rachel discreetly into Lucius Voland's palace party. They had an intense time-crunch because the party was taking place that Saturday night. To make it happen, Rachel was forced to use her own money. She could have justified using her expense account, she reasoned, but Murray's reception to the idea was lukewarm at most. Better to not draw any undue attention by racking up several thousand dollars in wardrobe, limo rental, creating a fake identification card, and whatever additional equipment Abe thought he might need. Best to just put it all on credit cards and deal with it later.

On Saturday night, as Rachel – dressed in a beautiful navy-blue sequined evening dress and sparkling with brand new jewelry – stepped into a limo out front of the hotel, St. Joseph's Catholic Church in Jerusalem was holding a special Saturday evening Mass in remembrance of the lives lost in the tragedy that struck earlier in the week.

The church was built two centuries ago but had been forever updated as technology and construction technique improved. It was breathtaking and ornate, with rows of pillars, statues of the Saints, and stories-high stained-glass windows depicting Biblical scenes in such detail that they looked like stills from big budget Hollywood movies. The ceiling was covered in small colorful tiles which created a massive mural of more Biblical scenes as if it were the world's largest, most detailed and well-crafted cave painting. It was so far above the floor that staring at it too long could be vertigo-inducing. This evening a crowd of churchgoers packed the place to its capacity with standing room only. People of all ages and races attended.

Outside, the mass of people wasn't any thinner. The streets were closed off for blocks to accommodate the crowd of thousands. Huge projection screens were mounted in front of the church showing the altar area within. Enormous speakers were set alongside the screens.

Father Marco Rossi stood before a mirror in the sacristy and adjusted his priest's collar. Though he was in his early forties, he was the youngest priest to ever be appointed to this grand, respectable church. It was the happiest day of his life when he got the assignment two years ago.

Raised in a devout Catholic family, being a priest was something he set his sights on even as a little boy. After completing seminary and being ordained into the Catholic ministry, he requested a transfer from Rome – where he was born and raised – to Israel. He wanted to be as close to God as possible and he believed living in the Holy Land was the place to do it.

After a decade of being moved from one church to another, he landed the job of head priest at St. Joseph's. He didn't think it could get better than that.

But that was back when he still believed in God. Today, his belief in God was gone. His loss of faith didn't follow a tragedy or a personal crisis or anything dramatic or interesting like that. He just simply quit believing because it didn't make sense to him anymore. His faith didn't leave him all at once. It was slow and gradual, like succumbing to a lengthy but terminal illness. No one in the church hierarchy knew. Neither did his family. He could have, and probably should have, left the priesthood, but, quite frankly, he didn't know how to do anything else. So, he just went through the motions. Like someone staying in a marriage that was long dead.

There was a knock at the sacristy door.

"Come in," he said with a forced smile knowing parishioners expected him to look welcoming.

The door cracked open and Eric poked his head in. He was one of the church Deacons. At least ten years older than Marco, he once dreamt of being a priest himself. But he was just too timid and introverted. At least that's what Marco thought.

"Father Marco... it's time."

"Thank you, Eric." He smoothed his vestment front, checked his collar and rose from the chair. He took a few deep breaths, said a silent prayer out of habit, and readied himself.

"There are thousands of scared people out there. Looking for hope," Eric informed him. He always added unnecessary commentary to their conversations. It used to annoy Marco but he'd gotten used to it.

"I know," Marco said absently. Eric frowned, thinking Father Marco didn't really care. That was not true, Marco cared deeply. He just didn't know if he could do anything about it.

After Eric slipped out of the room and closed the door behind him, Father Marco picked up a crucifix and studied it. It was marvelous and hand-carved. The artist took a great deal of care creating this. *Probably a devout believer*, Marco thought with a sigh.

He held the crucifix and stared at his reflection in the mirror.

"When the righteous cry for help, the Lord hears and delivers them out of their troubles," he recited from the Bible. He didn't believe those words anymore, but he had a job to do. He hung the crucifix around his neck, sighed, and walked out.

He was taken aback at the size of the crowd when he entered the sanctuary. Though he'd preached to many large crowds, he had never experienced anything of this magnitude. He mounted the pulpit and began his prepared sermon.

"Jerusalem, and the rest of the world, has suffered a terrible loss this week. But we must not despair." His voice was calm, strong and loud. He knew that is what they expected.

He took a dramatic pause as he scanned the crowd and listened to his voice echoing for blocks. Though the massive speakers outside were pointed away from the church, the front doors were open, allowing people to come and go, or to peer in from outside.

The people in the streets focused their attention on the huge projection screens. They would rather have been inside, but it was the next best thing. Hundreds held up camera phones high above heads to record the sermon. Sure, it would be posted online later, but having a personal record of it was more valuable for some.

The crowd was quiet as Father Marco's voice boomed from the speakers in time with his image on the large projection screens. He looked regal, stately.

"As Christians, we turn to Jesus for strength and know he resides within our hearts and souls." He paused for the echo to fade.

A commotion suddenly flowed through the crowd like a wave over a body of water. People began looking skyward. Mobile phones were aimed at the object of their attention.

Inside the church, the congregation started to react to the flurry of activity from outside. Panicked screams and shouts reverberated in the stone and marble church as people feared another terrorist strike.

Father Marco stopped speaking and calmly focused his attention to the open doors at the front of the church. Though it was relatively dark outside, the ambient light was enough for him to see the huge crowd outside looking at something in the sky.

Could this be an impending airstrike, he thought?

CHAPTER FIVE – PARTY CRASHER

"CAN YOU HEAR ME, RACHEL?" Abe asked through the hidden earpiece Rachel wore.

"Yes, loud and clear," she whispered, relaxing into the soft leather seat as she gazed out the limo's window. She really didn't need to whisper. The limo's glass screen between her and the driver was closed tightly, making the cabin more or less sound proof.

"Move your purse a bit – let me check the camera," he told her.

Rachel obliged by pointing the clutch to give him an outside view.

"Good. It's working fine. You'll make it through Voland's security with no problem. The camera is sewn into the purse and the few metal parts will blend in with its zipper. Don't give it a thought, carry it like you normally would."

"Sounds good. Thank you, Abe, for taking such good care of me in this," Rachel said. She was grateful for his friendship.

"Hey, what about me?" Rick laughed in her ear. Even with his jovialness, Rachel could hear the worry in his voice. Not for himself, but for her. Rachel often found his over-protectiveness annoying and dated, but not tonight. She was very thankful these two guys were going on this journey with her. Not directly into the lion's den, but in their van of equipment, relatively close, seeing and hearing everything that she sees and hears.

"Yes, you too, Rick. I couldn't do this without either of you two."

"Teamwork. That's what we do," Abe said, then returned their focus to the task at hand. "Okay, it won't be long before the limo has you at the mansion. Just relax and enjoy the party. Don't overstep things but use your reporter's instincts. You got this, girl," Abe said.

Rachel glanced over her shoulder through the back windshield. She saw the headlights of the van as it followed the limo. It kept a discreet distance but was close enough not to lose sight of the limo. She took a deep breath to steady her nerves. She smoothed the skirt of her dress and checked her hair in the mirror of her compact, also touching up her lipstick. Rachel smiled at the routine, always sure to look the "right" image as a TV reporter.

She looked forward to having a glass of wine to quell any fears and take off the edge. She relaxed in the seat and tried to enjoy the view of Jerusalem passing by the window. She really loved the older buildings and their rich history. She tried to imagine all the drama and excitement that took place in and around them over the centuries.

Rachel suddenly became cognizant that there were very few people on the streets. She thought it was probably due to the terrorist attacks earlier in the week. People were afraid and staying home. In contrast to that, every now and then the limo passed bars packed with people, so full that the crowd flowed out onto the sidewalks. The groups of people were like islands in an ocean of emptiness. She mused that this too was driven by fear. Some people go all out, living life to the fullest when faced with their mortality. *And that's what terror attacks do to us*, she thought. *They bring our mortality front and center in our minds.*

The limo moved beyond the city limits giving her a view of the lush countryside beneath the moonlight. It too helped calm the fear she was feeling. A thought popped into her head as she enjoyed the view of nature. *We humans have really fouled up the world.* The thought was so unexpected it startled her. And her realization that it was true only served to depress her.

"Wow!" It was Abe in her ear, snapping her back from being lost in her own thoughts. "Even more impressive than the photos."

Rachel leaned forward to stare out the front windshield and saw it. Lucius Voland's palace. A triumph of architecture. A monument. She was impressed that it blended well with the surrounding hills and greenery and wasn't just another man-made monstrosity that was an ugly blight on the landscape.

"Earth to Rachel. You still with us?" It was Rick this time.

"Yes, Rick, I am. And Abe, you're right, the photos don't do it justice." She knew they could hear the awe in her voice.

She did a quick glance back through the back windshield and saw the van continue on past the driveway. She wasn't concerned. Abe and Rick were as competent as people could be. They would park at a secluded spot away from the palace but within transmission distance of her earpiece and the camera hidden in her purse.

As the limo approached the palace, Rachel was overwhelmed by its beauty. She again checked her lipstick in the small mirror from her clutch, looked at her hair one last time, and let herself feel the excitement of what was to come. *This is going to be some event. Mr. Voland, who are you? What is your goal here? Are you a player in what happened in Jerusalem?*

The limo driver pulled to a slow stop at the foot of the mansion's steps where a man dressed in a black suit and white gloves descended the stairs toward the vehicle. His salt-and-pepper gray hair shone in the lights from the mansion, and matched well with his uniform.

"Here it goes, hope your hack worked," Rachel said, softly and nervously.

"Don't worry, I know my stuff," he came back, reassuringly.

The man carefully opened the car door for Rachel. She handed him her identification card, and he checked the guest list on his tablet, confirming her name and invitation. She waited with trepidation, hoping it wouldn't show on her face or body language. After a moment, the man handed her ID back to her.

"Welcome, Miss Bowman. We are happy to have you," the attendant said as he bowed, his English accent a delight to Rachel's ears.

She relaxed. It worked. She wasn't Rachel Williams anymore. At least for this evening. She was Sheila Bowman, Director of the Old Jerusalem Preservation Society. *Abe did a great job pulling this off.* And considering how much she admired and enjoyed Old Jerusalem it was fitting. She stood tall, knowing she made a striking impression. She usually did.

"Please follow the other gentleman to the top of the stairs where you will be directed to the ballroom," the man said with a wave of his gloved hand.

Rachel tipped her head in thanks and held firmly onto the clutch as she mounted the set of stairs. As she got closer to the entry door, she heard lively music from inside. A male singer, reminiscent of Frank Sinatra, was singing a familiar tune as trumpets and violins accompanied him. She heard laughter and loud voices conversing from an outside patio located to the far left. Lights were strung from trees at the patio, and the lighting from inside the home through its beveled-glass door made it a festive sight. A cool breeze blew tree branches along the staircase, which were trimmed to create an archway over the steps at the home's entry.

"All's well," Abe whispered from the van. "Just take your time, take it slow."

Rachel smiled as she entered the room, feeling good that Abe and Rick had her back. A woman wearing a red-and-black dress who stood to the side of the entry door handed her a red rose, which she touched to her nose to inhale its aroma. She was emboldened as she picked up a small glass of red wine from a waiter's passing tray. Across the room a small orchestra was positioned on a stage built into the room's décor. Red velvet curtains flanked either side of the platform, and large white speakers hung from the ceiling, along with a projection screen built into the wall off to the side for a better, close-up view of the performers from across the room. The man singing had a wonderful baritone voice, and Rachel stood alone for a minute, taking in the sounds and ambiance of the room. She had never quite been in a place like this before.

Hundreds of people smiled, danced and ate hors d'oeuvres which were served by men dressed in black tuxedoes wearing deep blue cummerbunds and shiny black shoes.

Rachel took the time to look at the other guests and was overwhelmed with who she saw – world leaders, even a few business people whom she had interviewed in years past. Powerful people, wealthy heads of states. All laughing, smiling, here at the invitation of Lucius Voland. *Who is this man? Why the party?*

She slowly stepped from group to group, staying in the background, being sure to blend in with the other guests. She was sure not to stare as if she was on the hunt for something. After a few more sips of wine and two tasty hors d'oeuvres, alone near a server, she felt comfortable enough to ask him to point out Voland.

"Why, miss, you're standing not far from him," the waiter said. "He's the one talking to the group of sheiks right there," gesturing to Voland's back.

In her earpiece, Ali cautioned her. "Be careful, Rachel." He could see Voland through the clutch's camera, a tall man with dark hair, whose presence filled the video screen.

"Thank you," she said to the waiter.

Then she began her trek toward Voland.

"What are you going to say to him?" Abe asked.

She spoke softly, trying not to move her mouth much. "I've rehearsed a few things, but it'll probably all go out the window when I'm actually talking."

"Hope no one recognizes you." It was Rick. Rachel smirked and rolled her eyes. He was always the worry-wart. Sometimes she thought it was sweet, but other times she just found it annoying. This was one of those times. But she wasn't going to show it.

"Doubtful. In this crowd I'm a nobody." Yet she knew most noticed her good looks.

"Rachel Williams?"

"Ow! You jinxed yourself!" That was Abe, speaking in her ear as if he were her subconscious.

The voice that called her name came from her right. It was male. She stiffened and continued walking as she fought the natural desire to turn to the man who called her name. We all instantly respond to our name when called. This seems to be something instinctually programmed into each of us. To ignore it took a great deal of effort. But ignore she must; she was Sheila Bowman tonight.

"Rachel Williams." This time it wasn't a question. It was a statement. The person knew for certain who she was. Rachel heard his footsteps on the marble floor as he hurried toward her. Lucius Voland wasn't too far away. Best to just stop now and avoid the embarrassment of dragging this interruption right up to her conversation with Lucius Voland, which would blow her cover. This man, whoever he was, has just completely fouled up her plans.

She slowed and let the man get in front of her. He was handsome with blonde hair and a pleasant smile. Trim and in his thirties, his tuxedo fit him perfectly.

Rachel met his eyes with a neutral expression. She was like a crouched tennis player just before the serve, waiting to see which way the ball was going to go. Could she continue being Sheila Bowman, or was the jig up?

She tried a safe question. "Do I know you?"

"No. I recognize you from television."

She was just about to tell him that he must be mistaken, when he added, "You're the foreign correspondent for News World."

That settled it. He had way too many details. And the way he looked at her, she knew why. He was a bit smitten. This was the downside of celebrity, even a celebrity as low on the ladder as her.

She had no idea how to deal with him, so she just smiled.

"You covering Mr. Voland's party?"

"No. Just a guest." Her answer was short, bland, and curt. Hopefully that will help bring the conversation to an end so she could get on with her task. As crowded as the room was, if this gentleman disappeared into the crowd, she could conceivably return to being Sheila Bowman and get on with her "mission."

It wasn't going to be that easy.

"Oh, how rude of me," he said as he extended his hand to shake. "I'm Jason Carter. I work for Mr. Voland. Do you know him?"

"Not exactly," Rachel replied in the most disinterested voice she could summon.

"Well, I'll introduce you," Jason replied with a big, enthusiastic smile. He turned to lead her, but she anchored herself in place.

In some other life, this guy must've been a door-to-door salesman whose eagerness never waned, no matter how many doors were slammed in his face.

"Thanks, but I'm just going to mingle for a while. I'll talk to him when he's... less busy."

The persistent man was taken aback a smidgeon. She now saw what he was about. *He's a guy who was used to getting his way.*

"Okay. Would you like to get a drink?"

Abe chuckled in her earpiece. "You have no time for this, Ms. Bond. You're on a mission."

Rachel of course ignored Abe and stared Jason in the eyes as she raised her wine glass and planted a fake smile on her face. "Got one. But thanks."

"Maybe later then?"

Absolutely not.

"Sure." If her smile was more plastic her face would be a mask.

He nodded, having read her rejection properly, and slinked away.

Abe laughed in her ear. "Cold-hearted bi—"

"Shut up." She wasn't happy about it. Always hated hurting someone, no matter how minor the injury. If he really knew her from News World screens, he might be one of those who would prefer to tarnish her reputation if his feelings were hurt due to the rejection.

Rachel turned to continue walking toward where she last saw Lucius Voland and realized she'd lost sight of him. The group of sheiks he had been talking to was still in the same place as before, but Voland was nowhere to be seen. She reasoned he was probably off mingling with other guests. She figured she'd have to catch up with later. If at all. The way the night was going, it seemed less likely with each passing moment.

She continued to move about the room, people watching, when something caught her attention. Against one wall were a row of shelves behind glass. It was a massive display case built into the wall and filled with antiques. She wasn't a museum curator or an antiques collector, but she could tell the items on the shelves were old. Really old. Like centuries, or possibly millennia. Though every type of antique, such as vases, statuettes, and other trinkets were well represented, the display was mostly composed of weapons and armament. Spears, maces, morning stars, and every type of sword imaginable.

"Whoa!" Rick barked into her ear.

She grimaced. "Easy, pal, you're going to blow out my eardrum."

"Sorry. Could you walk closer, I want to check out the antiques."

"Sure." This was a side of Rick she hadn't seen before. In fact, it was a contradiction. He was such a gentle soul. Who'd have thought he liked weapons, ancient or otherwise. She strode over to the case.

"Keep your purse-camera pointed at it."

"Who do you think is the boss here?" She couldn't resist the push-back comment.

Rick and Abe just chuckled, but she complied and made sure the camera-end of her purse had a good view of the case. She slowly walked along it, admiring the antique items on display, focusing mostly on the pottery and statuettes.

"Hold up," Rick said. On the bottom shelf was a sword with an unusual curve in it. Almost C-shaped blade. "That's a sickle sword. A common weapon used in Israel during Biblical times. It is said that was the weapon used in verses such as Judges 1:8 'The men of Judah attacked Jerusalem also and took it. They put the city to the sword and set it on fire.'"

Rachel was amazed. "Wow, Rick," she said softly. "You are full of surprises tonight."

"You like my collection, Ms. Williams?" The voice came from behind and startled her. She turned, a little too quickly, and sloshed her wine in her glass as she came face to face with Lucius Voland. He was taller, more muscular, and more imposing than he looked in his photo. His smile had a predatorial edge to it and his piercing brown eyes were so dark they hovered on the edge of being black. For a moment, she wondered if he'd heard her talking to Rick, but if he did, he didn't let on. Then it dawned on her that he knew her name.

She smiled sheepishly. "How did you know?"

He nodded to Jason who was leaning against the bar with a drink in his hand. He smiled and raised it as if saying "cheers."

Images of handcuffs chafing her wrists filled her mind. Voland was not a public servant, someone she could grill – borderline bully – with tough, embarrassing questions. Her powers as a journalist were meaningless here. He was a private citizen and she was an uninvited guest – essentially trespassing – on his property. Private property.

Either she wore this concern on her face, visible by anyone looking, or Lucius could read her mind, because right at that moment he leaned in with a grin, and in a stage-whisper said, "It's okay that you crashed my party. I won't have security escort you out."

She visibly relaxed. Her cover was blown but it seemed like it was going to be fine. Lucius stepped up alongside her and swelled with pride as he gazed at his own antique collection.

"It took a long time for me to acquire all these items." His demeanor was similar to a father showing off his brood of beautiful children.

"How long," she asked, deciding it was best to just move him as quickly as she could past the fact that she shouldn't even be here.

"Centuries," he said seriously as he glanced at her with those piercing brown eyes. Rachel stared at him, stunned. Then he cracked a small smile, forcing a surprised grin from her. *He sounded so convincing when he said it, I almost fell for it. Well… no almost about it. I thought he meant it. Which would mean he was crazy.*

She scanned a row of swords and spears. "Considering all the philanthropy work you're known for the collection of weapons doesn't seem to be your style."

"It's a reminder of mankind's violent past. It tells me I have much work to do," Lucius said with a sigh. Then he faced her. "I would've approved your request to attend my gathering had you inquired. But somehow I think you wanted to stay incognito."

Here goes, she thought, and sighed deeply. "You own the security company that guarded the three holy sites. That could raise some curious questions."

He thoughtfully nodded. "Yes. My company, Sharp Eye Global Security was present. It's unfortunate that my people couldn't stop the tragedies. Some of my employees were victim to it, in fact."

"Oh… I'm sorry to hear that."

"Thank you." He nodded and for just a second, looked humble before his arrogance reappeared.

Rachel wondered why he would even be having a party if some of his employees just lost their lives. Then, to her surprise, he answered it.

"I held a private memorial honoring them earlier this week. It was kept from the press at the request of their families. And my board of directors insisted I go forth with my social event tonight as it would stand in defiance of the terrorist. And also convey world unity. Just look around at all the world leaders here – in government and in industry – and you can see what I mean."

"I know, I've seen your impressive guests." This time it was her turn show humility.

"As for suspicions of my involvement," he continued, "I've already opened my personnel records to the Parliament. If there's anything there to find, I'm more than happy to help. In the meantime, stay as long as you'd like. Enjoy the party. Now... if you'll excuse me."

And just like that, he nodded and walked away. Rachel stood motionless, not knowing what to do.

"Can we breathe now?" Abe asked.

"Yeah, Rachel," Rick chimed in. "If that had gone on any longer, I think we both would've passed out."

"That makes three of us," she said a little too loudly. Fortunately, with the huge crowd of people in the room talking all at once, and the band playing, nobody noticed her talking to herself. "Send the limo back around, please."

"You got it," Abe said.

She sighed and headed for the front door of the palace. *This was a waste of time. And I'm going to end up with a big credit card bill. Sheesh.*

Jack Snyder, Pamela Cosel, Syed Nadim Rizvi

CHAPTER SIX – A SECRET MEETING

"THAT TURNED OUT TO BE a dead-end," Abe said as he fired up his make-shift editing studio in his hotel room.

Rachel poured herself a glass of wine. "Maybe not. The Parliament might find something in his files. You want some wine?"

"No, thanks." He glanced over at her as she sat on the couch. Her glass was nearly filled to the brim. "You drowning your sorrows now?" he chuckled.

"Just easing myself back down from my failed spy mission tonight. What are you doing?"

"You know me, I'm a media junkie. Always have to catch up on what's happening in the world." He had four different news sites open on the various computer screens.

It was still relatively early, only 10:30 p.m. Rachel had arrived at Voland's palace at around 9 p.m. and left around 10 o'clock. Short and sweet, but nothing really learned. They had all been quiet on the ride back, each silently processing the adventure in their own way. Rick had already retired to his room.

Abe clicked between several of the major mainstream media news channels playing on his monitors, with alternative news showing in the mix. Rachel looked from monitor to monitor, then, with a wide grin smeared on her face, shook her head. "How can you even watch all of it? It would drive me crazy."

Abe rolled back a little in his wheeled desk chair and spread his arms as he scanned the monitors. "If you position yourself just right, you can take it all in, and if something really important pops up, you are sure to catch it."

"It all looks like a chaotic mess to me," she laughed. She took another sip of wine.

He shrugged. "Yeah, well, I've been doing it for years."

Rachel squinted at one of the monitors. While all the other monitors played professional news image, the type she was quite familiar with – talking heads, anchorpersons, interviews, field reporters – this one showed grainy, shaky, amateur footage of something going in and out of focus in the sky. It occurred to her that Abe was right – that if you viewed all the monitors just right, you catch the important footage. This might not be important – probably wasn't in fact – but it was certainly different.

"What is that?" Rachel pointed a finger to one screen, not touching it.

Abe leaned in closer to the monitor and turned the audio up. It was just the chaotic sound of a huge crowd, no distinct voices. Nothing to be learned this way. The image was on 'full screen' mode, so he reduced it and saw that it was YouTube footage with information beneath it.

"It's a YouTube video that has apparently gone viral. Apparently shot tonight, right here in Israel. I have a program that I wrote myself that searches for current viral videos. That's why it's playing."

"Can you play it from the top?"

"Sure." He scooted his chair closer to the desk.

Abe tapped away at this keyboard and the video started over. It showed a massive crowd standing in front of St. Joseph's Catholic Church with Father Marco Rossi on a huge projection screen, which was almost too bright for the phone's camera that it was being recorded on, so the image of the father was just on the verge of being blown out. The priest's sermon was distorted on the phones audio system, which mainly picked up the sounds of the amateur videographer's fingers gripping the phone and the small talk that occurred in the immediate vicinity.

Suddenly, a few people glanced skyward and shouted. Fingers pointed. More people looked. A commotion ran through the crowd as the priest's video image bantered on obliviously.

The camera swept in the direction everyone was looking. The videographer did a poor attempt of trying to keep a dot in the sky framed in the center of the phone. And it kept going in and out of focus, which didn't help the situation.

Abe and Rachel watched in silence as the dot took on the shape of a silhouetted man descending from the sky. The phone was abruptly yanked down, and the image froze on the last frame.

Rachel curiously wrinkled her brow in astonishment. "What was supposedly going on there?"

Abe used his computers touch pad and slid the vertical slider bar down, revealing the videos information. He quickly read it and turned to Rachel with a wide condescending grin.

"It says here that it's Jesus returning. A sign of the End Times. It's gotta be someone messing around with a special effects program. But I have to admit, it looks really good. Real in fact."

Rachel leans in over his shoulder and brought her finger close to the touch pad.

"May I ?" she asked.

"Sure."

She brought the slider bar lower to reveal more info, then points near the bottom of the screen.

"Look."

Abe casually glanced over. Beneath the information about the video was written: Posted by CT.

He locked eyes with Rachel. His smirk was gone.

***

It was a gray morning in Jerusalem as a storm brewed in the sky. It was one of those days where one just wanted to curl up on the couch in a robe with hot coffee or tea and watch movies all day or read a book. But that kind of day was for one with a normal life. Something Rachel hadn't had in a long time. She globe-trotted at the beck and call of Daniel Murray, his right-hand woman in the field, always on hand whenever he needed her to report from the scene. That was as long as she understood the pecking order of their relationship. She played second fiddle to him, and – if he got his way – always would. If she threatened the order of things – natural order as far as Murray was concerned – she'd find herself quickly unemployed. Replaced by some other young upstart ready to stand in the limelight. Behind Murray of course.

Right now, though, she laid atop her comforter on her bed at the Jerusalem Intercontinental Hotel. A place she'd been staying for a few weeks now. It was starting to feel like years.

She was still in her formal wear from the previous evening, minus the heels. She laid flat on her back staring straight at the ceiling. She had not been able to sleep. Probably just as well. Sleep would most likely bring a hangover. Though she could easily hold her liquor – been able to since college – she drank on an empty stomach last night, so she was pushing her luck. However, she'd learned a long time ago, by accident, that if one doesn't sleep after drinking, they can avoid the hangover entirely. The trade-off was sleep deprivation. She was in this predicament because her mind wouldn't settle down. *Was Lucius Voland or someone in his organization responsible for the terrorist strikes? Was the video posted by the same CT who sent her the emails, or was it just a coincidence? Either way, who was CT?*

So many questions. Not a single answer. Yet.

Her phone, on the bed next to her, buzzed with an incoming text. She fished for it without taking her gaze off the ceiling. She held it up and, with a little effort, focused her eyes on the screen. It was Daniel: *How'd it go last night?*

Oh, it went great, Mr. Murray. My undercover effort was blown immediately by someone who recognized me. And the only thing I learned about Lucius Voland is that he likes to collect ancient antiques, circa biblical era, especially weapons. I didn't even get an interview out of the meeting. Oh yeah, and I've racked up thousands of dollars in credit card debt. But hey, got a nice new dress and some jewelry out of it. Can wear on my next date. Whenever the opportunity arises. Heck, I can't even remember my last date. But... please... feel free to gloat now.

She sighed and keyed in a response with her thumbs: *Dead-end. Looking into another lead.*

Keep me posted, was his reply. It came quickly, and then nothing. She glanced at the bedside clock. It was 9 a.m. Sunday morning, which means it was 2 a.m. in New York. Either Murray was returning home from a late-night social event or was in bed and woke up to use the bathroom or whatever. He had no real time for her at the moment, for which she was glad. She didn't want to field a lot of questions which would just end with him saying "I told you Voland wasn't involved." Oh, he wouldn't just come out and say it like that. He had more tact than that. But that's what he'd be saying nonetheless, just in different words. And a lot more of them.

Rachel scooted to the edge of the bed, rubbed her face, then ran her fingers through her hair. Time to get back to work.

She meandered over to her laptop which sat on the desk by the window. On any other day the view would be great but today the gray sky was just an external reflection of her mood.

She opened her laptop and turned it on. It seemed to take forever for all the drivers and icons to load, then another eternity for it to connect to the hotel Wi-Fi. Once it had, she sighed and typed out a short email to the mysterious CT and sent it to all the email addresses for him that she had. The email was straight to the point, no reason to waste time on pleasantries. It read: Did you post the *YouTube video last night that went viral?*

Yes. The reply came so fast it startled Rachel. She thought she'd have time to fix herself a cup of coffee, take a shower, and go down to the hotel restaurant for breakfast before a response came. Assuming she got a response at all.

She tapped away at the laptop keys. *It was grainy, hard to see. What is it a video of?*

That question was one of those transparent lies that anyone would see through. CT would know she must've read the blurb beneath the video, so she asked a question she already knew the answer to.

What do YOU think? Or should I ask: WHO do you think? CT was putting the ball back in her court.

Okay, enough of this. She might as well cut to the chase. *Meet today in Jerusalem?*

The seconds ticked away while she waited, thinking that maybe she moved too fast and should've played along a little while longer. *I've blown it*, she thought.

But then... pay dirt! *Jonah's Café 5 p.m. No interview. No camera crew. Just you. I'll be at an outside table. I'll wave you over.*

He had the advantage of knowing what she looked like since she was semi-famous. She wondered if she was doing the right thing, meeting this person, this total stranger. But she reasoned it will be in public so it should be safe enough. Hopefully this Jonah's Café will be crowded. She quickly replied with a thumbs-up icon before she lost her nerve. A thought came from nowhere and flittered through her mind. *Maybe I should wear my new dress! Get my money's worth. Afterall, this is almost like a date. A blind date.* She laughed out loud in a morbid sort of way. She couldn't help herself. Then realized it was time to get the boys together. Another mission was afoot. Hopefully it would be a successful one this time.

***

Rachel was in luck. Jonah's Café was in a well-traveled area of Old Jerusalem. The café façade was constructed with Jerusalem stone as most of the buildings in the area were. It had a very spacious outdoor area with dozens of tables set on a deep sidewalk surrounded by a low fence designed to control foot traffic. It was the first Sunday after the terrorist attacks and there was quite a crowd as people finally started to feel safe enough to venture out. The Israeli military was present which added to the feeling of security. Soldiers patrolled the area with a watchful eye while sporting automatic guns.

A taxi rolled up to the curb and Rachel stepped out. The thought of wearing her new dress was not a serious one and she opted for jeans and an unassuming blouse which allowed her to blend in easily with the crowd. That's exactly what she wanted, to not be noticed. She carried her clutch; the same one she took to Lucius Voland's palace; the one with the camera sewn into it. CT knew what she looked like and she assumed he'd be looking for her. She was not disappointed.

As she scanned the crowd seated at small round tables beneath umbrellas, she caught an arm pumping back and forth, side to side. It was a man waving to her. He was thin, small and bald. She guessed him to be in his sixties. He wore an old suit, possibly decades out of date, and thick round glasses, also way out of date. He appeared to be a guy who didn't care a wit about fashion, or didn't get out much, or both. He was staring her right in the eyes as he waved. She returned a subtle nod and a small wave, and he lowered his arm.

Rachel began her trek toward him. She could smell the aroma of the delicious coffee and baked goods as she got closer to the building.

"You have me?" she asked softly, barely moving her lips. She was starting to feel comfortable with this spy game approach to investigative journalism. Many tabloid television shows used this approach, so why not her.

"Yep. Picture and audio are good," Abe came back in her hidden earpiece.

"Great," she whispered.

Abe and Rick were in a van about two blocks away. She imagined they were huddled around the monitor, both with headphones, enjoying the show. Unlike crashing Voland's party, they all felt very relaxed doing this. Being at the café wouldn't be trespassing and whoever CT was, he certainly wasn't one of the wealthiest people on the planet, like Lucius Voland. This was a cakewalk compared to infiltrating the palace.

Rachel made her way to CT's table and saw he was drinking what looked to be an iced tea. She stood on the opposite side of the table.

"CT, I presume."

He gave her a small smile and nod as he motioned for her to sit in the only other chair at the table, which was across from him.

She sat and plopped her purse on the table with the corner containing the camera pointed right at him. The move was so smooth and casual that one would have to be a professional spy to know she did that intentionally.

Rachel glanced around, and although she was far from being a spy herself, her journalism experience brought with it some of the same skills. She noticed a man standing not too far away, leaning against the wall of the café, looking at his phone, another sitting alone at a table pretending to read a book, a third looking at a tablet, and a fourth at a magazine. They were all looking in her general direction. She wondered if they could be private investigators, or maybe police investigators. Possibly Israeli Intelligence. Whoever they were, the old-fashioned term Gumshoe would apply. But the bigger question was: were these guys spying on CT? Or were they working for him? Maybe this was as dangerous as infiltrating Voland's palace.

She noticed that CT peeked at his watch. It was a subtle move, meant to go unnoticed but it didn't work.

"Would you like something to drink?"

"I'm fine, thank you."

They were like a nervous couple on a blind date. She remembered laughing about that exact thought back in her hotel room and smiled inside.

"What do I call you? CT or –?"

"Carl Thompson."

She was disappointed, expecting his initials to be a special code for something. He could see it on her face.

"That's my real name. The initials meant nothing more. Sorry."

"No problem. My mistake."

He took a sip of his tea. "You know," he began, while he swirled the tea with his straw, "reading too much into things can get you into trouble. It did me."

She gave him a quizzical look and waited for him to continue. She knew he would or why else would they be here.

"I was a Biblical scholar at a university. The name of the institution is unimportant. But they expected me to toe the line. And I did. For a while."

Rachel put her elbows on the table, steepled her fingers, and leaned forward. "Explain."

He took another sip of tea and checked his watch again. "Are you familiar with Saul of Tarsus from the New Testament?"

"Been a long time since Sunday school." She grew impatient but didn't want to let on. He seemed like one of these people that went around the whole block just to cross the street. She decided she could indulge him for a while.

"After Jesus's death, Saul persecuted His early followers. Then, on the road to Damascus, Jesus appeared as a bright light which left Saul blind for three days. When he regained his sight, he became Paul the Apostle, preaching that Jesus was the Son of God."

Rachel furrowed her brow. "What does that have to do with anything?" The question had a bite to it, more than she intended, and she immediately regretted it.

But Carl didn't seem to mind. If he did, he didn't show it. "Because I had a similar experience. And it opened my mind." He glanced away, letting that sink in for a moment. Then he returned his gaze to her. "Are you familiar with John of Patmos?"

"Is this a religious test? If so, I must tell you I'm not running for office, so..."

Though she clearly meant it in jest, there was an underlining trace of sarcasm that would be hard to miss. Carl gave her a small grin; he appreciated the humor. *He probably told long, rambling stories to his students back when he taught at the university, and got used to sarcastic, bored students,* she thought. *So, my biting comments mean nothing to him.*

He ignored her question, and her comment, and continued. "John authored the Book of Revelation. That's the last book of the Bible."

"I've seen enough apocalyptic movies to know that."

"John had divinely inspired visions, the meaning of which scholars have debated for centuries. But I've figured it all out."

"Oh, really? What makes you think so?" *Yep, old Carl Thompson is crazy. Or to be more specific, he suffers from Narcissistic Personality Disorder. But I'm not a psychiatrist so I wouldn't really know. But I gotta be close. What else would explain the 'everybody's wrong but me' scenario? What a waste of time this has turned out to be.*

"Because what I experienced left me with a gift. John wrote the book from these visions. And I decipher the book the same way."

Rachel decided to just go for it and let the cards fall as they may. "Maybe you're just crazy."

"Possibly. But then again, I knew the date of the Jerusalem attacks."

Rachel's features hardened. She wasn't going to play this game with him. Didn't have the time anymore, needed to get on with the real investigation. "Maybe you're part of those responsible. Much easier to believe than what you're selling."

"How do you explain the YouTube video I posted?"

A laugh slipped out of her uncontrollably. It was loud enough that it drew attention from the nearby tables. And for a moment, she could tell Carl was annoyed. Maybe even downright angry.

"Really? Trying to convince me with something that a teenager could make with a computer program?

He gave her a very stern look, but only for a moment. With his eyes softening, he blinked slowly as a sheepish grin crawled across his face. For the first time since she arrived, Rachel knew he was way ahead of her, like a chess master who had planned so many moves in advance, the pattern was impossible to discern.

"There's a huge crowd of witnesses that would disagree."

He had her there, but she wasn't ready to relinquish her views. "Mass hallucination," she said flippantly, realizing it sounded ridiculous. Mass hallucination as an explanation always sounded ridiculous.

"Really? And you're the one mocking me."

"Okay, fine, I can't quite explain it. But I once saw a UFO when I was fifteen. Daylight disc that was as clear as can be. It's stuck with me my whole life, but I'm still not ready to run off and join a saucer cult."

"Not asking you to."

"What are you asking me to do." She was ready for some coffee and glanced around to see if a waitress was serving the customers.

Carl sipped his tea and gathered his thoughts. Looking her in the eyes, he sighed and began. "It's the End-Times, Ms. Williams. I want you to do what you do best. Report on it."

"Why me?" she asked, amused.

"Because you're a renowned news personality." She couldn't deny she was flattered by the sentiment. Daniel Murray would have been unmoved. He received adulation from a higher class of people than Carl Thompson. In fact, he would've just been embarrassed by Carl.

"Thanks, but I'm going to need more than that."

"Okay. Because you're a non-believer your word will carry more weight. Like Saul of Tarsus, aka, Paul the Apostle. Besides, no turning back now. Just like Moses's radiant face after seeing the Lord."

She scrunched her nose and cocked her head to the side. "I don't even know what that means."

He chuckled as he reached down, lifted a briefcase, and set it on the table. He popped it open, retrieved a worn Bible, and held it out to her.

"Everything you need is in here," he said.

She glanced at it but made no move to take it.

"I can get one of those anywhere. Got one in my hotel room right now, courtesy of the Gideon family."

He gently waved it at her. "Not like this one." The leather cover was worn from wear.

She reluctantly took it from him. Flipping through it, she saw it was filled with hand-written notes in another language, which, having spent so much time in Israel, she recognized as Hebrew. Most of the notes were in the Book of Revelation.

"I can't take this, it's your personal Bible. Besides, your notes are in Hebrew and I can't read that."

She handed it back to him, but, just as she did to him, he wouldn't take it. He checked his watch instead.

"You need to be somewhere?"

"No. But you should go. We're being watched."

"Oh, you saw the guys who are pretending to be minding their own business too?" she asked, sarcastically.

"Yeah. Of course." He leaned in and lowered his voice. "But I wasn't referring to them."

She also leaned in. "Now you're just being paranoid, Carl," she said in a low voice with a smile.

"No. I'm not." His tone was so dead serious a chill ran down her spine. "Now go," he added with an authoritative firmness that couldn't be ignored.

He might be crazy but maybe I should listen to him now, she thought.

"Okay, Carl. Fine." She stood and stuffed the Bible in her purse, careful to keep the camera-end pointed at him. His eyes briefly wandered to that corner of her purse and he gave it a quick smirk. *Whoa! Does he know? But that would be impossible! Right?*

"I'll be in touch," she said as calmly as possible; she wanted to draw his attention back to her. She waited for his response, but he just silently smiled at her. She suddenly felt very uncomfortable, so she nodded to him and walked away. She never did get any coffee.

She passed through the gate and strode toward the curb. "You get all of that?" she whispered.

"Yeah," Abe came back in her ear. "Nut job. I'll pick you up at the end of the block."

"Okay." The hair on her neck stood up, and she reconsidered that maybe she was being watched by someone.

By walking as far as Abe requested, she would be out of sight of the café, which would put her out of Carl's visual range. That way he wouldn't suspect anything. However, Carl seemed to be of the paranoid variety so he most likely always suspected something. Rachel thought Abe was right. Carl was indeed a conspiracy theorist religious nut.

When Rachel reached the sidewalk, she dug Carl's Bible from her purse and casually paged to the Book of Revelation, and randomly stopped on a page. A verse jumped out at her: *The second angel poured out his bowl on the sea and it turned into blood...* She skipped further down the page and continued reading to herself: *and every living thing in the sea died.* She slammed the book shut and dropped it back into her clutch.

Rachel turned completely around and looked back at Carl. She wanted to make sure the camera in her clutch was aimed at him for one last video image. At least until they met again, *if* they met again.

"Wave to Carl, boys," she said softly, without moving her lips. She heard them laugh.

She gave him a little wave, more to justify why she turned around than for anything else. He returned it. But there was something odd in his demeanor. There was a sad sense of melancholy in his wave. As if they were a couple breaking up, or he was a person with a terminal illness saying goodbye for the last time. She noticed a longing in his eyes, of things unsaid. A desire to tell her more, if only there had been more time.

She thought it odd indeed.

Then the outdoor café exploded into a ball of fire.

Jack Snyder, Pamela Cosel, Syed Nadim Rizvi

CHAPTER SEVEN – SURVIVING
A BOMB

RACHEL WATCHED THE DUST AND DEBRIS as it came down from the overcast sky above her. Sounds were distant and dull with a persistent, muffled and annoying ring that ran beneath it. There was something cold and hard against her back. A slab of concrete. She realized she was sprawled on the sidewalk.

Her mind raced to try and figure out what just happened. She remembered looking at Carl. Then there was a flash of light behind him – so bright she still saw the afterimage of it – then the ear-shattering concussive blast, followed by a powerful gust of wind and wave of heat.

Everything after that was a jumbled mess in her mind. Rachel planted the heels of her palms on the sidewalk and tried to push herself to a sitting position. Sharp pain from her right palm stopped her and she fell onto her back. She looked at her palm and saw shards of glass dug into it. Blood streamed from the wounds. Rachel listed her head to the side and saw people stumbling about, dazed and bloody. Some were screaming but the sounds were still muted. Bodies laid everywhere, twisted and broken. Some writhed and moaned, but most were motionless. Amongst them were customers, Israeli soldiers, and a few of the men she thought of as Gumshoes. Flames licked up the front of the café. Distant sirens grew louder with each passing second.

The thought occurred to her that Carl Thompson must be dead. If the blast did this to her, all the way out to where the sidewalk met the street, then he must've been blown to pieces. *And with that look on his face just before the blast – he knew it was coming!*

A big, white rectangle came into view in her peripheral vision. It was a van. Moving fast. Screeching to a stop. The side door rolled open and two men hopped out. From her angle they were upside down. One had a small frame, olive skin, and a beard. The other was tall and lanky. Abe and Rick. They grab her under her arms and legs and pick her up. She makes fists and notices her hands are empty.

"My purse!" She looked left to right, not seeing it.

They hoisted her into the van and set her on the floor. The sirens of the approaching emergency vehicles were deafening.

"My purse!"

Rick disappeared as Abe's face filled her view.

"We're going to get you to the hospital," he said.

"No, no, I'll be fine. I just need my purse."

"That's crazy talk."

Rick appeared at the edge of her view, holding her purse. He handed it to Abe, then he clambered behind the wheel of the van and sped away. Her right hand, the bloody one, felt the air for her purse, and Abe placed it in her hand.

"Carl blew himself up," Abe said.

"I don't think so." Rachel didn't feel Carl would do that, though she couldn't explain her thoughts.

"What do you know? Your bell's been rung."

She fumbled with opening her purse with the coordination of someone three sheets to the wind. Her fingers finally got it open, and she pulled out Carl's Bible. She squeezed Abe's hand around it.

"Hide it. Keep it safe."

He was conflicted, didn't want it, didn't know what to say, but took it, nonetheless.

Rachel could barely see Abe as he scrounged around the van. He briefly disappeared, came back with an empty backpack. He bunched it up and placed it behind her head. The makeshift pillow wasn't very comfortable, but she appreciated the effort anyway.

She felt herself fading and gladly gave into it. Her last thought was hoping she could be gone for a while. She needed the break.

***

Rachel comfortably floated in blackness and silence. A distant rhythmic sound drew her attention. Hard to tell where it was coming from. The sound became sharper and louder.

Beep – beep – beep.

The blackness gave way to a crack of brightness.

Her eyes fluttered open. She was in a hospital bed with wires and tubes criss-crossing everywhere, connecting various parts of her body to machines and bags of fluid. She and the machines were one.

It was hard to focus, and everything too bright. A rectangle high in the corner flickered colorful images. A television. Muted. Two men in dark suits stood at the foot of the bed. Their edges were fuzzy; they were ghosts with ties. She blinked and they sharpened up. Two mouths – just slivers actually – floated beneath beady eyes.

One of the mouths spoke. "Ms. Williams. We're with Israeli Intelligence." A badge was held up for her to view, but it was just light glistening off a piece of metal. He could have held up a belt buckle for all she knew. "Where is the Bible Carl Thompson gave to you?"

She blinked again, her bearings slowly moving back together. "Is he all right?"

"He's dead. Along with a dozen other people. The Bible. Where is it?" There was a trace of impatience in the voice.

"Didn't I have it with me when you brought me in?" It was an honest question. She didn't remember much. Flashes of Abe and Rick.

Then she remembered the Bible being pressed into Abe's hand. No reason to tell these guys.

"You were brought in by…," he checked a small pad, "Abidya Goldman."

"Abe," she cracked a painful smile. Good 'ole Abe. Her friend.

"He didn't have it." The man's voice was stern.

"Have what?" Now she was just messing with him.

"The Bible," he said in hurried, slightly raised voice.

"Then it must have been lost in the explosion."

The two agents exchanged skeptical glances. Even in her current state, she clearly caught their expressions. They didn't believe her. Time to play investigative journalist now, right from her hospital bed.

"Why do you want it? It's just a Bible."

The second guy finally spoke up. "It's a security matter. Why did you meet Carl?"

Rachel thought these guys were like twins. They certainly dressed alike, and sort of looked alike, and definitely thought alike. She didn't have any idea what drugs the hospital had her on, so as far as she knew, there might only be one guy standing before her, and her mind split him into two.

But she answered his question. In her way. "I was interviewing him for a puff piece... on religious faith." She thought that sounded credible. After all, she was a journalist and Carl was a religious scholar. Emphasis on was. And these two guys were in the Intelligence business, so they would know that too.

They exchanged glances again and it was obvious to her they no more believed that answer than they did the one about the Bible being lost in the explosion. As much as she hated to admit it, these guys were pretty darned good at their job. It was also obvious there was not much they could do about it. At this time anyway.

"Okay, Ms. Williams. We have no further questions," one of the them said. She wasn't sure which one spoke since they sounded alike too. They turned and marched out single file into the hallway.

The room was still except for the flickering of the television. She squinted at it and saw footage of the blown-up café with a female news reporter standing in front of it. Rachel fished around through the wires and tubes draped over her and on the bed until she found the box with all the buttons. She could call the nurse from it or work the television. Her thumb depressed the volume button and the audio came up.

"... identified the suicide bomber as Carl Thompson," the reporter said.

"Nonsense," Rachel said, though she only intended to think it.

The image switched to a news anchor's desk where a man with jet black hair sat staring out at her.

"Thank you, Monica," he said as a window appeared over his right shoulder showing a sunny beach clogged with dead fish for as far as one could see. Bathers walked about, gawking at them. "Thousands of dead fish have washed up on Whitehaven Beach in Australia. Authorities don't know the cause."

The sandy beach image filled the television screen where a young twenty-something female bather in a skimpy bikini was being interviewed. *Of course,* Rachel thought, *they always go for the female eye-candy. It's as if the program directors don't realize women watch too.*

"It was the strangest thing I ever saw," she began as she thoughtfully looked out to sea. "The ocean appeared to turn blood red for a short time, then cleared up. Probably just a reflection of some sort, but it sure was weird."

Rachel muted the television and laid her back on her pillow. She thought back to the moments just before the café bomb exploded. She was paging through Carl's Bible, specifically the Book of Revelation, when she stopped on a verse. It was about an angel pouring out a bowl of...something...and turning the sea blood red, which killed everything in the sea. Well, she knew everything couldn't be dead; that would have been a bigger story than thousands of dead fish washing up on a beach in Australia. Still, very weird.

Rachel took a couple of deep breaths and closed her eyes. *What happened to Abe and Rick,* she thought? Then sleep reached up and grabbed her, pulling her into its depths.

***

Rachel hurried down the busy and crowded New York City sidewalk. She was exhilarated to be back in the states, in a town that felt like home to her. Daniel Murray set up an early meeting to debrief her on everything that went down in Israel. Rumors buzzed around the office that she was to even get her own show. A seat behind the Anchor's desk. Finally. She earned it and deserved it.

She thought back to her time in Jerusalem. The terrorist attacks. And the café explosion. Wow. Craziness. How long has she been back now? Just a few days? No... it's been weeks. Right? Or has it been months?

Stopping dead in her tracks, she realized she couldn't remember how long she'd been back. In fact, she didn't recognize any of the buildings. Actually, she did. But they were laid out wrong. The landmarks made no sense. The Statue of Liberty stood in Times Square. She couldn't gather her bearings, had no idea where the News World offices were.

The white van screeched up to the curb with Abe behind the wheel. He grinned at her. The side door slid open and Rick poked his head out. For some reason, his camera was on his shoulder.

"Hurry up, Rachel," he shouted. "You're going to miss the meeting."

She tried to take a step toward the van but couldn't move. Abe and Rick shrugged at her at the same time and the van sped away. She looked down and saw that she didn't have any shoes on. Her bare feet were suddenly very hot on the pavement. She looked up into the blindingly bright sun, but she didn't have to squint against it, nor did it hurt her eyes.

There was something else in the sky near the sun. It was bowl-shaped.

I saw a UFO when I was fifteen and it was forever burned into my mind.

The bowl hovered above the sun. No, not hovered. It had two wings. No, not wings, they were hands. Giant hands tilted the bowl and a liquid poured onto the sun. It got brighter. Way too bright for her to look at it now.

She grimaced in great pain as her feet boiled in the increasing heat. She looked down as her toes blistered on the sidewalk. The smell of burnt flesh wafted up to her. She covered her mouth and nose and looked away.

Charred human bodies sizzled on the streets and sidewalks all the way to the horizon.

***

Beep – beep – beep.

Rachel jerked awake. She was still in the Jerusalem hospital beneath a blanket of tubes and wires. Considering her dream – or was it a nightmare – her disappointment quickly gave way to relief.

Rick sat in a chair near her bed, his elbows propped on the chair's arms, his fingers steepled before his closed eyes. She surmised he was praying. She'd worked with him for some time now but had never seen him like this before. *Is this another dream?*

"Rick!"

His eyes snapped open and he quickly lowered his palms as if embarrassed. "Sorry, didn't mean to startle you," he said.

She laughed weakly. "You didn't startle me, but it looks like I startled you."

He solemnly shook his head no.

"Didn't know you were the praying type."

"I keep my beliefs to myself. Jesus said to pray in private."

She threw him a surprised grin. "Didn't know you were a Jesus freak either."

"I'm a believer. Don't know if 'freak' applies."

"I didn't mean to offend you. Just making a little joke. A bad one apparently." She pulled the covers up closer to her chin, feeling the chill of the hospital room.

"I'm not offended." His smile was genuine.

She relaxed and scooched herself backwards into a sitting position as best she could with the wires and tubes. From her new position she could look out the window. She guessed she was on the third or fourth floor of the building. She couldn't see much of the city from here but what she did see looked tranquil enough. Unless one already knew, nothing she saw would indicate the city had suffered four terrorist attacks in the past week or so.

She looked herself over. One IV line in her left arm and several monitoring machines. Simple enough but she didn't like the feeling of confinement.

"How long have I been here?

"A couple days. Rick ran his hands through his hair, tired but happy that she was awake.

"Anything happening in the world I should know about?"

"Nothing like another terrorist attack or anything, if that's what you mean." He shot her a quick smile.

She thought a moment, then made a decision. Facing Rick, she looked him sternly in the eyes. "I need to get out of here. Got things to do."

"What?" Just the thought of it panicked Rick.

Rachel labored to the side of the bed and dropped her feet to the floor, careful not to dislodge the tubes in her arm. She straightened her back and took a deep breath. No pain. Well, not much anyway. Mostly soreness. The kind one gets a few days after an overly ambitious workout where you know you overdid it.

"Find a wheelchair," she was polite but stern in her request.

"Probably not a good idea. I should get the nurse."

He was stalling and she wasn't going to have any of it. She stared daggers at him. "Are you going to help me get out of here or not?"

"I... I..."

"Please...go get a wheelchair," she commanded.

He tried to resist but, in the end, he did what she demanded. As he always did. She was the boss, he was the grunt. That was the pecking order from the moment they started working together. While he went in search of a wheelchair, she called Abe from his phone. Didn't want to use her own for fear that the Israeli Intelligence Twins might be listening in. She told Abe to meet them out in front of the building with the van. Rick returned with a wheelchair he'd found abandoned by the elevator. He was covered in nervous sweat, which Rachel found endlessly amusing. Together they figured out how to set the monitors to silence so they wouldn't be heard after she disconnected all the wires. Sure, the nursing staff would discover her missing shortly after escaping but, with a little bit of luck, they should be gone by then.

With the equipment silenced and the wires disconnected, the last thing Rachel needed to do was pull the IV. Rick stood by with a dry washcloth from her bathroom, ready to hand it to her so she could apply it to the IV site after she removed the needle. In case she bled.

"Be sure to grab my clothes in the bag on that chair – I'll change in the van."

With that accomplished, Rick rolled her into the hallway in the wheelchair and they headed for the elevator. She still wore the hospital gown and hoped the nurses thought they were just going for a stroll around the wing.

"We're going to get in so much trouble," Rick moaned.

"Shut up and live a little." Though her clothes were dirty from the blast, she needed to get out of the hospital gown once out of the hospital.

The trip to the patient pick-up location in front of the hospital was uneventful, for which they – Rachel and Rick – were both thankful.

The always reliable Abe waited for them in the white van. He opened the vehicle's passenger door and he and Rick helped Rachel into the passenger seat. She groaned as she got herself situated. She didn't feel great, but all things considered, she didn't feel too bad either.

They left the wheelchair on the sidewalk in front of the hospital, something Rick felt bad about doing, and they drove off the lot. Rick looked out the van's back window as Abe and Rachel scanned the side-view mirrors. They were looking for any signs of pursuit. Hospital security, police, Israeli Intelligence, anybody. But no one was after them. When they got a good mile from the hospital, they relaxed. She was able to pull on her jeans beneath the gown, and turning her back to the men, her tattered shirt.

"Covert operation successful," Abe laughed. "I love it!"

He dug Carl's Bible from a hidden compartment near the driver's seat and handed it to Rachel.

"Thanks for not giving it to Israeli Intelligence."

He shrugged. "The questioning got pretty intense, just short of physical, but it was all right. Hope it was worth it though."

"Yeah, me too."

They drove back to their hotel in silence, each with their own thoughts. Rachel pondered the Book of Revelation verse about the angel pouring a bowl of blood red liquid into the ocean, and then seeing the news report on the thousands of dead fish washed onto the beach in Australia. Her mind moved from there to her nightmare of the charred bodies in New York after a bowl of liquid was poured onto the sun.

Was that just a dream? Or was it something else?

She relaxed against the headrest and starred into the sky, alone with her troubled thoughts.

CHAPTER EIGHT – THE BOOK
OF REVELATIONS

RACHEL RELAXED ON THE COUCH in Abe's room as he viewed the footage of her and Carl at Jonah's Café. He had postponed looking at it until she was out of the hospital. That wasn't the only reason, however. After his grilling by Israeli Intelligence, he wanted to keep a low profile, so he went about his normal routine for News World. Though he didn't really think he was being watched, he found no reason to risk doing something that would draw their attention. That included visiting Rachel in the hospital. He dropped in on her once with Rick while she was sleeping. They sat in the room for about a half-hour making small tall, then left. Rick visited a few more times alone. He was like a lost puppy without Rachel.

Right now, Rick was in his own hotel room. As much as he liked hanging out with Rachel and Abe, he liked his alone time.

Rachel nursed a bottle of water. She usually had a glass of red wine in her hand at this time, but she thought she'd give it a couple more days before she would do that, having been just "released" from the hospital. There really didn't seem to be anything wrong with her. The explosion rattled her teeth, for sure, but there didn't appear to be any real injury. Being at the far edge of the blast radius, she was one of the lucky ones. If there were any lucky ones. She viewed it the same as being in a car accident that leaves one with some muscle strain. Painful, no doubt, but anti-inflammatories and physical therapy usually fixed a person right up. Not always, but she was darned resilient. At least that's what she kept telling herself.

"Look at this," Abe said from his patched-together editing suite.

She walked slowly to him with her bottle of water and peered over his shoulder at the main monitor. It showed a frozen image of Carl Thompson sitting at the table looking slightly above the camera. Carl was about thirty feet from the camera. As usual, all of Abe's other monitors where filled with moving images. How he wasn't distracted by them, Rachel didn't know.

Abe hit the space bar and the footage on the main monitor played. The image bobbled closer to Carl. This must've been when Rachel first arrived. Abe paused it.

"You see it?"

"No."

He shuttled it back to the point where he had it before. He tapped the top of the screen on the monitor. "Watch here," he said as he hit the space bar again.

The footage played and she saw it this time. A man strolled past the entrance to the café and subtly set a backpack down behind a trashcan and strode on. The move was smooth and subtle; the man's stride never slowed. Just a quick dip down and the backpack he clutched was gone from his hand. Anybody watching the footage would conclude the move was meant to deceive.

Rachel rolled it around in her mind. "So, then what—?"

"I'll show you," Abe said. He was way ahead of her.

He shuttled the footage at high-speed. Once the purse hit the table, it held a steady shot of Carl. At the speed Abe shuttled the video Carl's movements were herky-jerky as he and Rachel spoke. It would've been humorous had it not ended so tragically. Abe had the volume muted to spare them both the words of a dead man. The words were there to be listened to whenever they needed or wanted, but the event was so recent it was better to get some time in between before listening to Carl again, assuming it was necessary.

The image swished off the table into indistinct blurriness.

"This is where you picked up the purse and walked away."

The footage somewhat stabilized and bobbled its way past other café customers at tables and staff serving food and drinks. A shot of the street followed that. Then another vertigo-inducing swish which settled on a shot of the café from the where the sidewalk met the street. Carl was near the center of the shot. He raised his right arm and waved a final – absolutely final – farewell.

Abe hit the space bar, pausing the image. Rachel, completely engrossed in the footage, was caught off-guard by it suddenly freezing.

"Wait! What—?"

"Just watch."

Abe advanced the footage a single frame at a time. *Click – click – click.* Carl's arm advanced a little with each wave, leaving a blurred afterimage trailing it.

"Here it comes," Abe said with anticipation as he continued advancing the frames.

Click – click – click. The next click brought a small flash from the backpack. In the one after that the flash grew to fill half the frame. The next frame was nothing but an entirely white screen.

Abe's chair creaked as he rotated around to face Rachel. "You were right. Carl wasn't a suicide bomber."

"I already knew that," she said, annoyed at ever being questioned about it.

"I'll have to give a copy of this to the police. It's evidence."

But she wasn't listening. Her mind was a thousand miles away. She walked over to the couch and sank into the cushions.

"The things he said to me. His behavior. It's like he knew it was coming."

"Maybe he did, and it was part of his plan. Suicide by proxy."

"I don't think so." She ran her fingers through her hair. "Hell, I don't know what to think anymore."

She took a big swig from her bottle of water, then stared off lost in thought. They were both quiet for a moment.

"Don't know about the Wailing Wall or the Church of the Holy Sepulchre," she began, "but many believe the destruction of the Dome of the Rock will signal the start of the End Times."

Abe crossed his arms and regarded her as one would a person who said they just saw a leprechaun. "Do you believe that?" he asked, with more than a little condescension.

She ignored his tone and continued. "I was raised in a mildly religious family for the most part. Like many families in middle America. It was intensely religious for a few years after 911, which led to discussions about the end of world back then. But when my father died, that kind of talk went with him. Haven't thought much about it since. And besides, the End Times scenario doesn't make any sense. Think about it. Wouldn't the Devil read the Bible and know how it's going to end. When you get right down to it, the whole thing is pretty darned stupid."

"Good point," Abe said with a laugh. "If you don't mind me asking... what do you believe?"

"I believe in myself," she responded without hesitation. The thought had become so rote over the years, that she never questioned it. But the look on her face showed she questioned it now. "At least I used to. Not sure anymore. What about you?"

"I was raised in an Orthodox Jewish family. Like you, I don't believe in such things anymore. But I believe there's purpose to life. And we're here to discover it. I think it's all about the searching. I definitely don't believe in the End Times."

Rachel solemnly nodded and took another swig of water. One of Abe's muted monitors grabbed her attention. It showed Daniel Murray babbling away at his News World anchor desk. Above him and off to the side a window showed a scene of smoke rising from a leveled building with the word SYRIA beneath it. *It's night here,* she thought. *So, it's early evening in New York. That footage is most likely live.*

She pointed. "Could you turn that up?"

Abe quickly did what she asked.

Daniel took what he did seriously, and it showed in his broadcasts. But today he ramped it up a couple notches. "The Great Mosque in Syria was leveled today by what the Syrian government is calling a terrorist attack from Israel. Israel released a statement denying it. Tension between the two countries continues to escalate."

Rachel and Abe exchanged nervous glances.

***

Rachel was back in her hotel room and she was a wreck. It was very late as she laid back on the bed and regretted her decision to leave the hospital. Maybe she should go back to the medical facility and lose herself in whatever drugs they were giving her. Probably morphine. She knew she didn't need it for any physical pain, she was past that, but a nice respite from everything else would do her good. She grinned at the irony of it all. While at the hospital she wanted nothing more than to get out of the place. But out here – in the real world – with café bombers and possible military attacks on Syria, she longed for the break.

Laying on her side, she looked out the window into the Jerusalem night sky. With the curtains completely drawn open, one entire side of the hotel room was nothing but a giant window. There were patches of stars here and there amidst patches of total darkness that must've been cloud cover. One thing completely missing were the Israeli military choppers from a week ago. Whether it's a missing person or a criminal, all searches are abandoned after time.

Or maybe everyone is just looking in the wrong place, she thought.

She got up with a moan and walked over to the desk, where Carl's Bible sat. She picked it up and flipped through it, stopping on a page in the Book of Revelation with a 3X5 photograph taped to it. The photograph wasn't digital, it was taken on real film. Rachel grinned at it. Though she had just met Carl and couldn't in any real way say she knew him, it didn't surprise her at all that he'd be taking photographs using an old film camera. The picture was of a tall, narrow four-sided structure, with a square base and a pyramid-shaped top – an obelisk. It was in a clearing on the top of a mountain, and although there were no people around it to give it scale, she guessed it to be about five-stories tall based on the trees nearest it.

Next to the photo was the Verse 13:4. It was circled in red ink with an arrow pointing to the photo. And a portion of Verse 13:5 was also circled with a line connecting it to the previous verse.

Rachel furrowed her brow and absently read the first verse out loud. "And they worshipped the dragon which gave power unto the beast: and they worshipped the beast, saying, who is like unto the beast? Who is able to make war with him?" She skipped down to the portion of the next verse that was circled, and continued reading. "And power was given unto him to continue for forty and two months."

Three and a half years, she thought as she stared out at the quiet cityscape beyond the window.

Rachel pried the photo loose and studied it. Nothing exceptional about it. It looked a bit like a miniature version of the Washington Monument, only darker and possibly in the middle of nowhere. But that's just a guess since she couldn't see beyond the edges of the photograph.

She flipped it over and hit pay dirt. Well, sort of. There was Hebrew writing on it, which she couldn't read. For all she knew it was Carl's special recipe for hamentash.

She set the Bible and photo on the desk and fired up her laptop. Then she pulled up Google Translate, set it for Hebrew to English, accessed the virtual Hebrew keyboard, and – after remembering the sentences in that language went right to left – she keyed the symbols in.

It read 'Abomination of Desolation, Mount Scopus, Daniel 12:11.'

She paged to that verse in Carl's Bible. Like the ones in the Book of Revelation, it was circled in red ink. She read it aloud, but at a whisper. "And from the time that the continual burnt-offering shall be taken away, and the abomination that maketh desolate set up, there shall be a thousand and two hundred and ninety days."

Rachel set the book down and pulled up her computer's calculator program. She keyed in 1290, and divided it by 365, and got 3.534 followed by more numbers.

About three and a half years again, but what does it mean?

She shook her head in frustration because this was not her area of expertise. But she knew someone who might know.

CHAPTER NINE – THE OBELISK

THE NEXT MORNING, RACHEL TEXTED Daniel Murray and let him know she was out of the hospital but remained vague on the circumstances of her "discharge." She informed him she planned on just "chilling" for a few days in her hotel room if that was alright. She figured putting it on him – in terms of asking for permission – would insure he'd approve it and then leave her alone. It was a good Chess move on her part, because if he denied her request he'd look like a monster. He approved it of course. She thought if this exchange had been a real conversation, and had not been taking place over text, she would've heard reluctance in his voice as he was granting her rest time. She obviously didn't know for sure but that certainly was Dan's style.

She signed off with her final text indicating she was tired and wanted to get some sleep. This was nonsense as she had other plans and didn't want him disturbing her with a phone call or text.

Rachel took her rental car to News World's Jerusalem affiliate and parked alongside the network's production truck. The door was locked so she knocked on it and was relieved when Rick answered. It would've been all right if Abe had answered also, but anyone else and she might have to field a dozen questions about being 'blown up' and ending up in the hospital. And her being there could make its way back to Murray which would only lead to trouble.

"Rachel!" Rick barked with wide-eyed surprise. "Mr. Murray said you weren't coming back for a few days."

"Yeah, well, let's keep my whereabouts between me and you for now."

"Okay," he said, confused. "You want to see Abe? I'll get him."

"No," Rachel said, stopping him before he could walk away. "I'm here to see you. I have an assignment that's right up your alley."

That piqued his curiosity. Usually, Rachel just told him to grab his gear and follow her. But this time she spoke to him as an equal.

***

The road to the top of Mount Scopus was treacherous and winding. Rachel clutched the wheel and kept her eyes on the road as Rick explained how the mountain was a strategically important location in ancient times for attacking Jerusalem. He told her the Twelfth Roman Legion used it as their base to carry out the final siege of the city, and ultimately for the destruction of the Jewish Temple in 70 A.D. And the Crusaders also used it as a base of operation in the 11th Century.

When Rachel had shown Rick the photo of the obelisk, she assumed the structure was on the peak of Mount Scopus, considering – as far as she could tell from the photo – it appeared to be at the top of the mountain. He informed her that Hebrew University was on the peak. He let her stew in disappointment for a moment before he added – with a knowledgeable wink – that the university was actually on one of the ridges of the mount that was rebranded as the peak for political reasons. He went on to proudly proclaim he could take her to the original peak because he knew its location. Though she was annoyed and impatient with how he boasted about his knowledge and took his good 'ole time explaining everything, she played along and let him bask in what little glory he got out of it.

Rick spent most of his life relegated to second fiddle in every work relationship he ever had – and probably personal relationships too, she surmised – so she thought it would do him some good to enjoy being on equal footing in this particular endeavor. In reality, she had few options. Unless she wanted to seek out some scholar at one of the local universities, Rick was the closest person she had to an expert when it came to the Bible and the Holy Land. And she had a gut feeling that time was of the essence. This feeling was inexplicable which unnerved her, as she usually could trace the reason for her intuitions.

Rick's knowledge was a Godsend so to speak and she was thankful for it. As close as she worked with him, this was a side of him she'd never realized existed. It did make her wonder if there were other sides to him she should be aware of. Possibly darker sides. Especially driving up the side of a mountain alone with him when her boss thought she was napping in her hotel room. She quickly put the thought out of her mind, realizing her imagination has been working overtime since her brush with death and her creepy dream. Rick was harmless, and as honest and loyal as anyone she'd ever known. Abe too. She appreciated both men and knew the three of them made a wonderful team.

Rachel spotted the top of the obelisk first. It was visible through the trees when they were about half a mile from it. It disappeared briefly as they drove through a canopy of oak trees, then it came into full view as they began a final climb up a steep road to a clearing. The rental car's engine whined in protest and Rachel worried it might give up the ghost and leave them stranded out here. If they couldn't get a cell signal, they'd be in real trouble. She sighed in relief when the road leveled off – for the most part – and the engine returned to its normal purr.

They parked near the obelisk and got out of the car. There wasn't a soul in sight. Rachel walked to the edge of the rise and peered down on Jerusalem. The view took her breath away.

"I didn't realize we'd be able to see the whole city from up here."

Rick stepped alongside her. "It's beautiful, isn't it?"

"Why isn't this a major tourist attraction," she said, glancing back at the obelisk. "Between the monument, whatever it is, and the view, you'd think vacationers would be clambering up the mountain."

"Good point," Rick said as he strolled over to the obelisk. He studied it and ran his hand across it. "Hmmm."

"What?"

"I believe this thing is brand new. At least it looks it. And it also would explain why I had never heard of it before."

She teased him. "Aren't we full of ourselves?"

"No, really. I'm no expert, but I know my way around the Holy Land. You'd think this would be fairly well known. I mean, look at it."

He stepped back to take in as much of it as he could.

"I'm just messing with you," she said with a smile. "And you're right. It looks new, which would explain why it's not crawling with tourists."

Rick walked halfway around the base, Rachel lingering behind him. He suddenly stopped dead in his tracks and faced her. "So, you think this could be the Abomination of Desolation from the Bible?"

The question was delivered so seriously she was completely caught off guard. "I have no idea. It's just a photo from Carl's Bible. And he references Mount Scopus as though it's significant, as well as circled some Biblical verses, which I've read repeatedly and can't make any sense of."

Rick wandered over to a flat boulder and sat on it. "Join the club. The meaning of the Abomination of Desolation has been debated for centuries. A more modern day... eschatological interpretation... that means study of the Last Days—"

"I know what it means. I might not know anything about the Bible, but I'm not stupid," she said with a little more bite than intended, and immediately regretted it.

"Sorry." He was a puppy dog and it made her feel even worse.

"No need to be. I'm the one who's sorry. Please, go on."

Rick nodded appreciatively and continued. "Some End Times scholars think it's a person, and some think it's a structure of some sort."

Rachel pointed at the obelisk. "I guess Carl fell into the second camp, because I believe he thought it was this."

Rick glanced around at the mixture of dirt, boulders, and trees that composed the top of the mountain.

"But this doesn't make any sense," he said.

"What do you mean?"

Rick spoke as if reciting something. "So when you see, standing in the *holy place* 'the abomination that causes desolation' spoken of through the prophet Daniel – let the reader understand, then let those who are in Judea flee to the mountains."

Rachel stared at him caught between impressed and creeped out.

"Mathew 24:15 and 16," Rick said with a shrug.

"You sure you're not a Jesus Freak?"

Rick laughed heartily which reassured Rachel that he was still the same 'ole Rick she knew and worked with. He motioned to the area with of his arm.

"But this isn't a holy place. At least as far as I know."

Rachel rolled it around in her mind for a moment, then strolled over to edge of the rise again and gazed down upon Jerusalem. "Israel is called the Holy Land. Maybe the 'holy place' referenced in the biblical verse means the entire country. And this thing," she pointed at the tall, thin obelisk, "is 'looking down' on Jerusalem. A sign of things to come perhaps? Bad things. An omen."

Now it was Rick's turn to be impressed. "That's good, Rachel."

"Being able to connect the dots is part of my profession."

"We're guessing that this thing is new, but when was it built? And by whom?"

She faced him. "I don't know; I can't really find anything on the internet about it. But this land must be in Israel's Land Registry Bureau."

***

Rachel dropped Rick off outside the News World production truck, which was still on the lot of their Israeli affiliate station. Then she began her hour-long trek to Tel Aviv where the Land Registry Bureau was located. Rick really wanted to go with her so badly he practically begged, like a child, but she insisted that if he was gone too long, someone might start inquiring about him, which could lead to her, and get them both in trouble. She was hoping to get another day at least before she'd have to take on an assignment from Dan.

If Jerusalem was a city anchored to the past, Tel Aviv was moored to the future. With its many, tall glass and steel buildings, it reminded Rachel a little of New York, making her feel more at home.

The Land Registry Bureau was a boxy and bland government building in the downtown area of the city. Rachel felt that showing up unannounced might be the best way to go. Had she called ahead they may have given her an appointment later in the week, or next week, or even later than that. She had a strong feeling she just didn't have the time, she needed to act now. She thought being there in person and announcing she was a journalist with a major international network might get a better response. Harder to turn someone away when they're standing right in front of you. Besides, oftentimes people would rather deal with people in the present moment and just get them out of their hair. And as Rachel expected, it paid off this time.

Mr. Gray was the government clerk that helped her. He was an older man, bald with glasses too big for his face, and a dark suit that hung on him as if it were draped over a skeleton. He looked like he could've been years past his retirement but just wouldn't leave. Probably just as well. Continuing to work kept many people alive. Though the office building was fairly new, Mr. Gray's office was furnished in an older style. An old oak desk filled the center of the room, and wooden shelves crammed with dusty books lined one wall. Rachel guessed that none of which have probably been opened since sometime before the millennium. Why, when you could find anything on the internet these days?

Even with his large glasses, Mr. Gray had to squint at the computer screen in his office. He didn't seem comfortable with the device. Even though he must've worked with computers for many years, it had to have been paper files and metals cabinets for decades prior to that. Some people get stuck in their ways and have difficulty with change no matter how long they're exposed to new technology.

"It's called the Selah Obelisk and it's government property, that's for sure."

"Is Selah the person it was named after?" Rachel asked.

"It doesn't say," Mr. Gray said as he scrunched his nose at the screen. "Interesting," he added.

Rachel perked up at that. "What is?"

"The construction was approved by the Prime Minister himself."

"Is that unusual?"

He glanced over the top of his glasses at her, with a look an adult might give a young child. "Of course. The PM has better things to do with his time than approve the use of government land. For something like this anyway." He looked back at the screen. "And it says here that it was paid for by a third party."

"Is that odd?" She knew that question would get her that look again but she didn't care; she needed to know.

Mr. Gray shrugged. "Not very common, but I wouldn't say it's odd. Sometimes financial donors like to keep their identity hidden for political reasons."

Rachel nodded. It seemed reasonable, but it still struck an odd cord in her. As a journalist, she often discovered that secret financial donors usually had something to hide. And more often than not the reasons weren't benign.

"Can you tell me when it was built?"

"Yes," he said, paging down on the document on his computer screen. "January 15th, three years ago."

"So, that would make the obelisk about three and a half years old?" she asked.

"Correct. July 15th will be exactly three and a half years."

Rachel's eyes subtly widened. *And the abomination that maketh desolate set up, there shall be a thousand and two hundred and ninety days.*

"Excuse me?" he said, looking over his glasses again.

She must've muttered it out loud. "Nothing. Thank you."

Rachel hurried across the parking lot hoping to get on the road before rush hour hit. It already took an hour to get here, she didn't want to grow roots on the highway stuck in traffic on her way back to Jerusalem.

"Rachel Williams?" It was a familiar man's voice. She glanced in the direction of the sound and spotted the man hurrying toward her. He looked familiar but she couldn't quite place him.

"I'm Jason... Jason Carter," he said breathlessly. "We met at—"

"Lucius Voland's party," she said as she realized who he was.

"That's right, my employer's party. The one that you crashed," he said with a grin.

She laughed. "Does everybody know that?"

He grinned ear to ear. "No. Only the privileged employees."

They both shared a good laugh.

"What brings you here?" he asked in a businesslike manner.

"I'm always chasing down a story. You?"

He could tell it was a dodge, but also knew that it was a common answer in her profession, so he didn't press the issue.

"Getting building permits for Mr. Voland. He's adding an addition to a hospital here in Tel Aviv. They're naming it after him."

"Nice," she nodded. "So, that's the kind of work you do for him? Run errands?"

He smiled quietly, not knowing if that was a jab, but he gave her the benefit of the doubt. "I do a little bit of everything for Lucius."

Lucius? It was Mr. Voland before. Is he really on a first-name basis with one of the wealthiest men on the planet, or is he trying to impress me?

"Kind of his right-hand man, huh?" She was messing with him, but in a fun way, which bordered on flirtatious.

Jason picked up on it and saw it as an opening. "He's got another social function coming up. Would you like to attend?"

Is he asking me out on a date, she thought? Either way, she wanted to go. Another shot at Lucius Voland and she might come away with a nice interview, whether or not it was related to what she was currently researching. And it was appearing more and more like it wasn't.

"Sure," she said as she found a business card in her purse. "Here's my cell and email."

He ran the card through his fingers before pocketing it. "All right. I'll be in touch. Good seeing you again."

"You too."

He smiled and nodded to her and strolled toward the building. She watched him for a few seconds before continuing to her car.

***

Rachel poked her head into the production truck and waited a few seconds for her eyes to adjust to the windowless interior. Too cramped and dark for her tastes, she was glad to be on-camera talent which almost always placed her in bright and open spaces. She saw Abe at the far end of the narrow center corridor with his nosed buried in equipment with glowing screens. He was completely comfortable in this environment and she was convinced he'd by quite happy – possibly exhilarated – if he could just turn this truck into a mobile home and sleep on a cot on the floor.

Rick was quietly talking shop with a few other cameramen gathered near another workstation. *A geek-fest*, she thought, and immediately felt bad. Especially since it always seemed to be the geeks that everyone else relied on. At some time or another anyway. She was there because she needed his help now. A short wave caught his attention in his peripheral vision. He glanced over and she motioned him out of the truck. Rick excused himself and followed after her. The other cameramen watched with envy. Rachel was beautiful and intelligent with a dynamic personality and he was her cameraman. In the other guys eye's they were practically married.

Outside, the parking lot was empty. It was late in the day and most of the station's employees were gone for the day. The news ran twenty-four hours, but the evening and night shifts were skeleton crews.

Rachel told Rick what he'd learned about the Mount Scopus structure – the Selah Obelisk. The name grabbed his attention and she confirmed the spelling of it for him.

"Selah is a mysterious word in the Bible," he said. "It appears dozens of times in the Bible, mostly in Psalms, and its meaning has been debated by scholars over the centuries. It usually comes at the end of the verse, such as Psalm 140:8 'Grant not, O Lord, the desires of the wicked; further not his wicked device; lest they exalt themselves. Selah.' Some scholars think it simply means 'end', like using the word 'stop' to mean the end of a sentence in telegrams back in the day."

"What do you think it means though?"

He shrugged. "I also think it means 'end.' And three-thousand years ago when the Psalms were written, maybe it just meant the end of the verse. But I think whoever commissioned the construction of the obelisk is using the word 'Selah' in its name for a different reason."

"Which is?

"End Times."

She looked down and shook her head with a light chuckle. She just wasn't ready to go there yet; it sounded too much like giving into the beliefs – and madness – of a cult.

"You laughing at me now?" Rick wasn't upset or angry. Just curious.

"No, I'm not, Rick, not at all. I'm just so out of my comfort zone I don't know what to think anymore."

"That's okay. Nothing wrong with having your world shaken. I went through it myself."

She solemnly nodded and told him about the verses circled in red in Carl's Bible that mentioned three and half years in some form or another. Rick was well aware of those for which she appreciated as it saved time. Then she mentioned that July 15, which was two weeks away, marked three and half years since the obelisk was constructed.

"Do you think that has any significance?" she asked.

"Yep," he said without hesitation.

"Well, don't keep me waiting in suspense. What does it mean?"

"The coming of the Antichrist." He said it so quickly and with such conviction, he half convinced her of the truth of it right then and there.

But she was not quite ready to give up on the universe that she came to believe she lived in. A universe devoid of purpose; at the very least, devoid of a spiritual purpose. So, she pushed back.

"How can you be so certain?" It was easier to just start with a question. Especially one that was non-offensive, one that wasn't attacking his beliefs, one that was just requesting clarity.

"I believe in it."

"That's not a very convincing answer," she said with a disappointed frown.

"Fair enough. Besides just believing in it, I did some digging on my own."

He pulled his mobile phone from his pocket. Rick was one of those that had an oversized phone, one that could barely fit in his pocket. This way he didn't have to carry his tablet everywhere, though he always had one of those nearby. Rachel guessed that right now his tablet was packed in his camera case on the truck. He could've traipsed inside and been back out in seconds, but then he might be grilled on what he and Rachel were discussing. Since Rachel just discovered his religious convictions in the last week, a stunning revelation after working with him for a few years, it would be fair to assume his camera guys had no idea. And Rick apparently liked to keep it that way.

Rick found what he was looking for on his phone. "Here's the Selah Obelisk's bigger, older brother." He showed her the image on the phone. It was the Washington Monument. One of the many standard publicity stills found online. Yeah, without a doubt, it was shaped just like it. Nonetheless, Rachel was unimpressed.

She mustered up a simple, "so?"

Rick was unflapped with her skepticism. She was learning he was quite the patient teacher.

"According to some, the Masons were involved with its construction. And there's supposedly a stone with a date inscribed on it. The stone is up high, around the five-hundred-foot mark, so it can't be seen from the ground."

She saw were this was going long before he got there. "Let me guess. July 15th, this year."

"You got it." He slid his phone back into his pocket.

She paced back and forth, letting this information sink in. She glanced at the road just off the parking lot, and at the passing cars. Most of the cars had no one other than the drivers in them. Probably people heading home from work. A few had more people and there was even the rare car with a family packed in. Going to dinner maybe, or parents dropping their kids off at relatives or friends for a play-date, so mom and dad could go to dinner.

And here she and Rick stood on a nearly empty parking lot talking about the coming of the Antichrist and the end of the world. An event that would change everything for everybody on every part of the globe. Nobody would be going to work, or home from work. There would be no more dates, or school, or anything. The term 'new normal' wouldn't nearly come close to describing the shape of life once one crossed the threshold separating 'before the end of the world' from 'after the end of the world.'

Rachel turned to Rick and rubbed her face as she spoke. "Did you already know this when we visited the obelisk?" The question came out as if asked by an exhausted lawyer at a day-long deposition of a hostile witness.

Rick's answer came out about the way one would expect from such a witness. "No. I looked into it because of the similarities of the shape between the two."

He wanted to say more but took a long pause to roll his thoughts around in his mind first. He was clearly hesitating for reasons that became apparent to Rachel when he spoke again. "Also, I'm kind of a fan of... conspiracy theories. And the Washington Monument has its fair share." He looked at Rachel to gauge her reaction. Now she knew; he was embarrassed. She found this reassuring. People who spouted crazy stuff without a shred of embarrassment had usually walked so far off the path of reality they couldn't see the path anymore. Rick was not one of those. He stood solidly on terra firma, even if he had some eccentric views.

"I love a good conspiracy theory," she told him. "I also love ghost stories. Doesn't mean I necessarily believe them, but I'm a fan. You have nothing to be ashamed of. So, you mentioned the Masons. What do they have to do with the Washington Monument?"

He visibly relaxed, glad to see she was onboard with at least hearing him out. "Some say the Masons put the date on the stone because they're Satanic. Others say they're divinely inspired and God gave them advance knowledge of the Antichrist's arrival."

She digested all of this or tried to anyway. Still, everything they'd discussed – the Biblical reference to the name of the obelisk on Mount Scopus, a stone in the Washington Monument that, allegedly, had a date inscribed on it that corresponded to the three-and-a-half-year anniversary of the construction of said obelisk – was all conjecture. Nothing solid. Granted, the July 15 date was enough to make one pause, but it could still be nothing more than a colossal coincidence.

Since Rick was so knowledgeable on this topic, however much a waste of time it might turn out to be, Rachel decided to ask him a pointed question. Put him right on the spot.

"Who do you think the Antichrist is?"

"I have no idea," came his immediate response. "Nobody does."

"Yet, you believe the Antichrist will come without a doubt on July 15th?"

"Absolutely. I read about that date on the Washington Monument before you told me about it regarding the Selah Obelisk. So, I'm convinced."

She pressed him, not satisfied with his answer. "I get that, Rick, I really do. I'm not religious but I know that it is a common response that nobody knows who the Antichrist is—"

"Right."

"– but... if he's right at the doorstep, which he would be if he's arriving in a couple weeks, then there would have to be some pretty convincing candidates for the position."

"I would agree with that."

"So, do you have any candidates in mind?" she asked, exasperated.

"I told you no," he laughed.

"Okay. Follow me."

She led him across the parking lot to her rental car. They walked in silence. She tabbed the door locks and removed her laptop case from the backseat. Pulling the laptop out, she set it on the hood of the car and fired it up. When it was up and running, she used her phone as a Wi-Fi hotspot and got an internet connection. She Googled for videos of Israeli Prime Minister Rubin Gellman. As they came up, she thought about the last time she saw him and spoke to him, which would've been during the signing of the Peace Accord and on the grounds of the Dome of The Rock. It had been only a little over a week since that fateful day, but considering how much had gone down since then, it felt much longer. She couldn't hardly wrap her brain around the fact that since the accord signing, she'd witnessed three terrorist explosions and been nearly at ground zero for a fourth one, barely surviving it.

She pulled up a video of Rubin Gellman speaking before a group of Orthodox Jews. As usual, he wore a crisp, expensive suit and had perfect hair and teeth. "I always do extensive research on a subject before interviewing them," she said. "Check this out."

She hit the space bar and the PM started immediately speaking as the video jumped into motion. "Achieving peace is my highest goal. As it says in the Torah, 'And they shall beat their swords into plowshares, and their spears into pruning hooks; nation shall not lift up sword against nation, neither shall they learn war anymore.'"

She stopped the video and pulled up another one. It was a very recent press conference, one that took place in Parliament the day after the signing of the Peace Accord. The PM shared the stage with the President of the United States, Greg Wright.

"Watch this," she said as she hit the space bar.

"The Peace Accord will not be derailed through this hateful terrorist attack," the PM said from her laptop screen. "President Wright and our allies stand with us. We are on the brink of a new millennium of peace."

"I've seen enough," Rick chimed in, before the PM could continue.

She paused the video and eyed Rick intensely, waiting for his reaction. Rick didn't disappoint.

"'And no wonder, for Satan himself masquerades as an angel of light.' 2 Corinthians 11:14."

She busted out laughing, couldn't help herself. "Have you memorized the whole book?"

"Hardly. But any references to the End Times or Satan seems to stick with me."

"So, you think the Prime Minister is the Antichrist?" She was working hard to try to pin him down, to force him to commit to an answer one way or the other.

"I'd say he's a good candidate."

It wasn't the decisive answer she was hoping for, but maybe there was absolutely no way to know until the Antichrist was breathing right in your face. Until then, 'a good candidate' might be the only reasonable response a believer could give.

"Okay. I'm playing journalist here, so bear with me. I'm trying to gather information."

He patiently nodded, understanding.

"What about the Prime Minister makes him a good candidate?"

Rick ticked it off on his fingers as he spoke. "He's Jewish, like Jesus was. He talks about peace – which was my 'angel of light' reference. And he has a formidable military at his beck and call."

"I'm going to play Devil's advocate, pun intended. Why couldn't the Antichrist be President Wright? He's pretty chummy with the PM."

"He's a good candidate too. In fact, almost every U.S. President has had that accusation thrown at them at one time or another. What do you think?"

"Honestly, I think it all sounds crazy," she said.

Rachel absently glanced over at the production truck as cameramen and techs poured out of it. It was getting late and they were calling it a day. She was feeling the curtain of exhaustion falling over her now and wanted nothing more than to get back to her hotel room and rest before getting some dinner.

Abe was one of the technicians who came out of the truck.

"I think we need a different perspective."

Rick followed her gaze to Abe.

"Him?"

She nodded.

"I don't know, Rachel. Abe's a great guy, but he's pretty much an agnostic or atheist."

"Exactly," she said with a wide grin.

Jack Snyder, Pamela Cosel, Syed Nadim Rizvi

CHAPTER TEN – IS HE REALLY JESUS?

ABE CHOSE THE RESTAURANT FOR DINNER. He lived in Israel and knew the best places to eat, whether it was a hidden hole-in-the-wall place for lunch or an elegant place with candlelit tables where the clientele tended to dress formally. No one was ever disappointed with Abe's choices. The bill might pain their wallet, but the food always left them with a smile. The place he picked to dine with Rachel and Rick was called Tiberian Steakhouse. A popular place in Jerusalem with rooftop dining that had a great view. One usually had to make reservations a few days in advance but Abe was friends with the maître d so he got them in that evening.

The tables on the roof ran along the railing and were spaced for enough apart so as not to feel squeezed in, and to more easily enjoy a private conversation. The view was of Old Jerusalem with buildings made of Jerusalem stone and mountains rimming the horizon. Though Jerusalem stone had a range of colors, the most common favored by builders was a soft yellow. The nighttime lights scattered across the city really brought out the color and gave the city a warm, inviting feel.

Set away from the tables were a row of couches covered in pillows for one to relax after dinner and enjoy a glass of wine.

Abe sat across from Rachel and Rick at a table near the roof railing. He had a medium-well entrecote steak in front of him. What would be known as a ribeye in the States. Rachel had a grilled chicken salad and Rick opted for a burger with steak fries. Rachel picked at her meal, which was quite the contrast to Abe, who tore into his steak like a hungry wolf.

He looked from Rachel to Rick and back to Rachel as he chewed a juicy piece of steak. After following it with a sip of red wine he set down his utensils and perched his elbows on the table.

"There is a much more logical explanation for the coincidences regarding the dates," Abe said. "Maybe some wealthy religious idiot – there are plenty of those in the world – spent God knows how much money on having this Selah Obelisk built three and a half years prior to the date on the Washington Monument. All because he wants to start Armageddon."

Rick took a drink of diet soda. "If that's the case, then nothing will happen on July 15th."

"Right," Abe said with a shrug and he cut another bite-sized piece of steak. "So, there's nothing to worry about. This bonehead will slink off disappointed and hopefully just check out their stock portfolio and move onto other things."

Abe chuckled at his own joke. Rick reluctantly joins in. He doesn't want the end of the world to come but being a Christian, he feels uncomfortable with Abe's complete dismissal of the possibility. Nonetheless, if he was honest with himself, he couldn't deny the veracity of Abe's logical approach to the situation.

Rachel, on the other hand, was not amused. She regarded the two guys with a deadly serious look. It did not go unnoticed by Abe.

"What's on your mind, Rachel? Spill it."

"There's a darker side to what you're saying. A far more dangerous scenario that hasn't been considered."

Abe enjoyed another bite of steak. "And what would that be?" he asked after swallowing it.

"If someone spent who knows how many millions to try and force a prophecy to come true... a prophecy about the end of the world... how far would they go to make that happen?"

That put a damper on the conversation. She was right. The guys quieted down and considered it.

"To figure that out, we'd need to know who 'they' is," Abe said.

"Well... I know a good place to start," Rachel replied.

They looked at her curiously, but she just smiled back knowingly.

Rachel and Rick gathered in Abe's hotel room the next morning, each with steaming cups of coffee. Another mission was in the planning and, considering Rachel was nearly killed during the last one, a worrisome pall hung over the meeting.

Abe sat before his work station like a NASA engineer nervously awaiting a launch. Rachel annoyingly hovered over his right shoulder as if she were an instructor examining a student's work in her classroom.

Rick leaned against the wall in the background, looking uncomfortable in his own skin.

On the main monitor, which had everyone's attention, was the frozen image of a young Israeli woman clutching a microphone. Behind her was a massive crowd standing before a huge, ancient Catholic church. The crowd filled the distance between the woman and church and flowed around the sides of the church and down the streets as far as could be seen. It was like a flood composed of people. It was so big, in fact, that it didn't quite look real, as if it were some kind of digital effect.

"I recorded this yesterday afternoon," Abe said.

"Do you record everything?" Rachel asked.

Though the question wasn't serious, Abe's response was. "I try to. You never know when we might want to reference something for a news story we're doing."

"But it's all on the internet anyway."

"Yeah, but not at the quality I like it."

He hit the space bar and the recording played. Crowd sounds roared from Abe's audio system, but the woman's voice – she was clearly a reporter for a local station – rose above the crowd since she had a microphone.

"The crowd is estimated to be over a hundred thousand at this point. People coming from all over the world. Looking for meaning. Looking for hope. A chance to see Jesus Christ. Most believe it's an internet hoax as no one has come out of the church since Jesus's supposed arrival. But the true believers—"

Abe paused the video and swiveled his chair around to face Rachel and Rick. "That's St. Joseph's Catholic Church. It's only five kilometers from here."

"It's interesting that this... 'event'... this 'return of Jesus'... has occurred a few weeks before July 15th. Awfully convenient when you factor in our other discoveries," Rachel said.

"You think staging this return could be another part of our theoretically wealthy nutjob's attempt to bring about Armageddon?" Abe asked.

"Possibly."

"What are we going to do about it?"

Rachel just grinned mischievously. Abe knew what she had on her mind.

"Time to wire you up again?" he asked.

She nodded. Abe retrieved a black leather pouch with a small lavalier mic in it, and expertly went to work, wiring her up, as she stood with her arms spread.

Though Rick was nervous when Rachel went undercover to enter Lucius Voland's palace, and then did it again when meeting Carl Thompson, he was downright beside himself at the thought of her entering a Christian church this way. And he couldn't keep his thoughts to himself anymore.

"I don't like this," he said.

"What's the big deal?" Rachel asked. She knew if Rick was too resistant, they could do this without him, but she wouldn't feel right about it. Rick was part of their team and it would seem like something was missing without his presence in the van, alongside Abe. The reality of it was, she and Rick worked together so often, she simply felt more secure knowing he was around.

"I don't know," he said after a moment. "It just feels wrong. It's a church, a place of worship, of celebrating one's faith. This just strikes me as... blasphemous."

Rachel felt stung by that word. In and of itself, it didn't mean anything to her, but she knew how powerful the word could be for believers. And it unsettled her to think Rick would use such a strong term to describe what they were trying to do.

"We are not disrespecting the church or the faithful. We just need to know if there's a sinister element in their midst. Someone who is just using them. Wouldn't you want to know?"

He shrugged and shifted uncomfortably from his position against the wall. Whether he liked it or not, Rachel's reasoning made sense.

"If we find nothing alarming, we'll move on and leave the people alone. Deal?"

He solemnly nodded.

"Good. Then let's do this."

The crowd was even more impressive in person. Breathtaking in fact. The alleged descent of Jesus took place the previous Saturday night, the same night Rachel went to Voland's palace, and the crowd had been growing steadily since.

She stood at what sort of passed for the edge of the crowd. There were plenty of people behind her, and more showing up, so it wasn't really the edge, but the crowd was much thicker in front of her.

Rachel was dressed casually, with athletic shoes, which was good since it was long trek to get to this point. She had to walk about a mile and a half – Abe would say two point four kilometers – because the guys said if they tried to get the van closer, it would take a few hours to get back out as they worked their way through the mass of people.

"Abe, you read me?" Rachel spoke softly with hardly moving her lips. Something she was getting good at having done this a few times already.

A few miles away, Abe and Rick sat in the back of the van. They were on a parking lot with so many people around them walking toward the church, it made them feel claustrophobic. The owner of the lot charged them double because, he claimed, they were taking up two spots he could rent to cars. To add insult to injury, he doubled his prices the way people do when a huge sporting event or concert came to town. So, they essentially paid four times what they would've under normal circumstances. Rick had no reaction since he didn't want to be there anyway, but the whole thing put Abe in a foul mood. Rachel had motioned for him to relax and that she'd take care of it, which she did with one of her credit cards. Then there was the surcharge for using the credit card. Abe sarcastically commented to the man, a big round guy who didn't look like he walked much, that he should just bonk them all on the head and take their wallets like an honest criminal.

This set the mood for the whole adventure.

Abe was staring blankly at the monitor when Rachel asked if he was reading her.

"Yeah, loud and clear. Not getting much of an image though."

The view on the monitor, from the camera sewn into her clutch, was just showing a passing mass of bellies and backs.

"Something wrong with the signal?" she asked, alarmed.

"No," he chuckled. "It's just the crowd is not much to look at with your current angle."

"Gotcha," she softly laughed. "Working my way to the church entrance now."

"Great. Wake us in a couple days when you reach it."

That got a laugh out of Rick, lightening his mood.

It only took Rachel about fifteen minutes to reach the front of the church, though, from all the bumping into and squeezing around people, it felt like days. However, it gave her a chance to take in the crowd up close, and she was impressed with the cultural and religious diversity. There were the expected people who, based on the Bibles in their hands and crosses around their necks, identified as Christians. Along with them were people wearing Middle-Eastern garb because of the part of the world where this church was located. But she was surprised to see the many Muslims, Jews, Sikhs, Hindus, Buddhists, and others that had come to the church. People gathered in groups and were chatting up others from different cultures as well as religious faiths. There appeared to be no tensions between them. Just lots of laughter and joy. So, if this thing turned out to be a hoax, some kind of con, it created some unintentional interfaith harmony between very diverse people. Rachel found her views on religion softening at the sight of it.

She hiked the stone stairs to the church's entrance where she encountered an older, small man leaning against the closed church door, with the casualness of someone waiting for a bus. He was wearing a white robe with a blue stole over his left shoulder and fastened at the right side of his waist. She racked her brains to try to determine the type of clerical vestment he wore. She'd done a few interviews with clergy in the past, so she had some foundation to work with. Deacon was what she concluded. But regardless of his title, in the end, he was the gatekeeper, the person she needed to get past to enter the church.

Might as well go for the friendly approach. "Hi," she said with a nice smile and extended hand. "I'm Rachel."

He awkwardly shook her hand. It seemed to her that this was something he normally didn't do. "Hi."

He's going to make me work for this. "What's your name?"

"Eric," he answered blandly, with a trace of boredom. He's had to go through this hundreds of times in the past week.

"Eric, I'm a foreign correspondent for News World."

"No one's interested in being interviewed."

"I'm not here for that."

"What are you here for?" He asked this in such a way that she thought he was just humoring her. All week long he'd heard a million reasons from people for why they should be one of the lucky chosen ones allowed access to whatever awaited inside. In his mind she was no different.

"The same reason everyone has come here. I'm seeking answers."

"Aren't we all?"

She thought he enjoyed this more than he was letting on. What else did he have to do but lean against the door and chat with folks?

He eyed her as something brewed in his mind. Then he slowly opened one of the huge church doors like a stage magician performing a trick to maximize the effect on the audience.

Rachel eagerly stepped up to peer inside. She was surprised to see that it was packed with people. Apparently getting inside wasn't impossible – far from it – it just seemed so when one calculated the size of the crowd outside. If everyone inside was packed shoulder to shoulder, violating every fire code imaginable, it would still probably be far less than one percent of the masses filling the streets for blocks. A mass that was growing every hour.

The people in the church formed a circle around a man standing in the center. He wasn't up in the sanctuary, or near the alter, or the podium. He stood in the middle of the center aisle and had everyone's undivided attention. He was too far away for Rachel to see any details. She could see he was dressed casually, wearing what could be bought at any department store in town. And he had short dark hair and a close-cropped beard. But that was about it.

Rachel pointed at him.

"That guy's supposed to be Jesus? The Son of God? Creator of the universe?" There was more than a touch of sarcasm in her questions.

Eric didn't care. "Yep."

In the van, Abe and Rick huddled around the monitor. The view from Rachel's clutch showed some of the floor, the backs of a row of people, and a few pillars. Abe watched passively but Rick was engrossed, hoping to see more.

Abe keyed the microphone for Rachel's earpiece. "Rachel, we can't see him at all. You need to get in a better position."

Rachel casually stepped onto the doorway threshold. Eric subtly motioned for her not to go any further. As much as she wanted to get a better shot for Abe, Rachel knew Eric the Deacon was being polite and going above his duty to even show her this, so she didn't want to push her luck and risk being physically shoved out of the church.

"Am I able to get closer?"

"No. Not at this time." *Not at this time? That's a good sign. At least the answer wasn't 'never.'*

She decided on the 'keep him talking' approach. "That's a shame. Can't see much from here."

"But you can see him, though," Eric said proudly, as if Jesus – or whoever he was – was his own child.

"I don't know," Rachel shrugged. "I expected him to be more... amazing. Or something. Glowing. Floating. Lightning bolts. Something."

"So did the people two-thousand years ago."

That surprised Rachel and she couldn't help but laugh. She stood on the tips of her toes to try to get a better view.

"Still can't see him," Abe sighed in her ear. He was frustrated. Nothing she could do about it though, other than holding her clutch above her head. That move just might be enough to get her kicked out. Eric didn't seem like a dupe; he would figure out something fishy was going on.

A middle-aged, frumpy man hobbled up to Jesus – or whoever he was – on crutches. Jesus put the palm of his right hand against the man's forehead. The man spasmed as if struck by lightning. He dropped his crutches and stood there unsure what to do, like someone standing on an unstable surface. Then he gingerly stepped forward, testing his newfound ability. He took another step and the crowd applauded and cheered. The man proudly strode away with a bounce in his step.

Rachel lowered herself from her tiptoes and looked at Eric skeptically.

"So, he's healing people," she said blandly. It wasn't a question; it was an observation. One that wasn't convincing to her.

"Yes. You sound like you don't believe it though."

"I don't, sorry. I've seen video of David Copperfield disappearing the Statue of Liberty. It's going to take more than a guy dropping his crutches to impress me."

"No one's trying to impress you."

"You know what I mean. I'd like to talk to him, one on one. Not an interview, just a chat."

"That might be difficult. It's a long line."

Rachel didn't get to where she was in life by being easily dissuaded. She wasn't going to let this guy, as nice as he was, stop her from achieving her goal. She smiled and played her ace.

"I think I know who the Antichrist is."

His head snapped around to her; his eyes so wide she could see the veins in them. She gauged from his reaction that of all the reasons people gave for their need to see Jesus, hers was a first.

"Nice," Abe chuckled in her ear.

She pointed to the so-called Jesus.

"That's why he's here, right? To battle the Antichrist?" She almost used the word 'fight' instead of 'battle', but it sounded too small, too personal. A battle between two beings that had universal ramifications would have to be a 'battle' or a 'war'. Of course, she didn't believe in any of it, regardless of what her and Rick had discovered. It was just too difficult to wrap her mind around.

Eric slowly nodded. With all the healing and joy going around, and blocks of people engaged in what seemed like a never-ending hallelujah party, it appeared that most had forgotten the purpose of Jesus's return. Maybe even Eric the Deacon.

"Wait here. I'll see what I can do. It might be awhile," he said as he motioned for another Deacon to take his place.

"That's all right. I got all the time in the world."

He stared Rachel in the eyes with a seriousness that sent a chill through her. "No, you don't."

"Owww. Two points for the Deacon," Abe chuckled.

But Rachel didn't think it was funny. She just stood there, not knowing what to say, as another Deacon took Eric's place. Her eyes followed Eric as he slipped inside the church, closing the tall, heavy door behind him.

Rachel walked along the front of the church, suddenly feeling very exhausted. She briefly longed for being back in the hospital in a drug-induced stupor.

When she was a dozen feet from the door, she leaned back against the cool stones of the church front and lowered herself to a sitting position to rest.

"I never got a good shot of the man they say is Jesus. Couldn't see him at all in fact."

With the sounds from the street crowd as cover, and no one close enough to hear her, Rachel was able to respond. "No worries," she said quietly, "I'll get a good shot when I'm inside."

"If you get inside." Abe was ribbing her. It perked her up a little.

"Hey, you better hope I do! We'll all benefit from this story if it pans out to be anything."

"Yeah, you're right. Sorry."

"No problem."

She leaned back against the wall and watched the crowd. The steps to the church were steep so her vantage point was higher. The crowd went on for blocks.

It looks like it's grown in the few minutes I've been here, she thought. *How big can it get? It would have to reach critical mass at some point. Then something would have to happen. But what?*

She had an overwhelming sense that time was running out, which filled her with dread.

Rachel walked along a sandy beach barefoot as glistening, foamy water rolled up over her feet. She was all alone. Just her, the ocean, the beach, and a mountain range further inland. The temperature was perfect all around; the sun on her skin, the sand and ocean water on her feet. Just perfect.

I want to stay here forever.

She felt pressure against her shoulder. Followed by a gentle push. Very confusing. It made no sense.

"Ma'am? Ma'am?"

She blinked and the ocean disappeared, replaced by the noisy gathering surrounding the church. Eric was squatted in front of her with his hand on her shoulder.

"He'll see you now."

Apparently having dozed off, she shook off her sleep and climbed to her feet.

Rachel followed Eric into St. Joseph's Catholic Church. He led her through the massive Nave. Jesus was gone but the crowd remained. They sat quietly spread out in the pews, deep in prayer.

Rachel and Eric reached the Sanctuary but stopped before entering. Eric walked her over to a massive pillar. "Wait here."

She gladly did what he asked. Talking him into bringing her inside the church took a lot less work than she imagined. She didn't want to blow it now by asking any questions. Standing alongside the pillar she listened to him quietly converse with a man who had a deep voice. She couldn't make out what they were saying. Eric appeared a moment later and silently motioned for her to follow him. They ascended a flight of marble steps to the Sanctuary. Once they reached the top, Rachel glanced back and was awed at the sight. From here, she could see the entire church in all its glory. It was from here the priests would address the crowd.

Eric led her deeper into the Sanctuary where a priest in his forties awaited. With him was an older man wearing a dark suit and a yarmulke – a Jewish man.

Familiarity crossed the priest's face as he looked at Rachel. "I recognize you from television."

"Should I be flattered?" She wasn't being sarcastic. Considering the bad rap the media got these days, she truly didn't know.

He answered her with a grin which didn't help. But he stepped forward with an extended hand, which was reassuring.

"I'm Father Marco Rossi, and this is Rabbi Noah Sable," he said, motioning to the other man. Noah nodded at her with a friendly smile.

"So, you think you know who the Antichrist is, huh?" Noah asked.

She looked back and forth between the men, settling on the rabbi.

"I'm confused," she said. "I thought the Antichrist was a Christian concept."

Noah gave her a knowing nod as he clasped his hands. "There is a Jewish equivalent called the Armilus. The Anti-Messiah. In Islam, the Antichrist is called the Dajjal. All three religions have a common heritage."

"I suspect who the Antichrist might be. Assuming he really exists."

The priest and the rabbi exchanged glances, then Father Marco turned to Rachel. "You're not sure he's real?" he asked her.

She couldn't deny how she thought, so why bother. "Well," she began with a little smirk, "in a world of modern medicine, instant communication, and space travel, believing in such things makes one... kind of an idiot. I guess. No offense."

She immediately regretted using the word 'idiot,' and grimaced as she thought about it. But it was too late to correct it now. She'll just have to live with the consequences, even if she's blown her chance to see Jesus.

Father Marco and Rabbi Noah stared blankly at her for a moment. Then, much to her relief, they busted out laughing. Considering the heads bobbing up from the Nave to see what the commotion was about, Rachel surmised the laughter was too loud.

"None taken," Father Marco said once he'd quieted down. "It's okay to have doubt. They don't call it faith for nothing."

He sighed and sat in a straight-backed chair, which, to Rachel, appeared to be a very uncomfortable.

"I went through that myself recently as a matter of fact," he said. "No reason in particular. No life crisis, no tragedy, no depression or despair. Just joined the millions of people who've lost their faith. It put me in a more precarious position than most, being a man of the cloth and all. Afterwards, I found myself just going through the motions."

"But your faith returned?" Rachel asked with a furrowed brow.

Father Marco stood with a wisdom-filled smile and pointed upward. "Because He returned. As He said He would. To our church. To a man who'd lost his faith. Because He didn't give up on me."

Rachel solemnly nodded as she digested this information. It certainly didn't sound like a hoax. If it was, she was certain Father Marco Rossi wasn't a part of it.

"What brought you here, Rachel?" the Father asked.

"A religious scholar... who recently died... inadvertently sent me, an unbeliever, on a quest. So here I am."

Father Marco gave the rabbi a knowing look.

"We all have our particular... and personal... path," Rabbi Noah said. "The night preceding the attacks on the three sacred sites, I dreamt the Messiah was coming."

"But Jews don't believe Jesus is the Messiah." Rachel didn't want to say that, to put the rabbi on the spot, but she couldn't let the obvious observation pass by.

Rabbi Noah grinned at her with a twinkle in his eye. "God's got quite the sense of humor now, doesn't He?"

He and Father Marco laugh at his little joke. Rachel wasn't sure what to make of this odd pair. Though she couldn't help but be amused by them.

Father Marco stepped before a door and waved his arm toward it like a butler or a servant. "Jesus awaits you."

After everything Rachel had to do to get to this moment – the hidden microphone, the earpiece, the camera in her purse, the long walk through the crowd, talking Eric the Deacon into it, dealing with the priest and rabbi comedy duo – she was suddenly nervous and hesitant. If she was being completely honest with herself, she'd have to admit she was afraid.

Her hosts could see it.

"You came to see him, right?" Father Marco asked.

"Yes."

"Then why do you hesitate?"

"Nervous. Anxious." She thought honesty would be the best policy at this point. She was in a church, after all.

"I'm sure Jonah felt the same way inside the belly of a whale."

"I'm still having trouble wrapping my brain around it."

"As do we all," Father Marco agreed, giving her an expectant look.

She took a deep breath, followed by a couple nervous steps that put her directly in front of the door. It was a simple, normal, wooden door. She glanced back at the two men, then, before she had a chance to talk herself out of it, she opened the door and stepped inside.

It was a quaint, humble room with a single window from which subdued light flowed in. It took a moment for her eyes to adjust, and during that time she thought she was alone in the room. The thought terrified her, the idea that she might've been willingly led to the back of a church and locked into a room by two crazy men for some nefarious reason.

Then she saw the silhouette of a man standing in the center of the room. The darkness created one of those optical illusions you see online. Was he looking away from her or at her? He moved slightly, destroying the illusion. Now she knew he was looking at her. From what she could tell from his silhouette, he was of average height, weight, and build. Nothing exceptional. Completely average.

"Rachel," he said in a soft, soothing voice. It wasn't deep, nor high. Just an average, mid-range pitch.

"Yes," she said expectantly.

He stepped toward her into a shaft of light that seemed to originate from nowhere. Now she saw his features clearly. He had perfect skin, not so much as a tiny blemish. His slightly long hair on his head, and closely cropped beard were perfectly groomed, not so much as a single strand appeared out of place. Though he wasn't overly muscular – very average as she noted before – his physique was perfect. Any medical doctor in the world, worth their salt, would place his height and weight ratio dead center on the chart, and grant him a clean bill of health. Barring any internal issues, which, she suspected, were none.

His eyes drew hers to them like a magnetic tugging on metal. She couldn't help but look deep into them as if he were a master hypnotist. But there was no sense of manipulation or malice. All she felt was love and warmth from him, and if one's eyes were the window to their soul, his soul contained more life than seemed possible.

Her head swam with a peaceful, content feeling, and the moment took on a dreamlike quality, as if reality had become fluid.

Time seemed to slow, and the walls appeared to fall away. They both stood on seemingly nothing but a small circle of floor with a white-hot spotlight from above, in an infinite void.

"Release your angst. There is nothing to fear here," Jesus said warmly.

And indeed, her fear did dissipate, leaving nothing but a sense of peace and tranquility. She felt intoxicated and never wanted to leave this place – wherever it was – nor his side.

"What's happening? I don't understand." She was surprised at her own words. A part of her mind, the part still anchored in the world, wanted answers.

"It's not important. Trust in me and do not lean on your own understanding. I will make your path straight."

"Did you bring me here?"

"You saw and you listened," he said with deep love in his voice. "Then came of your own volition. You were lost and now you're found."

Rachel was in a state of ecstasy, filled with love for everyone. Still, questions lingered. "Are you who people say you are?"

"What do you think?"

"Why do you have to speak in riddles?" It wasn't an accusatory question from her. Nothing like that emotion could even exist here. It was asked with amusement and playfulness.

"I just fulfill the word, as I've always done."

"If you're here to stop the Antichrist, why are you waiting? People are dying."

Just the mere mention of 'Antichrist' seemed to splinter the reality they were in. Just a tiny bit, but noticeably. Any negative emotions or connotations were unwelcome here.

"Everything in its own time, Rachel. The world knows I'm here. Even those that deny it, know it in their hearts."

He's talking about me, she thought. *But he's not judging me.*

"I'm waiting for all the faithful to come," he continued. "And for the undecided to decide. The time is short indeed. But it has not run out yet."

He's read my mind. Answered my concerns and inexplicable sense that time was of the essence.

Rachel became light on her feet and Jesus reached out and steadied her. The moment his hands touched her bare arms, she spasmed from what felt like an unbelievably powerful electric-like shock. But it wasn't painful.

Rachel is pressed between hot, sweaty, and smelly bodies, shouting in a language she doesn't recognize. She's out doors, beneath an overcast sky.

Where am I? Back on the street, outside the church?

The piercing crack of a whip snapped her attention to something happening in front of the crowd. She stood on her tiptoes and glimpsed pieces of it. A man, chained to a post, and so bloodied as to be unrecognizable, was being repeatedly whipped by a large man in a leather tunic and metal helmet. *A Roman soldier?*

She tried to study the bloodied man. He was a weaker, more vulnerable version of the man at St. Joseph's Catholic Church, but she knew in her heart, they were one and the same.

She grimaced and cried out as the soldier continued to whip him. Then something unexpected happened. The whip began to glow with an eerie aura. So bright she had to squint against it. No one else in the crowd seemed to notice. Nor did the soldier. Only Rachel. She knew she was sent here specifically to see that.

Rachel was jolted again and spasmed.

Another crowd, this one on a dirt path outside a high wall made of wood and stone. More shouting in the unidentified language. Rachel was a part of it, shouting along with everyone else with no understanding of the words that came from her mouth. She snapped out of it the moment her eyes found a bloodied, pitiful man who wore a crown of thorns and drug a huge cross of wood on his back. The crowd separated, creating a gauntlet for the man to pass through.

She didn't have to see him clearly to know him. It was Jesus. Though she wasn't a Christian anymore, hadn't been since she was a young teen, she knew the stories. Almost everyone on the planet did.

As he passed her, he glanced over. Through his painful injuries, he mustered a smile and winked at her. For one second, he was the risen version she was speaking with back at the church, two-thousand-plus years in the future.

Was this just a drama being played out for her benefit, she wondered? If so, to what end?

She mercifully flashed through the next segments of the drama, though it was still hard to bear. She watched helplessly as Jesus was laid on the cross and cried out in pain as soldiers drove huge metal spikes through his wrists into the wood. She tried to turn away from the blood and screams but couldn't. She was being forced to watch, to feel it along with him. But why? He was hoisted up, the base of the cross shoved into a hole. Blood streamed down his thin, nearly naked body as he looked skyward.

"Forgive them, Father, for they know not what they do" he said in a voice that was strained, yet loud enough for her to hear him. It should've been impossible. She was dozens of feet away and amidst the crowd that continued to scream and shout. And unlike everyone else around her, he spoke in crystal clear English. She wondered, again, if all of this was for her benefit. For reasons she didn't understand.

She watched as Jesus sucked in one final breath and said, "It is done." Then he went limp and hung loosely from the cross.

A Roman soldier stepped up and jammed a spear into Jesus's side to see if he was dead. Like the whip, the spear glowed with a bright and eerie aura.

Rachel was back in the present, in the back room of the church, standing before Jesus. The room had returned to normal, assuming it ever did expand to infinity. *Maybe it was all in my mind.*

Jesus was his perfect self again. No blood, no wounds, not even a scratch.

She suddenly became aware that she'd been crying but was now all cried out. Jesus regarded her with love and compassion. He understood her pain. He understood everyone's pain.

"Don't blame yourself for what's happened in Jerusalem. You couldn't have stopped the bombings. No one could have. It was prophesied."

With his index finger, Jesus touched her on the forehead. She felt peace and tranquility flow through her, almost as if sedated.

Then a blinding white light filled her vision.

What's happening to me now?

CHAPTER ELEVEN – A DATE
PREDICTED

RACHEL STOOD ON A SIDEWALK at an intersection. Groups of people walked past her, all heading in the same direction. The crowd was much thinner than that in front of the church.

How did I get here?

She was startled by a white van that quickly whipped up in front of her and stopped. She could see Rick behind the wheel grinning in anticipation at her through the open passenger window.

"Get in," he called out.

She pulled the door open and sluggishly climbed into the passenger seat. Rick pulled away from the curb, veering around a few people that threw them dirty looks for passing too closely.

"What happened?" Rachel asked.

Rick scrunched his face and glanced in the rearview mirror at Abe, who was just as perplexed by the question.

Abe, hunched over, moved away from his monitors and other equipment and hunkered up between the two front seats.

"What do you mean what happened? You called us and said to pick you up at that intersection."

"I did?"

"Yes!" Abe and Rick exchanged worried glances. Abe looked back at Rachel. "Are you all right?"

"Yes. I feel great in fact." She looked almost drugged. Now they were really worried. She went on. "Didn't you see it and hear it all?"

"No. We lost the signal when you entered the church," Abe said disappointedly. Rick solemnly nodded confirmation. "These old buildings are so overbuilt, with unnecessarily thick walls, that it's not unusual to not be able to get a clear signal through them."

"You saw nothing?"

"That's right." He grabs her clutch and held it up. "But the trusty chip in here would've gotten everything. We'll play it when we get back."

"Good!" she said, satisfied. "What you're going to see is amazing."

When they reached their hotel, Rachel impatiently prodded Rick to hurry into the parking garage and take the first available spot. She wanted them to see the recorded footage as quickly as possible. They thought she was acting like a spoiled child and Abe purposely took his good 'ole time loading his equipment from the van into a cart. Rachel felt the ride up the elevator to the floor Abe's room was on seemed to take forever. She was antsy as she paced back and forth watching the floors pass on the digital display.

Abe and Rick thought that if she was indeed drugged when they picked her up, the effects of whatever she was dosed with had faded.

Once in Abe's hotel room, Abe expertly attached a USB cable to the hidden port in Rachel's purse to his editing equipment and fired up the main monitor.

The chaotic image of people's torsos filled the screen.

"Rachel walking through the crowd," Abe said absently.

Rick and Rachel leaned over each of Abe's shoulders to get as close a view as possible. Their heads were like three pumpkins on a windowsill. Abe shrugged in annoyance.

"Hey, you both are crowding me."

They both moved a little back and to the side.

The image on the monitor bobbled its way up the stone steps that led to the front of the church. If it was a carnival ride, the passengers would be yakking up at the very least, maybe suffering whiplash even.

Erick the Deacon came into view as the image stabilized.

"Speed past this," Rachel said as she waved an impatient finger at the screen.

Abe's fingers tap danced across the keyboard and the image shuttled forward to where Eric opened the church doors and Rachel stepped up on the threshold. He let it play at normal speed at that point. Only the backs of a row of the faithful, along with a marble pillar, could be seen.

"This is where I told you to get a better shot, because we couldn't see... you know." Abe couldn't bring himself to say Jesus. Though he was raised Jewish, he didn't believe in any religious faith, certainly not in Christianity, that being once removed from Judaism.

"Keep going," Rachel said, adding a circular motion with her finger for emphasis. She wanted to get past all of this to the good part – her conversation with the Son of God Himself.

Abe dutifully continued speeding through the footage. We see imagery of the front of the church floating past, followed by a sudden swishing to the crowd as Rachel turned and sat against the church. The footage became rock steady as Rachel dozed, loosening her grip on the clutch. Eric's feet walked up. Rachel stood and was led through the church.

Rachel unconsciously bit her lip as Abe sped through the footage of her conversation with Father Marco and Rabbi Noah. The Father waved his hand toward the door leading to the backroom. The camera moved past him and suddenly stopped on an image of the door filling the frame. Nothing was wrong with the recording. The image seemed to freeze because Rachel hesitated at that moment.

"Stop it here!" she said a little too loudly, snapping the men's heads around at her. She glanced at them self-consciously. "Sorry. Just play the footage at normal speed."

"I was going to," Abe said defensively. Then he tabbed the space bar with an exaggerated hand motion.

They watch her hand enter the right side of the frame and clutch the doorknob. She turned it and slowly pushed the door open. It creaked, which surprised her as she watched the footage; she didn't remember that.

She stepped inside. The sound of the door closing behind her can be heard from the speakers.

The room was empty.

"Where is he?" Rick asked anxiously.

"He's in the middle of the room, in the darkness."

"I don't see him."

"Neither do I," Abe chimed in.

Rachel rolled her eyes in irritation at her complaining teammates. "Neither could I at first, give it a second."

So, they waited... and waited... and waited. At least thirty seconds passed. The guys were too nervous to say anything for fear of Rachel biting their heads off.

Another thirty seconds or more. No one was keeping count, but it had to be over a minute by now. The room still appeared empty. Not so much as a whisper of a motion from anyone or anything in the room. Just the image of the room gently floating as Rachel stood there holding her clutch.

Finally, after what must've been ninety seconds the camera floats in place as it turns back to the door. Rachel's hand appeared once again and turned the knob. Rachel gasped as she watched the footage, but Rick and Abe dared not look at her; they didn't want to be on the receiving end of her wrath.

The camera moved through the Sanctuary. The Father and Rabbi were nowhere in sight. The image bobbled along the center aisle of the Nave where praying people filled the pews. The front door of the church swung open into bright sunlight. It wasn't really that bright out, it was the camera overcompensating for the darkness within the church. Down the steps and into the crowd the image on the monitor went.

They heard Rachel make a mobile phone call as she walked.

"Hey, Abe, come and pick me up. I'll be at the intersection of—"

Abe tabbed the space bar, pausing the footage.

"That's it," he said as he rotated his chair to face her. "Then we picked you up."

Rachel stepped back, stunned and pale, as if about to pass out. Rick stood ready to grab her if she fell.

"That's not what happened. I told you and Rick the story." She plopped down on the couch in confusion and despair.

Abe was flustered but kind. "The video tells a different story. Are you asking me to believe you... on faith?"

"Yes... I guess I am."

"I don't know if I can do that, Rachel, I'm sorry. I'm really... really... trying to understand what could've happened here."

"Am I losing my mind?" she asked to no one in particular as she rested her forehead in her palm.

"If you were, you probably wouldn't ask that question," Abe said.

Rachel propped her chin in her palm and regarded Abe. "So, you *do* believe me?" She clung to the morsel of hope he tossed her.

"I don't know if I'd go that far," he laughed.

"It's not funny!"

"Well, I need to have some kind of response. Either laughing or screaming in horror. And the horror-thing seems like it would be an overreaction."

Rachel laughed weakly.

Rick's cell phone chimed with an incoming text. He pulled it from his pocket and looked at the screen; a concerned look crossed his face.

"Abe... could you pull up our network stream?" Rick asked.

"Sure," Abe said as he tapped at his keyboard. "What's up?"

"I told the other guys I was on a covert operation today—"

Abe threw an amused look at him.

"Well, we were," Rick responded defensively. "Anyway, I told them to keep me apprised of any major news developments."

U. S. President Greg Wright appeared on a secondary monitor, standing before a microphone-filled podium in the Rose Garden of the White House. The News World logo swirled in the lower left corner of the screen.

"... and we stand with Prime Minister Gellman and all our Israeli friends," he said with fiery conviction.

The image changes to Daniel Murray at his News World Anchor desk. "President Wright delivered that speech earlier today following the declaration by Prime Minister Rubin Gellman that Israeli Intelligence now knows Syria – and her allies – were behind the terrorist attacks which leveled three of their Holy sites. And Syria now claims that they too have evidence that Israel was behind the attack on them which destroyed the Great Mosque in Damascus. Both sides deny this. Nevertheless, lines are being drawn as allies of both countries gather their military might—"

Click! Rick reached past Abe and paused the video stream. Abe and Rachel are perplexed as he slowly sits on the couch as if distressed.

"What's wrong, Rick?" Rachel asked, concerned.

But Rick was a million miles, deep in his own mind, as he worked to process it all. After what seemed like minutes, but was only a few seconds, Rick shifted in the couch and faced them. He looked like someone about to seriously confess a deep dark secret.

"The world is taking up sides. This was foretold in the Book of Revelation. It's called Gog and Magog, which refer to two groups of nations that war against each other. I think the destruction of the three Holy sites right here in Jerusalem was the flashpoint that started it all."

Abe rolled his eyes. "Dude... The world is always going to war. It's situation normal for the human race. Especially in this region."

Rachel disconnected her purse from Abe's equipment and opened it. The move was overly large and loud so as to distract the men from getting into a full-blown argument that could never be settled. There was a deep, wide chasm separating them. On one side were the believers, on the other stood the non-believers. Neither side would ever blink or be persuaded by argument. A change tended to only occur through some kind of deeply personal experience or crisis. And it could go either way; neither the believer nor non-believer were on any more solid ground than the other. Crossing that chasm from one side to the other, and sometimes back again, happened all the time.

The guy's watched as Rachel pulled Carl's Bible from her purse.

"Rick, do you know what chapter of Revelation the Gog Magog stuff is in, or whatever you called it?" she asked.

"Not off the top of my head, somewhere around chapter 20 I think."

She paged through the Bible, searching for the verse.

"Rachel, is this really necessary?" Abe sighed.

"Can't hurt, Abe," came her curt response, shutting him up, which was her intent.

She found what she was looking for. "It's Revelation chapter 20 as you said, Rick," she commented. "I'll read from verses 7 and 8. '... Satan shall be loosed out of his prison, And shall go out to deceive the nations which are in the four quarters of the Earth, Gog, and Magog, to gather them together to battle: the number of whom is as the sand of the sea.'"

Rachel looked up and sternly glanced from one man to the other. Rick felt vindicated, but Abe just shook his head.

"I'm really disappointed in you two," he said as he leaned back against his editing table.

Rachel ignored him as she still studied Carl's Bible. There was something scribbled in Hebrew near the verses she read. She turned the book around and held it out to Abe and tapped a finger on the writing.

"What does this say?"

Abe reluctantly took the book, more to humor his friends than anything. He didn't care what was written there. It was all nonsense as far as he was concerned anyway. He glanced at it so subtly it would've been missed by a casual viewer, if it wasn't for the fact he snapped his eyes back to it. His olive skin slightly paled.

"What?" Rachel quickly asked, reacting to his sudden and alarming movement.

He brought the book closer to his face and run his finger beneath the writing as he spoke. "It says right here that these events will begin on... today's date," he said as he looked up at them mesmerized, like an audience member called upon stage by a magician to become an unwitting assistant in amazing the crowd.

Rick leaped at the chance to shove this revelation down Abe's disbelieving throat. "How do you explain that?"

Rachel quietly motioned for Rick to dial it back a bit. But it was too late. Abe shrank in his chair as if literally deflating. "I can't," he said, defeated. They all sat in silence, not knowing where to go from here.

It was late in Jerusalem and the nightlife was in full bloom. People were either trying to forget about the developments occurring in the world at that very moment, or they were so used to periodic and explosive violence in that region of the world, that they considered it business as usual. In any event, the bars were packed with people drinking, dancing, and living it up.

Outside St. Joseph's Catholic Church, the crowd continued to grow. People arrived every hour hoping for a chance to see Jesus. At the very least, they could enjoy fellowship with other believers, many of which were from other faiths. For a crowd that formed spontaneously, it was surprisingly subdued and well-organized. People brought and shared food, and tents and sleeping bags lined the sidewalks.

Due to the rattling of sabers between Israel and Syria, the Israeli government increased patrols on the streets of Jerusalem and Tel Aviv to discourage further terrorist attacks. Unlike the days following the destruction of the three Holy sites, this was done without publicity or any kind of fanfare. The PM felt there was no reason to alarm or further traumatize the citizenry. In keeping a low profile, he ordered no patrols by military choppers.

At the Jerusalem Intercontinental Hotel, Abe's hotel room became the unofficial base of operations for Rachel and her team. It was where all the electronics were set up, and although it wasn't as spacious as her hotel room, it was large enough. Besides, Rachel wanted her own room to be a place for her to escape to for some alone time and solitude if needed.

Presently, Rachel was curled up on Abe's sofa while Abe sat in a chair reading Carl's Bible under the only light on in the room. Across the room, Rick sat on the floor only a few feet from the television as a child would, with the volume very low. He stared unblinking at Daniel Murray's latest news report which he streamed from his tablet.

"The militaries for both Israel and Syria are lined up on their mutually shared border. And their allies have naval armadas on their way to the Mediterranean Sea leading world leaders fearing a military accident could lead to a major war."

As Murray continued, his normally detached professional veneer showed signs of cracking. Usually, when some conflict was developing in some other region of the sphere everyone lived on, called the Earth, it was easy to keep a healthy, clear-headed detachment. No matter what happened, even in this age of nuclear proliferation, it was unlikely the conflict would come washing up on America's shore. And if so, it certainly wouldn't come knocking on anyone's door. Absolutely not the door to Daniel Murray's house, where he lived with a closet the size of Rachel's apartment. But his strained voice indicated the currently brewing situation might challenge that view.

Rick, on the other hand, still maintained that detachment, even though he was practically at ground zero for the conflict. He held his faith close to his heart and – at least partially – expected this End Times conflict to come in his lifetime. He knew if it happened, his faith would be tested. What he told no one though, was that he worried how he would fare when that moment came.

Abe had other things on his mind which, too, brought him worry. His entire reality had been shaken earlier in the day and those ripples continued to keep him off balance. He paged through Carl's Bible with worry lines so deep in his forehead that he looked like he'd been slashed several times with a very deadly sharp knife.

He stopped on one page and read a verse over and over again as the lines on his forehead seemed to deepen even further. He stood and wandered over to the sofa and gently shook Rachel.

"Yeah," she said, disoriented, through cracked eyes.

"Sorry, but I have to show you something." Abe glanced over to the television. "Rick," he said, just loud enough for Rick to hear. "You need to see it too."

Rachel slid up to a sitting position, her face puffy and red. Rick traipsed over and sat on the edge of the couch.

Abe handed Rachel the Bible and tapped a verse. "Read this."

She flashed him a look that asked him why he didn't just read it, but, realizing it was a huge step for him to be even taking this book seriously, thought it was best to indulge him.

Rachel took the Bible, swallowed, then read as if she was reciting before a classroom. "Revelation 16:21. 'And huge hailstones, about one hundred pounds each, came down from heaven, upon men, and men blasphemed God because of the plague of the hail, because its plague was extremely severe.'"

Rachel expectantly looked at Abe. While staring her straight in the eyes, he reached around the edge of the book and touched the Hebrew handwriting in the margin near the verse. He didn't need to look to see where it was at. He knew.

"This is a date. July 10th, the day after tomorrow. And Carl included the time. 1:06 p.m."

"Considering the conflict developing between Syria and Israel, this could be a reference to an impending military strike," Rick said.

Rachel snapped fully awake and came to her feet. "We have to do something!"

"Do what?" Abe asked with a flustered shrug.

"Warn the people!"

"Warn who?" Abe asked in a calm, reasonable tone. "The verse is too vague. It doesn't say what's actually going to happen. Or where." He raised the Bible. "That's the problem with this book. Prophetic scripture is so open-ended that it can be interpreted in almost any way."

Rick nodded agreement. Abe smiled at him appreciatively. Considering their differences in views, Abe was glad for any support he could get. Especially from one as well versed in the Bible as Rick.

Rachel took the Bible from Abe and read the verse in question silently to herself. In the margin, beneath the date and time in Hebrew was another Hebrew word or phrase. There was enough space between the previous writing as to suggest it was separate from it. The word or phrase was circled in red ink with an arrow drawn to the verse.

Rachel showed it to Abe. "What's this say?"

"Sails."

"Sales? Like a sale at a store?"

"No... like on a boat. Not much help is it? Frustrating enough that the verses are vague, but so is some of Carl's notes."

Rachel realized he was right and dropped back into the sofa. She absently tossed the Bible onto the cushion next to her and put her face in her hands. After a moment, she glanced at her watch, then to her friends.

"Well, we have about thirty-six hours to figure it out."

How many lives might be lost if we don't, she thought?

Jack Snyder, Pamela Cosel, Syed Nadim Rizvi

CHAPTER TWELVE – MISSILE TESTING

REALIZING THEY WEREN'T GOING TO be able to solve it in the middle of the night, and sleep-deprived, Rachel and Rick retired to their rooms, agreeing to meet as early as reasonable to continue this discussion.

Abe was glad for the break. The discoveries of the day had disrupted his world and fried his brain. He needed at least a few hours sleep before he could try and unravel the knot that was tied into his personal views of reality.

Rick, on the other hand, was out cold as soon as he dropped into bed.

Rachel took Carl's Bible with her when she returned to her room. She fought the urge to continue reading it and set it on a table furthest from the bed before she climbed beneath the comforter. As had been her pattern in recent days, her dreams were restless with a few downright disturbing. Fortunately, she couldn't remember them when she woke at sunrise.

She had drawn all the drapes but with windows that wrapped around her hotel room, the sun found a way. It was as if it beckoned her to awaken. A reminder that time was short. That every second spent in bed was one second closer to whatever awaited the world on July 10 at 1:06 p.m.

Rachel thought a change of scenery would give her a fresh perspective, so she gathered up her laptop and walked two blocks to a popular coffee shop called The Mocha Hut. Unlike a lot of coffee shops these days where you can never seem to find a seat, this place was large with plenty of seating. Rachel people watched as she stood in line for her espresso. Most sat alone at tables as they sipped their coffees while engrossed with whatever they were reading on their phones, tablets, newspapers or magazines. She fought the urge to shout a warning of the impending disaster, whatever it may be. But such an outburst might get her thrown out. At the very least it would bring unwanted attention, and people would just think she was crazy. She wondered if this is how the prophets of old felt: having inexplicable knowledge that led to them getting ostracized. Or killed.

After getting her caffeinated drink, she managed to get a table near the window and set up her laptop. It only took a few minutes of searching the internet before she made a discovery that might be significant. Or maybe not. It was the same quandary that she, Abe, and Rick had with the scriptural verse itself the night before.

Rachel had searched with the keywords 'sails Israel' and found a colorful image that grabbed her attention. It was a sculpture of tall, triangular-shaped sheets of metal that resembled the sails on a boat. There were half-a-dozen of them. At least from what Rachel could see in the photos. The sculpture was titled Sails Square, putting to rest any thoughts that she was reading too much into it. The sculpture was near the coast of the Mediterranean Sea in a city called Ashdod, about sixty kilometers directly West of Jerusalem.

She called Abe's mobile phone, expecting to wake him up, but he too awoke at first light and wanted a change of venue. So, he went to his mobile workstation in the News World production truck. The day shift personnel would be arriving shortly, but for now he was the only one there. He was busy cataloguing footage, thinking the repetitive, rote activity would clear his mind, as meditation would do, to prepare for whatever lay ahead for him and his friends.

Rachel told him what she'd found on the internet.

"I'm familiar with Sails Square in Ashdod, but that's quite a stretch, Rachel."

"Agreed. But we have to start somewhere. What is Ashdod known for? And don't tell me stuff I can just find on the internet. I need to know something about it that only someone who lives here, like you, would know."

He chuckled. "Glad to know I'm good for something."

"You're good for lots of things, Abe, and we don't have time for self-esteem boosting right now. Do you know anything about the place?"

"Well... Israel conducts missile tests of Ashdod, in the Mediterranean."

Rachel's eyes widened. *That could be a jackpot!* She realized she was gripping her phone too tightly and loosened her grasp.

"That's all I can think of off the top of my head," Abe went on. "And that might even be on the internet, I don't really know. Have never had a reason to check."

"That's a good enough starting point. I'll look into it."

"Not much time left," Abe said with a trace of despair in his voice. Rachel could hear people arriving for their shift on Abe's end.

"Don't remind me," she said, then ended the call.

It was near midnight in New York when Rachel tried to reach Daniel Murray from her table at The Mocha Hut. Since the military build-up in the Mediterranean, the News World hours were all screwed up. People were working all hours of the day and night, and Daniel Murray, the big shot he was notwithstanding, was one of those people. But as she expected, she could only leave a voicemail. While Rachel impatiently waited for Dan to return her call, she got the shop's daily blend dark brew and a sesame seed bagel with cream cheese.

Dan still hadn't called back a half-hour later. She tried again but when it went to voicemail, she disconnected before leaving a message. Then she called his personal assistant, hoping she was still awake. She was, so Rachel, using her influence as an on-screen personality, talked the assistant into interrupting a meeting to pass a personal message to Daniel. He was irritated, but when he saw what was written on the message, his irritation dissolved, and he ended the meeting quickly with a sense of urgency.

Rachel was still sipping her coffee ten minutes later when Dan Facetimed her from his office. She took the call as voice only, not wanting to risk Dan reading her expression – something he was very good at – when she started laying it on thick.

"Why voice only?" he asked.

"I'm in the lobby of the hotel," she lied, to cover for the noise in the coffee shop, "and getting a terrible signal for some reason."

"So, you have information on a terrorist attack in Ashdod?" His voice was strained, as if he was in Ashdod himself.

"Well—"

"Don't well me! My assistant gives me a message from you that states exactly that. And also for me not to tell anyone yet."

She was shaking. Rachel hated to lie to anyone, even when trying to get past obstacles for a story, but she really despised lying to Dan. He was her boss and didn't get to where he was at by being a dupe. But she couldn't tell him she was following a lead she got from a Bible verse in the Book of Revelation, along with a scribbled note from a guy who was blown to bits in the café bombing. She had to go a different route, even if it meant bending the truth. Or more like shattering it to pieces in this case.

"Remember the Israeli Intelligence officers I told you about that visited me in the hospital?"

"Yes."

"One of them came to see me last night at the hotel. You know, since I've been resting since getting out of the hospital." She was weaving quite the web and hating herself for it.

"Okay," he said slowly, waiting to see where she was going with this.

"The conversation started out as another question and answer session, then turned more personal. He wanted to know how I was recovering and such."

"Was he interested in you?"

Dan took the bait, but she didn't feel any better about it.

"Maybe," she said, "but I stopped it before it could go anywhere. Anyway, he strongly hinted at a possible terrorist strike Syria was going to try on Ashdod, so I wanted to pass that onto you to see what you can find out through 'official' channels."

"What was this agent's name?"

She was hoping he wouldn't ask that question. "I don't want to say right now."

"Come on, Rachel! I'm going to look like a fool unless I give my sources a little more info."

"Just ask if they know of anything going on in or near Ashdod tomorrow. Blame it on me. Tell them your crazy foreign correspondent got wind of something and you wanted to check it out."

He sighed louder than he would've had it been a video call. He wanted to make sure she got it through the audio only. "Okay. I'll see what I can find out."

"Thank you. And let me know as soon as you hear something, anything, one way or the other."

They ended the call. She was sweaty and her mouth was dry. *Time for a shower and a bottled water*, she thought.

Rachel filled Abe and Rick in on her conversation for lunch in the hotel restaurant. They were impressed with the tale she wove to get him involved. They decided there was really nothing more they could do about it but wait. Whether Dan found out anything, or even tried, tomorrow afternoon was coming, and no one was going to be able to stop it. They all spent the rest of the day in their respective rooms, alone with their own thoughts. Abe continued cataloguing footage, Rick cleaned and did routine maintenance on his camera gear, and Rachel took the opportunity to catch up on sleep and watch some non-news related television.

Daniel Facetimed her at 8 a.m. her time on July 10. She had been lying awake for an hour but didn't get out of bed. *Why? Today's the day something is supposed to happen, and I have failed to do anything about it.*

She snatched her phone off the bedside table so fast she almost missed grabbing it. She took it as an audio call only.

"Voice only again?" he asked, wondering what's going on. It was 1 a.m. in New York and she could hear the exhaustion in his voice.

"I'm still in bed. I wouldn't even let my mother, God rest her soul, see me first thing in the morning. What's up?"

"I got some info, Rachel."

She sat up so quickly in bed her head swam. "Tell me!" She scooted to a sitting position on the edge of the bed.

"Easy. It's nothing really. Not a terrorist strike certainly. Israel is testing a new missile guidance system at a base near Ashdod. They're testing it on a U.S. supplied missile-version of a bomb called the MOP: The Massive Ordnance Penetrator."

"What does it do?"

"It penetrates deep into the ground, then explodes, leveling buildings, and blowing debris into the air, where it rains down on the sea."

Rachel thought she felt her heart skip a beat, but surely that was just her imagination. She stared off blankly. *Hailstones. Coming down from heaven. Upon men.*

"They're testing it on a small island close to Ashdod," Dan said. "I've heard it's a show of strength against the military build-up in the region."

"Tell your contacts to call it off!" Rachel shouted.

Dan went completely silent long enough that Rachel thought they might've been disconnected.

"Hello," Rachel said.

"I can't do that," he replied with a mix of shock and annoyance at her outburst. "Why would they listen to me anyway?"

He had a point. Daniel Murray might be a recognizable face in the many parts of the world, but he was just a news person, like her, and carried no real weight in matters that dominated the world's political and military stage.

Still, she had to get him to try.

"Something is going to happen," she said without a trace of doubt.

"What?"

"I have intel of possible sabotage." Another lie to add to the pile. *It's okay. It's all for the greater good, right?*

"I need more than that. Names and such."

"That's all I can give you right now."

"Not good enough."

"Okay. No reason to continue this conversation."

"Rach—"

She hung up on him. This was something she doesn't think she'd done since she was a teenager. There was no good feeling associated with it. But this developing situation was by far bigger than either of their careers. Possibly tens of thousands of lives were at stake. Men, woman, and children. Husbands, wives, mothers, fathers, daughters and sons. Every human being is connected to others in various ways. Any loss of life was felt and mourned by the survivors no matter how isolated or how much a loner the deceased was while alive. Rachel couldn't stand by and do nothing as she did before the destruction of the Church of the Holy Sepulchre, the Dome of the Rock, and the Wailing Wall. She couldn't live with herself if she did. And it didn't matter to her if it destroyed hers or Dan Murray's careers. She had to take a stand. And she needed to do it now. But she couldn't do it alone.

After a quick shower she threw some clothes on and went down to Abe's room. She knocked a few times but there was no answer. She tried Rick's room. No answer there either. After calling them and leaving voicemails, she sent them both texts. No response from them after thirty minutes.

Did Daniel Murray call and tell them I was crazy? Now I'm just being paranoid.

She hopped in her car and headed off to where the production truck was last parked, which was on the lot of their Israeli network affiliate. It had been there for days, but if another major assignment came in – one that required the truck – and another correspondent was given it, the truck would be gone, taking Abe and Rick with it. She needed to get there as fast as she could. Traffic was slow, making her restless and short tempered. Two blocks from the affiliate station she got stuck at a red light. It seemed to last forever.

"Come on, come on, come on."

It finally turned green and she practically floored the accelerator. Buildings whipped past and the edge of the parking lot came into view. There was no reason to rush; the truck was still there. She sighed in relief as she screeched onto the parking lot. A couple of employees on the lot rubbernecked in her direction, relaxing when she got out of the car.

They recognize me and probably thinking I'm chasing a hot story.

She saw them go about their business. *Good! They're ignoring me.*

After mounting the few steps leading to the truck's door, she yanked on the knob. It was locked. She pounded on it. After an impossibly long moment, Rick sheepishly opened the door. He looked at her as if she was the last person he wanted to see.

"Hi, Rick," she said in an unassuming tone. *Maybe Dan did call him.*

"Hey, Rachel." Rick was bland and distant. "What's up?"

"I was looking for you and Abe."

"Yeah, ummm... Mr. Murray called us."

I knew it! "I know he's angry because I hung up on him, but—"

"He told us what you said."

Something in Rick's voice. "I thought it was important to try and—"

"We're on your side, Rachel, it's not that. We know you couldn't tell Mr. Murray anything. He'd think you were crazy."

Rachel was perplexed with Rick's odd behavior. "Then what is it?"

"It's Abe. He..."

"He what?" Rachel was getting aggravated now. "Is Abe here?"

"No," he said, his eyes locked with her. His face was slack and pale. "He left about an hour ago."

"Where did he go? Just tell me!" She wanted to throttle his throat if he didn't spit it out.

"He went to Ashdod to get his cousin out." Rick looked like he just confessed to murder. "He asked me not to tell you, but..." He started to tear up and Rachel's heart went out to him.

Rick was a great, sensitive guy; the kind that would give you his last dollar. She would've liked to ease any feelings of guilt he had for outing Abe, but a quick glance at her watch told her there wasn't time. It was 11:45 a.m. and whatever event was destined to happen in Ashdod, Carl placed it to occur in exactly eighty-one minutes from now. With Ashdod being sixty kilometers away, she should have plenty of time, depending on the traffic. But that's just to get there. To get Abe to safety – and who knew how far away they'd need to get from Ashdod to accomplish that – was another matter.

Without another word, Rachel bolted to her car.

Rick jumped down the short flight of stairs, shouting, "I'll go with you!" But she had already clambered into her car. Rick was stunned at how fast she started it and peeled off the lot. He wallowed in guilt as she disappeared around the corner.

Upon reaching the first red traffic light, Rachel programmed the rental car's built-in GPS system for Ashdod's city limits. It was 11:48 a.m. and the GPS told her it would take sixty-three minutes with her arrival time at 12:51 p.m. Exactly fifteen minutes before the event. Not much wiggle room. She debated with herself that maybe she should just stay put and continuously call his mobile phone and leave one voicemail after the next, each one more annoying and desperate than the previous one. She could even enlist Rick's help with both of them making call after call simultaneously. Abe is bound to return one of their calls just to get them to shut up. But what difference did it make? Abe wasn't answering as it was because he knew exactly what Rachel wanted: for him to turn around and head out of Ashdod as fast as his car would carry him. He already what he was heading into and made the decision to do it.

So, why was Rachel accelerating toward a potentially doomed city? For the same reason Rick wanted to go with her to Ashdod. Guilt. Had she not spilled the beans to Daniel Murray, he wouldn't have told Abe and Rick about it. So, in a roundabout way, she was responsible for sending Abe rushing headlong toward disaster. All because of her need to satisfy her demanding ego. She really told Dan off now, didn't she? Yessiree.

She wondered if she was driving straight to her own death. For the moment, she didn't care. Guilt will do that to a person. Snatching up her phone from the passenger seat, she made another call to Abe. It was going to be a long trip, so she might as well multitask. As expected, the call went to voicemail and she left him another message.

Rachel continued to leave voicemail messages every five minutes or so. The trip was going smoothly with light traffic, and she felt good about it right up until she hit seven kilometers out from Ashdod. Then it ground to a halt. It wasn't stop and go. It was a complete halt.

The car's GPS still showed blue all the way into Ashdod, not the expected red for slowed or stopped traffic. Five minutes later, traffic still sat stone still. Rachel swung the door open and stepped out onto the highway. Just one foot though as it felt unnatural to stand on a wide ribbon of concrete made for cars to move on at seventy-five miles per hour. Or rather one-hundred-twenty kilometers per hour as Abe would say. Abe. Poor Abe.

Standing outside her car, Rachel could see traffic at a standstill as far as she could see. She wasn't going to make it into Ashdod; she knew that now.

A car door opened somewhere behind her. A short, chubby woman pulled herself out of her car. She called out to Rachel in another language. She guessed it was Hebrew, but it could've just as easily been Arabic.

"I'm sorry, but I only speak English," Rachel said to the woman.

The woman switched to English without a trace of an accent. "Can you see what the holdup is?"

"I'm sorry, but I can't."

The driver's side door of the car immediately to Rachel's left opened and out stepped a man who Rachel thought looked too young to even drive. "I just heard on the radio there was a terrible accident about four kilometers ahead. Traffic is completely stopped."

Rachel and the short woman thanked the young man and got back into their cars.

This is it then, Rachel thought. *Stuck in traffic outside a soon to be annihilated city. How many of these people have relatives in the city that will die? Is the disaster going to reach us out here on the highway?*

She looked at the digital clock in the car and compared it to the one on her phone. They were the same – 1:04 p.m. Two more minutes. The wait felt both unbearably long, and not long enough.

1:05 p.m.

What if I'm wrong? Or at least misinterpreted what Carl meant with the word sails?

The car's clock clicked over to 1:06 p.m. Rachel looked at the screen on her phone. Still 1:05. She stared at it until it flipped to 1:06. The moment of truth had arrived. She leaned forward and looked at the city in the distance. There was a cluster of buildings in the center that reminded her a little of Los Angeles as seen from about ten miles away. But without the haze. The sky here was a clean, deep blue.

If we can just go another minute – just sixty seconds – without anything happened, we'll be in the clear. And Carl would've been wrong. He is only human after all. Come on 1:07, come on 1:07, come—

A bright flash high in the sky grabbed her attention. An explosion? No. A glint of sunlight off metal. She searched, her eyes darting about where she noticed the flash. Then she saw it. A missile ascending high in the sky, so far away it looked like a shiny silver needle. It climbed higher and higher, getting smaller with each passing second. Just when Rachel thought it would shrink out of view, it slowed and appeared to stop. For a moment it just hung there, then it flipped over and descended, picking up speed as it went.

"No...," she said so softly that she wasn't sure she actually spoke it.

The missile rocketed straight into the center of the city and disappeared. Several seconds of stillness followed. Than a fireball silently rose, throwing entire buildings upwards like toys in slow-motion. They came apart in the air. Not a trace of a sound from any of it; it would take several more seconds before the sound reached Rachel.

She watched in horror and disbelief as huge chunks of debris sailed to unimaginable heights above the city.

Must be concrete and asphalt from the city streets.

The debris arced and rained down on the city like a fountain of death. A cloud of black smoke formed and clung to the city.

Then the sound reached Rachel. It began low like rolling thunder, but quickly got louder beyond comprehension. It was the sound of the explosion. The sound people in the city heard the moment the missile went off after burrowing deep under the city. Rachel was hearing it seven kilometers away, after it had died down a bit. She couldn't imagine how loud it must've been at ground zero. That alone probably killed people.

Then the tornado level winds hit her car. As the car rocked violently, she realized she'd be dead now if she hadn't gotten back in the car.

Abe is dead. There's no way he survived this.

She put her head on the steering wheel and cried.

CHAPTER THIRTEEN – A LEARNED PROFESSOR

DANIEL MURRAY SAY AT HIS anchor's desk under the white-hot lights at 5 p.m. on July 11. Three remotely operated cameras were fanned out before him before him in an arc. He would know which one to look at when the time came; it would be the one with the lit red tally light just above the lens. It would start out as green to let him know the control room would be switching to that camera momentarily. It was established wisdom that switching between cameras during a broadcast made the show more interesting. He thought that was nonsense. It was the content that made the show interesting. And the news anchor, or course, was the most important part of the show. In his mind anyway.

The camera they always started the program on was the center one. He didn't need the green tally light to tell him that. Sometimes they even tracked in on him for aesthetic reasons.

None of this mattered to him today. In less than a minute he was going to go on the air and begin the hardest broadcast of his career. Those at the network knew how he felt, he had made that clear. One thing everyone knew about Daniel Murray is that he always told people what he thought.

Today would be a first, however. He was most upset about what he had to tell the world: that the tensions in the Middle-East has cost them the life of a colleague. What no one knew was this particular loss hit him harder than people realized, because he felt responsible for what happened. The guilt gnawed away at his guts like a cancer.

He just needed to get through this broadcast this evening. Then he could weep in the privacy of his home.

"Ten seconds, Dan," the director said in his earpiece.

At five seconds the green light on the center camera blinked on and the director counted down in his ear. "Five, four, three, two..."

The tally light turned red and Dan Murray spoke to millions of people watching on their televisions, computers, tablets, or phones.

"As the world already knows, an Israeli missile test, miles off the coast of Israel, went out of control yesterday and exploded in the center of the city of Ashdod. The loss of life is feared to run into the tens of thousands." His voice choked up, which he did his best to control.

With the routine part of the broadcast now out of the way, Dan fought back tears as he steeled himself for the part he dreaded most.

"This tragedy strikes us here personally at News World. Though only a few of the deceased have been identified, one of our broadcast engineers, who resides in Israel, was visiting a relative in Ashdod when the explosion occurred. He is among the dead. His name was Abiyda Goldman."

A file photo of Abe flashed on the screen behind Daniel.

"Our thoughts and prayers go out to his family and friends, as well as the families of all the victims. The accident has increased the tension in an already tense region of the world. That story next."

The red tally light blinked off. Dan reached for the tissue box that sat on the side of his desk and pulled one out. His eyes had teared up and his nose was running.

"Great job, Dan," the director said.

"Thanks. Has there been any word from Rachel?" He cleared his throat and threw the used tissue in the wastebasket nearby.

The director stepped out of the darkness behind the cameras and spoke to him directly. "No, did you want us to contact her?"

"Nah. I'm sure she's doing her job, chasing a story. She'll get in touch with us when she has something."

And next time I'll listen, he thought. He took off his microphone and slowly left the anchor's set.

Rachel watched Dan's broadcast streaming from the News World website on her phone while sitting on a bench in Teddy Park. It was 10 a.m. on July 12, the morning after his broadcast aired live. She went through the previous day in shock, overwhelmed by Abe's death, not knowing what she could do anymore, or if she could do anything. When Dan finished, she pulled out her earbuds and turned her attention to the splash fountain for which the park was known. Squealing children of all ages ran through the jets of water. She envied their ability to live in the moment. Not a care in the world. July 15 was only three days away. Would there still be a world for them after that?

Parents stood nearby watching their children play. The adults were in a daze, rocked by the event in Ashdod. Though it was an accident, it couldn't have come at a worse time. Israel didn't need its national pride shaken with the world's militaries descending on the Mediterranean Sea.

Rachel stood and gave Rick a hug when he strolled up. They both sat down on the bench and watched the children. The sorrow they felt from Abe's absence was so strong as to be felt by anyone walking past, forcing them to quicken their pace.

The distant rumble of a military jeep moving along a street just outside the park reminded them of the world they now lived in.

"There's nothing we can do about any of this, Rachel," Rick said. "It's been prophesied. In the big scheme of things, we don't even count."

Rachel spent her whole life trying to control everything around her, or at least those things that she had some influence on, so she refused to buy Rick's explanation. However, she didn't want to just dismiss him; he'd been a great ally on their recent adventures, as well as their more mundane assignments.

"If what you say is true," she began, "then everything is happening because of mankind. If it's about us, we can participate. That's what I think anyway."

"So, what do you want to do then?" He shifted his body, so he was turned toward her.

Good, he's willing to at least consider a course of action other than 'let's sit back and watch the world end.'

She too turned to face him. "Maybe I've been going about this all wrong. I've been relying solely on Carl's Bible for info. There has to be people that knew him. Worked with him. People who might be able to give us some insight."

He didn't outright dismiss her idea, but he couldn't fight the little smirk that creeped up on his face. "Yeah... sounds like a plan. But we only have three days. Two, actually, if you don't count the fifteenth itself."

She nodded in agreement, then propped her elbow on the back of the bench as her mind worked to solve this seemingly impossible problem.

"Maybe we need to narrow our focus," she said. "You know, many puzzles can be solved with just one key piece."

"Granted... but... what is our missing piece?"

"I thought instead of Carl's Bible, maybe the missing piece is Carl himself. I did an internet search for him, but do you have an idea how many Carl Thompson's there are in the world?"

"Did you try limiting it to just Israel?" Rick chuckled.

Something dawned on her and a smile lit up her face. "Wait a minute... Carl said he was a Biblical scholar at a university at one point but never mentioned the name of it. In fact, he went out of his way not to."

Rick shrugged and pulled his phone from his pocket. "Well, the clock is ticking." He punched the screen, searching for information.

Rachel scooted closer to him on the bench as he keyed "Carl Thompson biblical scholar university" into the browser's search engine on his phone.

Tons of hits returned, but nothing on the first page with their Carl.

"Add Israel to the search parameters," Rachel instructed.

Rick did as she asked. Again, lots of links returned but nothing with their Carl. At least, not on the first of thousands of pages. They could spend days going through the links. Days they didn't have.

They pondered what to do next in regard to searching the internet. Rick grinned mischievously.

"What?" Rachel asked.

He didn't answer. Instead he typed in "Armageddon" at the end of the list of search terms. Nailed it. A whole page of links to Tobias University in Jerusalem popped up. All articles about Carl Thompson and his Biblical studies. Spread across years. Most of them with photos of Carl. No matter what year or how young Carl looked in some of the them, Rachel recognized the man as the Carl Thompson whom she had met at Jonah's Café. It felt like months ago at this point, but in reality, was less than three weeks back.

Rick clicked through a few links, a little too fast for Rachel. It was an annoying habit Rick had cultivated over years of working in the news business. He made it clear he didn't care what others thought. His view was you shouldn't be trying to read over his shoulder, anyway. And if you didn't like his speed, do your own research.

His face lit up after scanning a link. "I think I've got something here!" he said with the excitement of a child, practically shouting it. "Aziel Kaplan was Carl's mentor."

He highlighted the name and pasted it into a new tab's browser. A relatively current photo of Aziel came up. He was a trim and in shape man in his seventies. And he lived right here in Jerusalem.

Rachel quietly sighed in relief. She was just happy he was alive. A dead mentor would do them no good. A pang of guilt stabbed at her for being glad a man was alive for strictly selfish reasons. There was no address listed for him, which was to be expected, but he taught at a place called the Institute of Scripture Studies.

"Are we going to pay Professor Kaplan a visit?" Rick asked with anticipation.

"Just me," Rachel said, trying to let him down as gently as possible. "Don't want to risk losing another friend."

"Well, I don't want to risk losing you."

"I appreciate that, but only one of should go. And I'm the journalist, which makes me the professional questioner."

"Fair enough. But I'm going to be close for you to text in case there's trouble. Deal?"

"Deal," she said with a smile. They sealed it with a handshake. With July 15 nearly upon them, they left for the Institute of Scripture Studies right after lunch.

The facility was about a 90-minute drive outside Jerusalem and difficult to find, even with the GPS in the rental car. They opted for the car over the van, because the van belonged to Abe and they just weren't ready to go there yet.

Rachel and Rick were silent as they walked past it in the hotel's parking garage on the way to Rachel's car, feeling Abe's spirit. The vehicle was still canted at an odd angle from the last time he parked it. He had taken a small economy car on his fateful final journey to Ashdod. He towed the car to the hotel behind his van, Rachel remembered.

Abe lived in Tel Aviv, an hour's drive from Jerusalem, and talked the network into putting him up in the hotel for two nights during the Peace Accord signing. He was their star broadcast engineer, so they didn't complain. But after the bombings sent the world into a tailspin, they just seemed to forget he was there, and he didn't bring it to their attention. Every day he waited for the notice that he had to vacate the hotel, but it never came. So, he kept his mouth shut and enjoyed staying in a luxury hotel. If it wasn't for that, he probably wouldn't be in Jerusalem at all, Rachel knew. He considered the place a city-sized museum and tourist trap that was anchored solidly in the past. He preferred the contemporary lifestyle and architecture of Tel Aviv, and she remembered the conversation where he'd mentioned this to her.

Rachel was a bit concerned with how far the GPS was taking them into the countryside, well outside the city limits. She thought maybe they should have hired a driver who knew how to get around Israel, but Rick assured her that they would find it. She was happy and impressed seeing him take charge and thought that she and Abe had rubbed off on him.

It took a little while, but they'd finally found the place. The Institute was a small humble building surrounded by lush greenery that was so thick it was as if the building was trying to hide. Rick dropped off Rachel in front of the gate to a waist-sized white wooden slatted fence that disappeared into bushes on each side of the building. Rachel thought it added to the charm of the surroundings. It was like someone's large summer home where they'd come and would never want to return to civilization.

"I'll be about a block away on the shoulder of the country road," Rick said. "Call or text me if you need me or when you want to leave."

"Sure thing. I'll do that," she said as she opened the gate and waved goodbye.

The gate creaked a bit as she passed through it. She took an old stone walkway up to the front door and knocked. As usual, she didn't call ahead to make an appointment. Rachel preferred to live life under the motto that it's better to ask forgiveness than permission. Yes, it bit her in the backside a few times with long drives to see someone only to discover they weren't there. Or getting doors slammed in her face, or threats of having the police called on her. But, occasionally, she came away with gold. Gold she'd never had gotten had she tried to make an appointment.

She waited. Nothing. Another rap of her knuckles and she waited again. Just when she thought she'd need to call Rick and give him the bad news, the deadbolt on the door unlocked and the door whined opened about six inches. A man stared at her blankly through the opening like he'd never seen a person before. She recognized him as Aziel Kaplan from the photos Rick found online, though he looked several years older.

"Professor Kaplan?" Rachel asked with a bright smile. She wanted to be as non-threatening as possible.

"Yes," he said after a few long and uncomfortable seconds. The door hadn't budged, and he looked poised to slam it in self-defense if necessary.

She needed to choose her next words carefully so as not to scare off this skittish man. Identifying herself as a television journalist for a major American network would probably not be the way to go. Nor would immediately inquiring about the impending emergence of the Antichrist. If he mentored Carl he probably believed in that sort of thing, but that wouldn't necessarily insulate her from being considered a nutcase.

Suddenly, the right words came to her. "I was the last person to see Carl Thompson alive."

Though he wore a poker face, his eyes widened. Her words worked as effectively as if she'd said a secret password for an exclusive club. He slowly nodded, then stepped back and opened the door all the way to permit Rachel to enter.

The Institute of Scripture Study was not a large facility, but a house. Aziel Kaplan's home. The front door opened into a warm and inviting living room with plush chairs, couches, and an ancient stone fire place. Two walls bore floor to ceiling built-in bookshelves. They were packed only with old leather-bound books. As Rachel moved closer to the shelves, she could see there were Bibles in a dozen different languages along with other religious texts. Scholarly works on the Bible and religion took up several shelves. Some of the books were written by Aziel himself. World history books, and volumes on ancient cultures and artifacts rounded out the collection. Hundreds of volumes. A history buff or someone interested in all the world's religions and ancient cultures could spend decades in this room.

It looked like that was exactly what Aziel Kaplan had done. Probably had been here and at Tobias University, from where he had retired, passing on his ancient knowledge and wisdom like a sorcerer passing on incantations to apprentices.

Is that what Carl Thompson had been to Kaplan? An apprentice?

Rachel told Professor Kaplan everything that had transpired in recent weeks: The meeting with Carl, and how he gave her his note-filled Bible; she and Rick discovering the Selah Obelisk on Mount Scopus and the significance of July 15 and the death of their friend Abe while following information from Carl's Bible.

As Rachel looked through Kaplan's impressive library, he prepared Israeli Mint Tea. He carried in two steaming cups of the brew from his kitchen. He handed one to Rachel. They sat on two sofas, facing each other.

"I was the only one at the university to give credence to Carl's End Times visions," he said as he took a sip of tea.

"Why just you?" Rachel sat on the edge of the couch, holding her cup and saucer in both hands.

"Carl's visions gave specific locations and dates. The standard view is that End Times prophecy speaks in generalizations. You analyze it through the preponderance of the evidence, so to speak. But I don't really think that's why he was ousted." He paused to let that sink in as he sipped his tea again. "I think the university just feared the ramifications."

Rachel blew carefully on the hot tea and took a sip. Being more of a coffee drinker, she was surprised at how good it tasted. "Were you also removed from the university?" She wanted to use the phrase kicked out but thought it might be too crude for him.

"No," he grinned. "I kept my mouth shut. Carl couldn't do that." He glanced down as his grin gave way to a melancholy look. "Carl and I worked together for many years. He was a good friend."

"I'm so sorry for your loss. I only met Carl the morning he...passed, but he seemed like a really likeable guy. And an interesting guy." Rachel's mind flashed on the minute the bomb exploded, and she shook away the vision.

"He was."

"Did anyone else work with you two?"

He nodded, deep in thought, then sat up and a leaned closer as if he was about to impart a deep, dark secret. "The world is full of people and organizations quietly seeking the truth, Miss Williams. Carl and I are members of many of these organizations. Such as the Masons, Eastern Star, and others."

"The Masons?" She was intrigued as that was the organization Rick mentioned to her. "I was recently told about their involvement."

"You know anything about them?" He asked the question as if he knew her answer.

Where is he going with this?

"Not really."

"Your father was a Mason. He achieved a very high level – called degrees – within the organization."

That hit her like a punch to the face. When Rachel was a little girl, her father often retired to his office in the basement where he spent many hours on the phone in quiet conversation to his friends. At least that's what her mother always told Rachel. Sometimes he left in the evening, and Rachel was long in bed before he returned. She asked him one time where he went at night, and he told her he was called into work. As a child she unquestioningly accepted that answer. It wasn't until she was older, after her father passed away, that she realized it didn't make any sense. Her dad had worked in IT so it wasn't unreasonable if there was a computer software problem that one would be called in late. But he was management. The person usually called in was a programmer or a technician.

Could he have been meeting up with people like Aziel and Carl?

"Your father being a Mason is why Carl reached out to you."

Rachel smirked. "So, it wasn't just because I was a world-renowned journalist?"

Aziel gave what must have been a rare smile for him. He didn't strike Rachel as the smiling type. "That certainly had something to do with it as well."

He set his tea cup and saucer on the wooden coffee table and walked over to one of the walls with the bookshelves. He proudly looked them up and down.

"The institute is the nerve center for the various organizations. All pertinent Biblical analyses and discoveries are sent here. Collected and collated." He stood a bit taller, proud of the significance.

She set down her cup and walked over to him. This was the moment she'd waited for. The moment everything that had happened was leading to. She had a burning question and hoped he was the man who had the answer. Rachel stared him straight in the eyes and asked the question. "Who is the Antichrist?"

Aziel's face flushed with disappointment, and her heart sank. "Unfortunately, we don't know. And time has almost run out on us. July 15th is just three days away."

"I know," she said as she plopped on the couch in disappointment. But she was also perplexed. "But this whole End Times thing doesn't make any sense to me. I mean...the Bible is clear that Christ defeats the Antichrist. If so, why would the Antichrist even bother?"

Aziel paced in front of her like the college professor he used to be. "If you faced a challenge that was inevitable – one that you couldn't escape – what would you do?"

"This isn't a trick question, is it?" she asked, going for some levity in the face of a dire situation.

"No," he said with a chuckle.

She thought a moment as she ran her fingers through her hair. "Try to get as prepared as possible, control what I could. Pick the place and time if feasible."

"That's right."

"Until you asked, I never thought of it quite that way, but it makes sense."

"The Abomination of Desolation – the Selah Obelisk – empowers the Antichrist. Strengthens him if he's within a certain radius of it. There are other things too. Our decoding of scripture indicates the Antichrist will collect weapons that were used on Jesus during his crucifixion. The whip the Romans used to give Jesus thirty-nine lashes. The spear that pierced his side as he hung on the cross. It's called the Spear of Destiny."

Rachel gasped as she remembered her vision, or hallucination, or dream, or whatever it was when she was in the presence of Jesus. Heck, as far as she knew, it was time-travel. Regardless, Jesus brought her to a place where she witnessed him being lashed with a whip. A whip that glowed. That image was followed by seeing his side pierced with a glowing spear. In both cases and based on the reactions – or rather lack of reactions – of the people around her, she was the only one to see the weapons glow.

That must have been Jesus's intent in showing me these scenes! To see these weapons up close! And understand their significance!

She was so lost in thought that it took her a moment to realize that Aziel had stepped directly in front of her and stared deeply into her eyes.

"You find the whip and the spear...and you find the Antichrist," he said with certainty.

CHAPTER FOURTEEN – MISSING ARTIFACTS

"RACHEL!"

The shout came from her left, and she recognized the voice. It was Jason Carter. Rachel was walking across the wide sidewalk leading to the entrance of the Israeli Parliament. Jason jogged up to her, his dark blue tie whipping in the wind.

"We meet again," he said breathlessly. "You here for the press conference with the PM and the PLO?"

Rachel hid her surprise well. She was so caught up in her own pursuits that she'd fallen out of touch with other developments in the world and knew nothing about the press conference. So as not to embarrass herself, being in the news business, and all, she asked no questions regarding it.

"No. I am here on an unrelated matter."

"Really?" he asked, his interest piqued. "You chasing another story?"

She grinned wide and mischievously. "You should know I can't discuss it." *Actually, Jason, I'm trying to find out who the Antichrist is. Oh, what's that? You think I'm insane. Yeah, well, I probably am.*

"Are you here for the press conference?" she asked him.

"That would be much more interesting than what I'm tasked with. I'm meeting with his cabinet," Jason sighed. "Always have to keep government palms full of money to get what you want. Even when it's just to approve one of Mr. Voland's non-profits. Sad the world works that way, but it is what it is."

He looked up at the Parliament building. It was a block-shaped, gray and tan structure with rectangular support columns lining the perimeter. A large white and blue Israeli flag, with the Star of David in the center, was mounted at the edge the roof whipping loudly in the wind.

"This Prime Minister's administration seems to be particularly difficult to deal with. Very frustrating."

This grabbed Rachel's interest. "How so?"

"He's a big talker on peace but he's built up the military more than any PM I know of."

"Really? I didn't know that." She genuinely was surprised. Though she and Rick had already leaned toward him being the Antichrist, and she did the proper research before the Peace Accord so she could ask good questions, she had no idea of his proclivity for increasing the military in relation to his predecessors.

"It's not surprising. He's done a good job keeping it out of the news." He grinned proudly. "I guess being a lobbyist makes me privy to *some* things. Anyway, I should get in there." He was anxious as a schoolboy to run outside for recess. He hurried toward the entrance but glanced back before getting too far and shouted, "I think you still owe me a drink!" He disappeared inside.

"Okay," she laughed. "You got it."

She, too, made her way toward the entrance, but at a more relaxed pace. Once there, she had to pass through the security checkpoint.

"What's the purpose of your visit?" the heavily armed guard asked her.

"I have an appointment with Mr. Marks."

The guard acted like she'd said the secret password and motioned for her to proceed. She placed her purse on the conveyor belt, glad that she was using a different purse than her clutch. It would just be her luck that the sewn in camera – which was still in the clutch – would look suspicious on the x-ray monitor and be discovered. That would definitely get her in big trouble. Not now though. The purse made it through the x-ray without incident, and she walked through the metal detector with nary a beep. Slipping the purse onto her shoulder, she crossed the foyer toward a spacious hallway, her heels clicking on the floor.

Rachel rounded the corner and nearly collided with the leading edge of a huge crowd coming her way. She was surprised she didn't hear the approaching group way in advance. Journalists clustered around and barked questions as they orbited two men in the center. Next to the journalists, video camera operators and photographers danced about as they jockeyed for the best positions to get their shots.

The subject of their attention were the two men in the middle of the gathering: Prime Minister Rubin Gellman and PLO President Ahmed Rahal. Two men Rachel hadn't seen since the day of the terrorist attacks. Black-suited men with obvious earpieces and sunglasses formed the immediate circle around the political leaders. They held out their hands to keep the journalists at bay.

Rachel had to fight her cultivated drive to jump right in and shout questions along with her colleagues. But she was on another mission. And if the world was heading in the direction that she thought it might be – one that Rick definitely believed – then she may never return to her old life.

She stepped off to the side, close to the corridor wall, to let the crowd pass.

As she stared at the PM, he swiveled his head and looked her right in the eyes. It was slow and deliberate without any searching. He knew right where to look to pick her out through the crowd, as though he felt her staring at him. The thought unnerved her, and she glanced away.

Too late. He stopped, the sudden ceasing of motion drug the crowd to a halt. Silence fell over the crowd as they turned in unison to see the object of his attention. Rachel stood wide-eyed and motionless like someone who had just woken up under a hot spotlight on a Broadway stage on a sold-out Saturday night. She opened her mouth to speak but nothing came out.

The crowd parted as the Prime Minister meandered over to Rachel with his security detail flanking him. The PLO President tagged along.

"Miss Williams, I remember you from the Peace Accord signing," he said.

Just like that day on the roof of Herod's Palace, Rachel was shocked and impressed that he knew her name.

"If I recall correctly," he continued, "you asked the most questions."

He must think I'm part of this journalistic entourage. No reason to waste the opportunity.

"It's my nature, Mr. Prime Minister," she grinned. "Are you certain Syria is behind the terrorist attacks?"

She could feel the other journalists around her bristling. They were relegated to shouting questions from a distance, separating by the stiff arms and hard stares of the security team. But her she was, standing face to face with him, in an encounter he initiated.

"We are about as certain as can be," he said.

"We?"

The Palestinian President stepped forward. "Yes. We," he said as he slightly adjusted his Keffiyeh. "The attacks have strengthened our resolve to come to peace."

"To end all conflicts," the PM added. The two men spoke as one.

Armed with new information she had received from Jason Carter, she fired her next question like a bullet at the PM. "But isn't mobilizing the military sending the wrong message then?"

She hit her target and he didn't like it. He sternly narrowed his eyes at her and fired back. "Peace through strength, Miss Williams. That's the way of the world."

His eyes unnerved her. "Indeed," was all should could muster.

One of the PM's aides quickly strode up. "Mr. Prime Minister. The press conference is scheduled to begin."

The PM acknowledged the comment with a nod while maintaining his hard stare at Rachel. Then he crisply turned and walked away, with the PLO leader following, as security wrapped around them. The journalists and camera people followed as if being towed. The journalists shouted their questions like yapping dogs.

Shaken by the encounter –which was more of a confrontation – Rachel watched the crowd disappear from view as it moved down another corridor. She continued in the direction she was initially heading until she reached a thick wooden office door with a frosted window that was stenciled with the number 171. There was no other signage on the door indicating the name of a particular government department. Nothing like that. Just the number.

After leaving the Institute of Scriptural Studies the day before, Rachel spent the rest of the afternoon searching the internet and making phone calls in attempt to locate where the artifacts of ancient Israel were kept. Not those that could be found in one of the country's museums. But the artifacts that had controversial histories. The type of past that might challenge certain religious dogmas. By late afternoon, just before the end of the business day, she found such a place. Room 171 on the first floor of the Israeli Parliament. This was not the kind of place where she could show up unannounced. She had to make an appointment, something she was loath to do.

At 4:57 p.m., three days before who-knows-what was going to happen, she made a phone call and reached a man named Mr. Marks in room 171. He was happy to see her the following week. She had to bite her tongue to keep from demanding he see her the following morning. Instead, she gave him a sob story regarding a news piece she was doing for a small Israeli publication that was owned by the Prime Minister's aunt on his mother's side, whom he was very close to. His aunt always dreamed of being a publisher and wanted to give the PM a special issue on Jewish antiquities for his birthday. So, if Mr. Marks would be so kind as to see Rachel the next morning, that would be splendid. Well, Mr. Marks certainly didn't want to disappoint the PM or his aunt so he said he could squeeze her in at 10 a.m.

At precisely the stroke of 10 in the morning, Rachel knocked on the frosted window of the door to room 171. She saw a shadow floating toward her through the glass and the door opened. Mr. Marks was a big bald man with a red tie that was too wide, a dark blue suit that was too tight, and forehead that was too sweaty.

"Rachel Williams, I presume?"

"Yes. And you must be Mr. Marks."

"That's correct. Please, come in."

He stepped back for her to enter, then closed the door behind her. "I have what you inquired about up on the computer screen," he said as he led her to his desk.

The desktop computer's flat screen was on a swivel that could pivot 180 degrees. He rotated the screen around for Rachel to see. A horizontal line ran through the middle of the screen separating two images. An ancient-looking whip made of cracked leather was the top image. The bottom image was a spear that appeared very old and lacked the consistency of something that was machine made. She knew in an instant these were the authentic items she was looking for. She could feel it in her soul.

"These items are here?" she asked Mr. Marks.

"Yep. They've been in the possession of the Israeli government for...," his head bobbed back and forth as he tried calculating it before giving up. "Well, long before my time and I've been here forever. Seems like forever anyway."

"May I see them?"

"Sure!" Mr. Marks said enthusiastically. He was in his element and Rachel guessed this was the most excitement that had happened to him in a long time. Possibly since Mr. Marks started working there. Which might be forever, at least according to him.

Rachel followed Mr. Marks to an elevator at the back of the building. It was an old, creaky, ride down into the basement. It seemed ridiculously long as if the basement were really deep. In reality, Rachel thought it was probably just a very slow, hardly used elevator.

Mr. Marks flipped a switch in the nearly pitch-black basement and rows of fluorescent lights flickered on, a few audibly protesting, while others refused to come on at all. The lights illuminated aisles that ran between cabinets with wide but shallow drawers.

"The artifact cabinets," Mr. Marks said with a wave of his arm.

He wobbled over to a dark, metal file cabinet containing index cards that were so yellow Rachel guessed they'd been there since the middle of the previous century. After a couple minutes of searching, he produced two index cards and off he and Rachel went down one of the aisles.

He stopped before one of the artifact cabinets and compared the number on one of the index cards to the drawer number on the large cabinet.

"The Spear of Destiny is in this drawer," he said in awe. Rachel couldn't tell if he believed in such things or if he was just being overly dramatic for effect.

He opened the drawer and they both peered inside in anticipation. The drawer was empty! Mr. Marks was perplexed. He checked the number on the card again against the one on the drawer. They were the same.

"I don't understand," he mumbled, more to himself than to Rachel.

"Could someone have...checked it out, for some reason?" Rachel felt her heart pounding, afraid to think about what this meant.

He glared at her like she was an idiot. "This isn't a library, Ms. Williams."

"When was the last time you checked on it?"

"Never!" He was downright irritated. The missing item disturbed him, and her questions didn't help the matter. "Had no reason to. Who knows when the last time this drawer was opened? Probably decades ago."

"Let's check on the whip."

He threw her a fearful look. He didn't want to know if it was there or not, but of course he had to check. They ambled to another aisle where they stood before another artifact cabinet. After the routine of comparing the numbers on the index card to those on the drawer, Mr. Marks pulled the drawer open. No whip. Completely empty. His heart sank. With a handkerchief from his back pocket, Mr. Marks dabbed the perspiration from his brow.

"I will have to inform security."

She nodded in sympathy, but then got back to business. "May I have copies of the photos of these items?"

"Yes."

Back in his office, he gave her the photos, then placed a call to the Security Office, palms sweating.

***

Rachel stood by the window of her hotel room watching a rare summer storm brewing in the sky as Rick sat at the desk and examined the photos of the whip and the spear.

"Though Rubin Gellman has only been Prime Minister for six years, he's been in the Israeli government for over twenty-five," Rick said. "He could've taken those artifacts at any time over those years. And you said the PLO President was with him?"

"Yes," Rachel said absently, still staring out the window. Like the storm in the sky above, something brewed deep inside her.

"They've known each other forever," Rick continued. "Been inseparable since the Peace Accord. He could even be the Antichrist."

She didn't respond. Rick looked over at her with narrowed eyes. "What's wrong?"

Rachel pulled herself away from the window and the view of the hypnotic swirling of the grey storm clouds. "Something doesn't seem right. Those artifacts look familiar to me."

"Okay," he said, drawing the word out as people do when they're waiting for more information to get some context.

Rachel's eyes flew open wide. "I've got it!" she said in a vocal level reserved for those who have just won the lottery.

Even though it was noon, Abe's hotel room was dark. The curtains were drawn closed. He always kept them that way, and Rachel had ribbed him for it, saying that he was really a vampire. He had explained he closed the curtains because it was hard to see the monitors during the day, even on an overcast day. That's something he would have said about today, were he still alive. The real reason he kept the curtains closed was he was used to working in the production truck or in the control room at the network or one of its affiliates. Places that didn't have windows. When habits formed, good or bad, they tended to be hard to break.

The lock on the door to the hotel room clicked and the door opened forming a rectangle of light with two human silhouettes. Rick and Rachel. They entered and Rick flipped on the light switch.

Abe had been the last person to touch his editing system. There was a fourth full cup of coffee on the table near the keyboard. It turned cold days ago. At the edge of the table was a wine glass with just a trace of red in it. Abe couldn't be bothered to carry his used drinking glasses and cups the ten feet to the kitchenette. Not until there were at least four clustered on the table.

Rachel and Rick stood before the editing system like it was a holy shrine.

Rick sighed. "No one at the station wants to deal with Abe's death right now so they just keep paying for his room and leaving things as is."

Rick slowly worked up the courage to turn Abe's equipment on like a cop on the bomb squad worrying that the next wire he cuts on an explosive will be his last. Finally ready, Rick leaned in and flipped the main power switch as he held his breath. Lamps popped on throughout the equipment and monitors came up with blue screens, patiently waiting for a signal. The monitor tied to Abe's computer system formed a digital desktop filed with files.

"Think you can find it?" Rachel asked with the hope of a child on Christmas morning.

"I'll try." Rick rolled up Abe's chair, sat in it, and went to work browsing through Abe's video files. "This could take a while."

And it did. Rachel went down to the hotel restaurant to get them both deli sandwiches and drinks. She added a couple after-lunch coffees to the order. She could have easily used the coffee maker in Abe's hotel room but felt that would be disrespectful of the deceased, a violation of his personal space.

When she returned to the room, she found Rick beaming, a smile across his face.

"Got it!" he proudly said.

It was footage from Rachel's purse-camera, taken at Lucius Voland's palace party. Rick had it cued to where Rachel stood before Voland's glass cases with the antique artifacts in them. Rachel set their lunch and drinks down on the coffee table. It could wait. This was much more important.

She pulled up a chair and sat next to Rick.

"Okay. Let's do it," Rachel said with anticipation.

Rick tapped the space bar and the footage came to life. Unintelligible crowd sounds filled the hotel room as if the crowd was really there. It was so loud it startled them both. Rick grabbed at the volume controls and lowered the audio to a reasonable level.

The camera image was wide but not quite fish-eye. It swished back and forth as Rachel casually turned to-and-fro and walked along the glass case. An imposing tuxedoed man appeared but they could only see his midsection.

"That's Lucius Voland," Rachel said to Rick, narrating the footage.

"I know. I watched it live, remember?"

The man's posture suggested he moved in close to whisper. "It's okay that you crashed my party. I won't have security escort you out."

Voland and Rachel turn their attention to the glass case as the image on the monitor gently floated back and forth taking in the old items.

"This collection doesn't seem to be your style...based on everything I've read about you," they heard Rachel say from the monitor.

"It's a reminder of mankind's violent past. It tells me I have much work to do."

Rachel wasn't listening to the recording of herself or Voland. She was busy studying the video image as it floated about, sometimes jerking this way or that. She found it quite irritating in fact, wishing she had stayed still or moved much more slowly. Then she spotted what she was looking for.

Her finger shot out like a bolt of lightning striking the monitor screen. "There! Freeze it!"

Rick hit the space bar, a little too hard, he thought. The image stopped. Near the lower left corner of the image were two items fairly close to each other. A whip and a spear.

Rachel reached into her purse and produced the two photos she received from Mr. Marks. One was of the whip used on Jesus on the last day of his earthly life. The other was the Spear of Destiny, used on Jesus by a Roman soldier to confirm he was dead.

The similarities between the images in the photographs and the one on the television monitor were so striking that any differences were negligible.

Rachel and Rick locked eyes with a direct gaze at each other. She repeated what Aziel Kaplan said to her. "Find the whip and the spear and you find the Antichrist."

Lucius Voland was the Antichrist, she thought. *No doubt about it now!*

Jack Snyder, Pamela Cosel, Syed Nadim Rizvi

CHAPTER FIFTEEN – THE ANTICHRIST

"RIGHT UNDER MY NOSE AND I didn't see it," Rachel said as she nervously paced back and forth. She glanced up. "Thank you, Abe. You're helping us from beyond."

She walked over to the window and looked out over the city. The view wasn't as good as what she got from her room, nor as high up, but it'll do. She often liked staring out at the city from her New York City apartment when she needed to think. Any cityscape would do, or even the horizon of an open field. It helped her get into a meditative or trancelike state to clear her mind and process what needed to be done next when faced with an issue or a decision.

Rick knew this about her. Sometimes he found it reassuring and welcomed it. Sometimes it alarmed him – this was one of those times.

"What are you thinking, Rachel?"

"Something needs to be done," she said softly as she continued to stare out at the city.

He gently shook his head in worry and took a step toward her. "If Lucius Voland is indeed the Antichrist, there is nothing you can do about it. This cosmic drama is much, much greater than either of us."

She faced him and he could see in her eyes that she was resolved to a course of action and wouldn't be talked out of it. He knew that about her. She was a stubborn woman and when her mind was made up, nothing could change it.

"Maybe just letting the 'powers that be' know about Mr. Voland will be enough to change the course," she said.

Rick eagerly nodded in relief. He was on board with that. At least she wasn't going to pursue what he would consider a hairbrained scheme of trying to confront Lucius Voland himself. That would be a failed operation at the very least, or suicide if it went really sour. Nonetheless, he was skeptical that anyone she contacted would move against Voland if she told them he was the Antichrist. Sure, Rick himself was convinced, but he knew how the world worked. Stories about the Antichrist might sell books or make truckloads of money for Hollywood but mentioning that you truly believed in such a being beyond a close circle of believers, or above a whisper in public, would certainly get you branded a nutcase. He feared that would be Rachel's fate. But at least she would be safe.

***

It's definitely a much better view here, Rachel thought as she looked over her laptop screen to the cityscape beyond her hotel room's window.

She was on a Skype call with Daniel from her hotel room desk. She told him, via text, earlier that it was urgent they speak. She didn't want a simple phone call or for them to Facetime or Skype on their phones; they both needed to be on their computers. That would force him into his office and ensure a private conversation. It was risky asking him to do that, because he could always put her off, saying he didn't have the time, but telling him it was urgent paid off. It didn't hurt that the temperature of the world political environment was currently very hot and rising.

It was 4 p.m. on July 13 in Jerusalem, which made it 9 a.m. in New York. Rachel had just finished telling Daniel her story. Or rather, a *version* of the story. She waited for his response as he mulled it over in his mind.

Daniel sighed. "Okay. Let me see if I got this straight. You're saying that Lucius Voland *thinks* he's the Antichrist and is trying to bring about Armageddon?"

"Yes. On July 15th. Two days from now."

"You're saying he's responsible for all the recent terrorist attacks because he owns a security firm that has infiltrated sensitive sites around the entire globe?" Daniel's tone was skeptical.

"Yes."

"And that he has stolen religious artifacts from the Israeli government?"

"That's correct?"

"How do you know he just didn't purchase them?" Again, Daniel was hesitant to go along with what he was hearing.

"Because, besides being priceless and not for sale, the Israeli government thought they still had possession of them. I know this first-hand. I discovered it during my research." Rachel explained her visit to the museum where the artifacts were believed to be stored.

Daniel sat back in his desk chair and steepled his fingers. Rachel heard the chair's springs creak. She tired of waiting and decided to go in for the kill. Speaking slowly and decisively for effect, she said, "Lucius Voland is a super-rich crackpot and plans a major terrorist attack on July 15th. Again, that's only two days from now. And seven hours closer for us here in Jerusalem than it is for you. Since he lives here, I'd assume that's the timeframe he's using."

"I'm sorry, Rachel, this is all circumstantial evidence and conjecture. My contacts would think I was crazy if I came to them with—"

"I was right about Ashdod, wasn't I?" Her voice insistent, she leaned forward in her chair.

Daniel had no reply and looked up toward the ceiling.

"And you did nothing about it," she said, glaring at him, "which resulted in the deaths of at least ten thousand people." She *needed* him to act on this information. She was happy to make him feel guilty, even if it meant he might think of putting a noose around his neck or down a bottle of pills. It was a risk she could live with. The entire world – all of humanity – depended on it.

He sat there motionless, like a digital image on a computer.

Might as well go for the knock-out punch. "Among the dead lies our friend and colleague, Abe Goldman...Abiyda Goldman. Don't forget that."

Dan glanced down at his keyboard, too ashamed to meet her eyes. He shook his head.

Rachel pushed on. "Lucius Voland's resources and influence make him a formidable and dangerous man. You need to inform your DC sources of what I told you. We can't risk another catastrophic...*mistake!*" She thought to use the word "event" but changed it to "mistake" to put it on him. She felt badly about that but pushed it from her mind. No time for her to feel guilt; too much was at stake.

"I trust you'll do the right thing." Rachel closed her laptop fast and hard knowing he would see it but made sure she didn't slam it shut. She sat way back in her chair and exhaled, feeling exhausted as if she had just given an award-winning performance. She looked across the room to Rick, who lounged on the sofa, safe from the computer camera during the Skype call.

His grin was so wide he looked like he wore a clown mask. "Saying Lucius *thinks* he's the Antichrist was brilliant!"

"Yeah, if I said I *thought* Voland was the Antichrist, Dan would definitely think I was crazy, and not act on the information, regardless of what happened in Ashdod."

She thought a moment. "Actually, I probably am crazy."

"If you are," he laughed. "I'm right there with you."

Her demeanor took a somber turn. "Now we just wait and see if he does something with it. He'll have to act fast if he does do anything."

Rick quietly nodded.

***

Rachel's gamble of playing on Dan's guilt paid off. At 10 a.m. he met with two intelligence officers in a parking garage in Times Square. He'd met with these men before on more than one occasion. He didn't know their names – they just told him to call them Bob and Tom – or what three-letter intelligence agency they worked for. They didn't hide their faces but were careful not to let him photograph them. Without names it would be very hard for Daniel to find them online if he'd tried. They were both in their forties with no defining facial characteristics. He guessed he could pass them on the crowded sidewalk of 5th Avenue and not recognize them even after just having a meeting. Maybe some of the more covert government agencies purposely recruited people with non-descript looks for certain types of meetings, such as with journalists. Dan once tried to record a meeting, but they had equipment that detected his attempt and they castigated him for it like parents with an errant child.

He knew these men only because they had reached out to him four years earlier to grill him about one of his sources on a story about toppling the government of a small Middle-Eastern country. It was a country that didn't generally make the news. He refused to give up his sources, so they rattled off a list of ten names to gauge his response. Three of the names on the list were indeed his sources. The men exchanged glances, thanked him, and left. Within a week, those three informers were brought up on espionage charges. Dan concluded he'd subconsciously ratted them out. He thought these two men – Bob and Tom – were the kind of guys who could accurately read a person's facial reaction to key words. That must have been one of their talents that interested the agency they worked for.

They contacted him a second time concerning his coverage of a kidnapped U.S. Ambassador. Bob and Tom told Daniel what he was to say on his next broadcast. It was a series of key words that must be peppered throughout his broadcast. When he refused, they mentioned some of his questionable tax deductions over the last ten years. That persuaded him. He did what they asked, and within 24 hours the Ambassador was released. During that visit, they had given him a plain white business card with a phone number on it, printed in block numbers on the center of the card. Nothing fancy. A pretty dull card, in fact, something a businessman would be embarrassed to hand out. But not these guys. The less you knew about them, the better. The card had all the necessary information the recipient of one needed. They told him at the time to call in the future with any story he thought they might be interested in.

This was one of those times.

They met at the same parking garage where they always met. Daniel proceeded to pass on all the information that Rachel had shared, regardless of the vagueness, or how crazy it sounded. Initially, Dan was going to withhold her name but realized they either knew who his source was or would figure it out quickly. Dan and Rachel's conversations were never covert or very secret, easily traceable by anyone with some know-how and a little time on their hands. Dan had no idea how much time these guys did or didn't have, but he could see know-how all over their faces. They were not to be trifled with.

The men thanked him for the information and left the same way they always did. Which is to say, they got out of his car – they always sat in the backseat of his car during their meetings – and walked through the garage's exit door. Dan then drove off down the ramp – they always met on the third floor – paid for the parking, and headed out into Times Square traffic. He really, really hated that part. It didn't matter what time of day or night it was, Times Square was not the place one wanted to be if needing to get somewhere quickly. He thought they did that to him on purpose, and he always hated them for it. Another instance, they had made him meet during evening rush hour traffic. He hated them a lot after that.

They probably won't do a darn thing with that intel, he thought as he drove back to the office. *Who would? It sounds crazy.*

But Daniel Murray was wrong. Bob and Tom took his intel seriously because they took their jobs seriously. So seriously, in fact, that they had no life outside of work. By 11 a.m. on July 13, they passed the intel onto their superiors, who passed it onto their superiors, and so on, until a phone call alerted the Secretary of Defense who, in turn, alerted all the senior military leaders who make up the Joint Chiefs of Staff. After a hastened meeting at the Pentagon, a call was made at 4 p.m. to the White House Oval Office where President Greg Wright was browsing Intelligence Briefs he had received earlier in the day.

While Daniel Murray was on the air at News World at 5 p.m. Eastern Time, thinking Bob and Tom promptly forgot about their meeting, Rachel Williams was having a glass of wine in Jerusalem. It was midnight, and Rick was dozing off with the Bible opened to the Book of Revelation on his chest, at the same hour President Wright was giving the kill order on Lucius Voland to his Secretary of Defense.

Wright had a reason to take seriously the warning about Lucius Voland. There were more than 2,500 billionaires in the world. Almost all of them private citizens. Every one of them was on the radar of all the first-world governments. Most everything was known about each and every man and woman on that list. Where they hid their money. What businesses were shell companies for other businesses. Which ones were cheating on their spouses and the names of their secret lovers. The governments knew just about everything. Private citizen or not, if a person had enough money, they could move mountains like chess pieces on a board. But there was one billionaire they knew almost nothing about.

Lucius Voland.

They knew he was a philanthropist and owned tons of companies – not very secret to most. His personal life was another matter. No matter how much sifting through material the intelligence agencies of the various countries did on Voland, they always came up empty-handed. They didn't know who his parents were, where he came from, nor what year he was born. As connected as the world was, Lucius Voland was a black hole of information – no matter what went in, nothing came out.

What they did know is that he lived primarily in Jerusalem. The city where three major terrorist attacks occurred at the same time a few weeks earlier, and about 60 kilometers from a missile accident that many believed was sabotage. All of these events had the collective governments of the world on edge.

One billionaire's life was now being weighed against more than seven billion people on the planet. It was decided by those in power that even if they were wrong it was a fair trade.

President Wright gave the order over the phone from the Oval Office at 5 p.m. Eastern Time. He followed that with thirty minutes on the treadmill, then a shower, and dinner with his wife and children. He returned to the Oval Office for two more hours of phones calls and reviewing briefs. No other world governments were involved in the decision, nor even notified. It was decided that alerting anyone else would slow the process down, and with the fifteenth of July just a few days away, better to just do it and be done with it. Being a world leader certainly had its perks. Ordering the death of someone wasn't one of them.

***

At 7 a.m. on the fourteenth of July, Lucius Voland marched out the front door of his palace in the lush countryside of Jerusalem surrounded by security personnel and aides. He descended the steep stone steps toward a waiting limousine. He had a full day scheduled and he was energized for it.

A half a mile away on a grassy hillside a man laid hidden in the brush with an MK 11 sniper rifle mounted on a bipod. He was a U.S. Navy SEAL, but no one would know that by looking at the solid black outfit he wore. He peered through the telescopic scope and centered as best he could the crosshairs on Lucius Voland's heart. With the guards and aides walking all around him, getting a clear shot wasn't easy. The SEAL was one of the U.S.'s best snipers and he always accomplished his missions. Every job had its challenges, but he always overcame them, and felt this would be no different. All he needed was a clear shot for a second and it would be done.

Through the scope, the so-called frogman watched Lucius reach the limo and stop. This is it, he thought as he started to tighten his finger on the trigger. Sudden motion, and his shot was obscured. An aide had stepped in front of Lucius. The SEAL relaxed his finger. The aide opened the limo's door and stepped aside. Lucius moved to duck into the vehicle, which blocked any chance the sniper had at a torso shot. Before his target was out of range, the soldier quickly brought the crosshairs to Lucius's head and pulled the trigger. A puff of crimson filled the air and Lucius dropped from view. The SEAL focused on the scene through the scope. He watched panicked guards and aides cluster around their fallen employer. The frogman couldn't see Lucius Voland, who was blocked by the limo. Satisfied with the result, he expertly packed up his weapon, and jogged down the hill away from the palace. He reached a dirt path with a motorcycle parked on it. He loaded his gear, hopped on the bike, and sped away to a waiting Black Hawk chopper, which spirited him away to parts unknown.

An ambulance arrived at the palace twenty minutes later and carried Lucius Voland to the finest medical center in Jerusalem. With the victim showing a gaping head wound spewing blood, the emergency room doctors immediately assessed him as deceased. Being told he was one of the richest men in the world, they had no choice but to employ all live-saving efforts despite his condition. They worked feverishly to stabilize the bleeding billionaire as the surgical team readied a suite to receive him.

He never made it to surgery. At 7:42 a.m. Israel Standard Time, on July 14, Lucius Voland flatlined and was pronounced dead.

What happened next would be called a miracle by many people around the world.

At 7:43 a.m., before the ink dried on the chart where the doctor wrote the date and time of death of Lucius Voland, the heart monitor still hooked up to his chest beeped, bringing all activity in the ER to a disquieting halt.

"Maybe it's just a final surge of bioelectricity shooting through his body," a nurse said. "His final gasp at life?"

Then it beeped it again. And again. Strong, loud, as if it had never stopped. Faster and faster it beeped, until it had achieved the normal sinus rhythm of a living human being.

Not possible, they all thought. The medical personnel around him gasped in shock when Lucius Voland's eyes shot open, filled with life and energy. They didn't flutter – something one might expect from a person in trauma such as Voland had suffered. His eyes glared with anger.

Lucius Voland sat up and looked around at all the wide-eyed doctors and nurses. Some showed fear in their eyes. Lucius sneered at them, enjoying their fright, their shock. He hated them. He hated everyone, all of humanity.

"Well," he said, basking in his audience's range of reactions, from the merely curious, to completely terrified. "I guess my time has come. Might as well get on with it."

He swung his legs off the ER bed, stood, then strolled toward the exit like someone going for a leisurely afternoon walk. Everyone was so distracted at what they just witnessed they didn't notice that his head wound had healed, and he didn't have so much as a drop of blood on him.

Voland grandly stepped out through the hospital's front door. Even though it was early morning, this was the largest and busiest hospital in Jerusalem, so there was a large crowd of people in the vicinity – some having just been discharged, waiting for rides; others getting out of vehicles, sitting in wheelchairs. Some were being taken out of ambulances on stretchers and wheeled inside.

Lucius understood that for secularists, humanitarian aid is what is needed. But for the religious, a more direct approach worked better. A supernatural approach.

Nearby, a mother pushed a young girl in a wheelchair. She was hunched over from years of pushing the bulky unit, her eyes sad with worry. Lucius Voland walked up to the pair and began talking to them. He asked about the girl's condition and expressed genuine concern.

"How would you like to be able to walk again?" he asked the girl, bent down on one knee to be at her eye level. The mother and daughter exchanged glances, both saying, "Yes! Of course. Who are you?"

"You shall see." Voland touched the girl on her head as he closed his eyes for a minute. He opened them, stood and stepped back a bit. He motioned for her to stand. The young girl hesitated, then held herself steady on the wheel-chair's arms while her mother supported the chair from behind. "I can stand!" she shouted with joy, as she rose from the seat. "Look at me!"

The mother wept and hugged her daughter. "It's a miracle! The doctors told us she would never regain the use of her legs!" The crowd who witnessed the scene clapped and cheered. Many pulled out phone cameras and began record-ing the scene as Voland walked on.

Soon, videos of my miracles will be all over the internet, and the world will know. He smiled to himself, looking for similar opportunities – for it was his time to come out into the limelight, behind the scenes no more. *I have waited for this, when the world is connected by technology. From the comforts of home, work, in restaurants or coffee houses, they will see me. They will know. And many will turn to me as planned through the ages.*

Jack Snyder, Pamela Cosel, Syed Nadim Rizvi

CHAPTER SIXTEEN – AN ABDUCTION

AT 4 P.M. ON JULY 14 in Jerusalem, Rachel sat at her hotel room desk watching the News World live stream on her laptop. Rick crouched behind her peering over her shoulder. They were watching Daniel Murray's morning report. He was on an hour earlier than his normal morning broadcast. He bumped the 9 a.m. anchor's spot, much to that man's annoyance, but Daniel was the network celebrity, so he had carte blanche to rearrange the network's schedule as world events dictated.

Rachel thought he looked as if he hadn't slept a wink and she could tell he was rushed through make-up that morning. *He's trying to get on the air with the news before the competition.*

A "Breaking News" banner lit up the bottom of the screen as he spoke. "In what some are calling a miracle, billionaire Lucius Voland has survived an assassination attempt in Israel and left the hospital minutes after arriving. Hospital staff reported that Mr. Voland received a serious head wound, one they believed fatal at the time, and, in fact they say, he died in the emergency room but was successfully revived—"

Rachel muted the broadcast. Dan's voice was strained and shaky. It could have been just lack of sleep and the rush to get on the air, but she didn't think so. This assassination attempt on Voland was a direct result of her information about him, which Dan successfully passed on to his government contacts. Dan must have thought one of the U.S. federal agencies, the CIA perhaps, would arrest Lucius Voland, or detain him for questioning, basically hold him in some way until the fifteenth came and went. He never thought they'd attempt to kill him. The thought tore him up, just like it did her.

"You didn't expect them to try and kill him, did you?" Rick knew her so well it was as if he could read her mind.

"No...I didn't. I thought they'd try to get intel on him. Monitor him. Maybe detain him. But that's all."

"You glad he survived?" Rick asked, his head cocked to one side, trying to read her expression.

"Not much to be glad about today." She too looked tired from the ordeal.

He nodded earnestly. "Are you *surprised* that he survived?" The question sounded like something an attorney would ask during a cross-examination or deposition of a witness the lawyer was trying to trip up.

Where's he going with this? "A little. Aren't you?" she asked.

Rick picked up Carl's Bible off the desk and opened it to a page in the Book of Revelation. He didn't have to flip through it; he knew right where to go. He handed her the book with his finger on a verse.

"Read this."

She read aloud. "Revelation 13:3. 'And I saw one of his heads as if it had been mortally wounded, and his deadly wound was healed. And all the world marveled and followed the beast.'"

Rachel felt she should be surprised, but wasn't. With everything that had happened in recent weeks, she wasn't sure she'd ever be surprised by anything again.

Next to the scripture verse was more of Carl's handwritten in Hebrew. She showed Rick and tapped on it. "You wouldn't by any chance know what this says, would you?"

He shook his head no. "That was Abe's department."

She sat at the small desk and opened up a browser on her laptop.

"What are you doing?" Rick asked, as he came around to view the screen.

"Google Translate." She opened the Hebrew keyboard and meticulously keyed Carl's Hebrew characters into the field. Rachel expected the result. "To-day's date. July 14," she said to Rick so casually it hovered around the edge of boredom.

"I ask you again: are you surprised?"

"Not anymore," she said. She wasn't bored but overwhelmed with what was happening.

He dug around in his backpack and pulled out his tablet. "I saw this a few hours ago. Was waiting until after Mr. Murray's morning report to show you." He pulled up a link on the device. She was still sitting in the desk chair, so he squatted next to her and held the tablet so they could both see the screen.

Rick touched the link and the video started playing. It was a silly entertainment news program called "Here and Now." It was the kind of program that was all about celebrities and sensationalized stories. Its silly logo bounced around the bottom of the frame, changing colors with each bounce. The hosts, Sally and Sam, both fresh-faced and barely out of high school, stood before a set so busy and colorful as to be distracting. They were bubbly and overly excited to the point of being annoying.

"Here is what is going viral right now across the internet!" Sam shouted as the camera zoomed in and out on him at a nauseating speed.

The screen suddenly filled with clips of various quality, some out of focus, some shaky, all of it amateurish, of Lucius Voland healing people of various ailments. The crippled drop their crutches or stood up tall from their wheelchairs. The blind squealed with delight as they miraculously regained their sight.

Sally and Sam jarringly reappeared obnoxiously laughing and laughing. Rick and Rachel would have stopped the video if they weren't so horrified at the implications, which were completely lost on the kids who hosted this internet show.

"Who is that guy in those clips?!" Sally shouted in a scripted performance so poorly executed she wouldn't have been selected for a role in a neighborhood production.

Sam spread his arms like a circus ringleader announcing the trapeze artists. "Straight from Jerusalem! It's billionaire, industrialist, philanthropist, whatever-ist, Lucius Voland! And I guess we can add miracle healer to his list of accomplishments now!"

The kids delivered some more over-the-top guffaws.

"I guess he's competing with that guy from the church who's also supposedly performing healing miracles in Jerusalem! The guy people claim is Jesus!" The pair was irreverent.

The camera zoomed in and out on them as they belly-laughed.

A cold chill ran through Rachel's body.

"Please, Rick, stop it," she said as she turned away. Rick did as she asked while she lowered herself to the sofa and buried her face in her hands. After a moment, she looked up at Rick, who leaned back against the wall and stared off.

"What are you thinking?" she asked.

"'And he doeth great wonders, and he deceiveth them that dwell on the Earth by the means of those miracles.'" It was a Bible quote he knew well.

Rachel shook her head, stood and walked over to the window. It was the same view she saw every day since she'd been in the hotel, except there was a noticeable increase in military vehicles – Israeli jeeps and personnel transports – rumbling through the streets.

The world is plunging toward disaster, she thought. *And there's nothing I can do about it. In fact, I may have made it worse.*

"None of this would've happened – Lucius getting a head wound, recovering from it and performing miracles – if I hadn't told Daniel about him." Tears welled in her eyes.

Rick referred to Carl's marked-up book. "But it's all right here in the Bible."

"I know. I'm just saying I'm a part of what's happening. I've become a thread in this prophetic tapestry." She shook her head in despair. "And I've been played for a fool."

Rick wished he could ease her conscience, explain that all of this was foretold thousands of years before they were even born. Convince her that all the events that have led to this point started before the universe was even created. But he'd already tried, and it yielded no results. She must deal with this in her own way. As everyone on the planet had to.

Rachel's mobile phone vibrated from her purse. She walked towards it, completely drained of energy, getting the phone from her purse.

"It's a local number, but I don't recognize it." She looked puzzled.

"Are you going to—"

She answered it before Rick finished his sentence. "Hello."

"Hey, Rachel," the person said weakly. "It's Jason."

Rachel frowned. "Oh, hi, Jason." *Why's he calling me?* She quickly lowered the phone and whispered to Rick. "It's that guy that works for Voland. The one I ran into a few times."

Rick was surprised at her words.

Rachel jerked the phone back up to her ear.

"What a crazy day," he said. Rachel thought he sounded defeated, beaten down by life. She also heard background sounds. *He's in a public place. A restaurant? A hotel lobby?*

"I know, right? You okay?" She was fishing and immediately felt guilty. The guy sounded distraught.

"Not really," he sighed. "I'm at a bar not too far from your hotel. Can you meet me here?"

"Sure. What's the name of the place?" Rachel couldn't take off her investigative journalism cap if she'd tried. This was an opportunity to get more info about Voland.

Rick could read it on her face, and he had to bite his tongue to fight the urge of shouting at her and not agree to meet Jason.

She jotted down the name and address of the bar on the small pad of paper hotels always placed on room desks. "Okay, I'll be there shortly." She ended the call.

Rick was flabbergasted. "Why are you meeting him?"

"I don't think he's part of anything. He sounded down and confused," she responded calmly. "I have to get ready. I'll meet up with you when I'm finished."

"Is this personal or professional?" Rick asked, stone-faced. There was an undeniable trace of jealousy in his voice.

She'd always thought of Rick as a brother or, at the very least, a good friend. She spoke gently to him, not wanting to hurt his feelings. "It's both. He sounds like he needs a friend. And maybe I can learn about Voland. And right now...I could really use a drink."

He nodded and slinked out of the room without saying a word, himself exhausted.

Rachel spent a few minutes freshening up and changed her clothes. She kept it casual with a pair of jeans, a loose blouse, and – considering she had a five-block walk – rubber-soled slip-on shoes. She could have taken the car out of the garage but the military activity brewing on the streets below unnerved her. Sticking to the sidewalks sounded much more appealing. She instinctively grabbed the clutch with the camera sewn into it and instantly became depressed thinking about Abe. What she wouldn't give to have Abe – and Rick – watching her back right now. They were a team, and although Rick was technically more than adequate to do what Abe did, he lacked the emotional make-up, the maturity, that Abe brought to the table. As a covert team they were truly crippled with Abe gone. She was about to switch out the clutch with another purse, then thought better of it.

It would be good to honor his memory, she thought as she put her wallet and mobile phone into the clutch and strolled out of the hotel room.

The walk to the corner bar was more harrowing than she expected. The military vehicles rumbling by, coupled with the occasional distant sound of sirens – *Police? Ambulances?* – reminded of her of when she would hurry down the sidewalk to the subway station from the network in New York during a brewing storm as the sun set. The urge to get home to the safety of her apartment was overwhelming. At those times the dread felt like an invisible weight pressing down on her. She knew it was irrational, a base fear driven by instinct, but she felt it, nonetheless.

The same fear and dread coursed through her right now and she found herself hurrying faster and faster with each step toward the bar. She wanted the safety of the indoors and in the company of a possible new friend. And of course, a nice glass of wine. Unlike the thunderstorms that brewed in New York City, she feared the storm that was right now sweeping across the planet was inescapable. No matter where one tried to hide.

She finally believed it now in every part of her being. Jesus was real. And he was on Earth at a Catholic church only a few miles from here. And the Antichrist was also real, in the form of a man named Lucius Voland. Also, only a few miles from where she stood. Should she tell Jason? To what end? She saw how the two teens on their internet show acted. And Jason worked for Lucius Voland. Been close to the man on a daily basis. Surely, he'd laugh it off, think she was a loon, then clam up and regret calling her. No, telling him would be a bad idea.

As a journalist Rachel always wanted to be in the center of the action – where the story was taking place at. But as the old saying goes: Be careful what you wish for. She thought about that now and wondered if it was too late to do anything about it.

Rachel reached the corner bar. She could tell it was an upscale place from the elegant signage and the polished wooden door that complimented the pleasant yellow hue of the Jerusalem stone that made up the rest of the building. This didn't surprise her. Jason Carter seemed like an upscale sort of guy. She'd only seen him three times, once in a tux and twice in a suit, and he wore those outfits as if he were born in them. Yes, this place was definitely the kind of bar he'd go for a happy hour drink.

She pulled the door open and entered. It took her eyes a moment to adjust to the darkness. Table lights dotted the room along with a few ceiling lights, nothing too bright. The lights behind the bar illuminating the glass shelves with rows of hard liquor were the brightest light source in the place. A musician played jazz on a piano in the far corner.

Though he was sitting at the bar with his back to her, Rachel recognized Jason Carter immediately. He was wearing another perfectly tailored suit. She realized each time she saw him he wore a different suit.

She wandered up and perched herself onto the barstool next to him. He had a glass of red wine on the countertop in front of him. It was nearly filled to the brim. That was not something a bartender would normally do unless a customer asked for it, to drown one's sorrows. Or drown something.

A bartender wearing a red vest and smile appeared behind the bar. He was an older guy and Rachel surmised he might have been filling glasses and serving cold bottles of beer since before she was born. She ordered a glass of their finest white wine. If the world was coming to an end, why spare the expense?

"You made good time," Jason said, brooding. He hadn't looked at her yet.

"I always try to be punctual. A habit one develops in my business."

He grinned, turning to face her. "I suppose one could lose out on some great stories if late."

"No supposing about it," she laughed. "I once lost a great scoop to another journalist by getting stuck in rush hour traffic. Never again after that. I'll arrive an hour early and twiddle my thumbs if I have to. Drives my cameraman buggers but what is one to do."

"Thanks for coming," he said, trying to hide his melancholy.

He didn't fool her, however. She shifted her body on the barstool to face him and propped her cheek in her palm, an elbow on the bar. "If you don't mind me asking, I realize we barely know each other, but what's wrong?"

"Where do I begin?" He shook his head and sipped his wine.

"Well...I always thought the best stories began at the beginning. But maybe that's just me." She nodded as the bartender placed a glass of white wine in front of her.

Jason waited until the bartender was out of earshot before he continued.

"I lost my job today." He finished off the last swig of his wine, motioning for another.

"I'm sorry to hear that." Rachel said with sincerity.

They were both quiet, deep in their own thoughts. In Rachel's mind, yes, she thought Lucius was evil incarnate. Spawned from outside space and time, and here to do irreparable harm to all of all of mankind. Still, Jason was just a guy, about her age, who had a job unwittingly working for the Devil himself. That is no different than anybody working for a corporation whose CEO is a psychopath in business, stealing or defrauding as many people as they can, she mused. Many of white-collar criminals have climbed the corporate ladder wrecking lives along the way. Some were demons masquerading as angels, she had learned. The only thing separating them from someone like Lucius Voland is he really was a demon.

The pianist switched from jazz to soft rock. Rachel recognized the song but couldn't quite place it. She hummed a few bars as Jason broke his silence.

"The whole world seems to have just turned upside down," Jason blurted out. Two businessmen at the far end of the bar glanced over as did a couple at a nearby table.

"I know. The military build-up in the Mediterranean keeps escalating. And it's right on our doorstep."

He shook his head, frowning at her. "Yes, but that's not what I'm talking about. You do know what happened this morning, right?"

Of course, I do, but I want to hear it from you. "Actually, I was up all night, on New York time, doing work in real time for the network. So, I slept most of the day."

"Really?" he gaped.

She loathed herself for lying to him like that. "Yeah. What's up?" The loathing bordered on a type of self-hatred at this point.

"My boss was shot today. In the head." He raised his hands toward her.

"What?" Rachel mustered up her best acting skills.

"Yes. But he...," Jason shook his head in disbelief, "... somehow... miraculously... survived. Then he just walked out of the hospital."

She stared at him, unblinking, eyes focused on him like lasers.

"You don't believe me, do you?"

"Why wouldn't I believe you? Yes, it sounds crazy, but, still, there's no reason to lie about it." She was cautious with her words.

"Well... you're not going to believe this next part. I don't even believe this next part." He checked her reaction and saw that she was waiting for him to go on. "I heard he – and there's news clips to back this up – that he was performing... oh, never-mind, it's just so stupid." He swallowed a big drink of wine as easily as one would swig beer.

"You should go easy on that," she cautioned him.

"What difference does it make? Didn't you hear the world was coming to an end?"

"Yes, I heard that too," she agreed. "It's the tension building in the world. It's brought the religious nuts out of the woodwork. I keep hearing about the 'end of the world' as foretold in the Bible." She laughed, wincing deep inside, feeling like she was betraying Rick, possibly the only real friend she had left in the world. She suddenly regretted devoting her entire life to her career, which cut so many people out of her life, and ruined all potential romantic relationships. With the potential for her death tomorrow, along with the rest humanity, she could see with crystalline clarity that her priorities were misplaced. Disastrously so. It was too late to do a darn thing about it now, she realized. The past was forever gone and could not be summoned back.

Her phone rang in her clutch. She remembered to turn the volume up a little before placing it in her purse. She retrieved her phone and saw it was Daniel calling her through Facetime. "It's my boss, I need to take it."

"Sure," Jason said, somewhat tipsy. "No reason for you to lose your job too."

That drew a spontaneous laugh from her. "Sorry," she said. "I don't mean—"

"No, no, it was meant to be funny," he chuckled. "You better take your call."

"Right. I'll be back." She stood and stepped away to have a private conversation. She answered and greeted Daniel. She noted it must have been a poor connection as his image kept breaking up.

"A storm just blew in here," he said. "It's messing with everything, even our broadcast signal. Lots of viewers have called in or emailed us. Weather patterns are going crazy all over the planet. Storms. Heat waves. Very strange."

She thought back to her dream with the enormous hands pouring a bowl of liquid onto the sun that charred the people on the New York City streets like bacon sizzling in a frying pan. *Is this part of the End Times scenario?*

"The reason I'm contacting you, Rachel, is things are turning really bad in the Mediterranean. There's already been warning shots fired between two aircraft that came too close to each other." His voice was quick and excited.

Her jaw opened with surprise. "I hadn't heard that."

The image of Daniel pixelated for a moment, then snapped back clear. "I got that from insiders who told me not to report on it yet."

Dan being told what to do? That's a first. It must be more serious than he's letting on.

The piano player switched to an instrumental version of an Israeli patriotic song. Rachel was familiar with it because Abe once played the music video of the song off his computer.

"The same source told me that Israel might start evacuating the coastal cities. And they fear Jerusalem and Tel Aviv might be imminent military targets. So, I want all News World employees to relocate south, outside the city. Immediately."

"Okay, Rick and I will pack up and get out tonight. Have you talked with him?" she asked.

"No, you're my first call. I'll text him and you can confirm our conversation. Contact me as soon as you both get settled inland."

"Will do." But he was already gone, the signal lost.

Rachel hurried to the bar where Jason was perched on his stool exactly as before, nursing his glass of wine.

"Things are heating up in the Mediterranean," she said. "I need to get back to the hotel, my boss wants me out of the city. You should go too."

Either he didn't take the ramifications seriously or didn't care. Rachel assumed the latter, considering how his own life was falling apart. She touched his shoulder. "Jason, you need to leave this place. It's not safe here."

He nodded and took a drink. "I will. Thanks."

"Good. I have to go." She turned to leave.

"I'll give you a ride," Jason said, his back to her.

Thanks, but it's not that far."

He spun around on his barstool. "Nonsense. I'll drive you."

It occurred to her he might not have any place to go himself. "Okay. Why don't you come with us, my cameraman and me?"

He flashed her a broad grin. "Sounds good! But first..." He points an intoxicated finger at her glass of white wine idly resting on the bar. "Don't let your wine go to waste. You never know. It might be some time before you get more."

It was a good point, she thought. And if that's what it took to get him moving, she reasoned, why not? She stepped over to the bar and downed her glass. There wasn't much in it, anyway. "Come on."

"Yes, ma'am." He followed her out the front door.

Rachel flinched from the sound of a military chopper passing by overhead as soon as they were on the sidewalk. She realized Dan was right to make the call to leave Jerusalem as she watched the machine head toward the sea. Jason didn't react in the least to the sound, nor so much as glance up at the helicopter.

He pulled his car keys from his pocket and pushed the remote key. A nearby black Mercedes honked as its lights flashed.

"Nice ride." Rachel was impressed.

"Company car," Jason said. "They're letting me keep it until the end of the week...then bye-bye." His words were a bit slurred.

If there is an end of the week, Rachel thought. "Maybe I should drive," she said, considering how much he'd been drinking.

"Thanks, but I can handle it." He comically bowed to her.

She didn't push the issue since it was only five blocks to the hotel, against her better judgment. They climbed into the car. It was spacious and the brown leather seats felt cool to Rachel's legs. As they pulled away from the curb, Rachel looked out the passenger window to view the people on the sidewalk shopping in the nearby stores on the block. Some people seemed alarmed by all the military activity; others went about their day either oblivious to what was happening or thinking it was business as usual since seeing soldiers on the street was indeed normal for this part of the world.

Fatigue suddenly rolled over her like a fog and she slumped back against the headrest. *I can't give into my exhaustion. I need to get Rick and get out of here. Jason can go with us. He lives in this country; he must know some small town we can hole up in.* She pictured them convoying – she in her rental, Rick in the van, and Jason in his Mercedes – through the beautiful Israeli countryside, far from the cities until they found a little village lost in time. Ignored by any marauding soldiers that make up Gog. Or is it Magog? She'd have to ask Rick. She tried not to picture explosions on the horizon as Jerusalem fell. But those images forced their way into her mind.

She blinked and looked out the windshield. She was still in Jerusalem, could tell by the architecture, but the streets didn't look familiar. She was so tired her head swam. *The wine must've hit me stronger than I realized.*

"Jason... I think you missed the hotel," she said.

"Yeah, we passed that a couple of kilometers back," he replied nonchalantly.

"What?" She jerked upright in her mind, but her body wouldn't cooperate. She tried to lift her arm, but it was as if it belonged to somebody else.

"This whole 'end of the world' thing really has me on edge, actually," he said with the casualness one typically used when discussing the weather. "But not Mr. Voland. He's been planning it for decades. And July 15th is tomorrow. That's when it all goes down."

Panic erupted within Rachel and she tried to reach for the door handle, but her body wouldn't move. It would've done no good anyway; the car was moving.

"What did you do to me?" she tried to shout, but her words were just a slurred whisper.

"I dosed your wine when you took the call," he said. His voice sounded echo-ey to her. Everything beyond the car windows seemed blurred. "We've kept an eye on you for some time now. Ever since we blew up the holy sites. Mr. Voland couldn't believe how much trouble one person could give him." He glanced over at her to see if she was still conscience. She was, barely. "You can't fight him, Rachel. He's Satan's son."

Blackness was closing in on her. *Got to reach Rick! Or Daniel! Someone, anyone.* She fumbled with her clutch to get her phone out, but her fingers weren't her own anymore. Her purse tumbled from her grasp to the passenger foot wall.

"Where are you taking me?" She didn't know if she asked that out loud or just thought it, until he answered her.

"To see Lucius Voland."

Then she slipped away, her last thought hoping she'd never wake up.

Rachel walked toward a man in a massive room. He wore a black suit and his back was to her. And he seemed so far away. She felt the presence of others all around her. Men in black featureless uniforms. There were insignias on their shoulders. An image of the world with a camera lens in the center. She'd seen this before. Yes, yes, Sharp Eye Global Security. There were men like these on the grounds of the Dome of The Rock right after the terrorist attack. They were escorting her toward the man. Sounds became muted and time seemed to slow down. Rachel didn't know if this was the result of the drug Jason put in her wine, or if it were caused by another reason. Whatever was causing it, it seemed to intensify the closer she got to the man. She glanced around to take in her surroundings. It was a ballroom. A familiar one. She'd been here before, and at that time it was filled with hundreds of people. World leaders, some of the wealthiest, most powerful people on the planet. The men escorting her stopped before one particular man. Rachel stopped with them but didn't know if it was of her own accord or if the men stopped her.

The man in control turned toward her, slowly and methodically, but not because he was affected by the slowed time that seemed to hold her, but because he chose to. It was Lucius Voland. Tall and intimidating, with a predatorial grin. He looked her directly in the eyes and she was forced to look away, cowering in his dominant and commanding presence.

"Hello, Rachel," he said. "Good to see you again." His words weren't evil or threatening. They were inviting. Quite inviting. Which made them far more frightening. And dangerous. "You were right to question the rationale of the End Times. Why would I fight if I knew I was going to lose? I know about this coming battle more than any human that has ever walked the Earth. I have read the holy books of the three Abrahamic faiths – in fact, in the original versions, not later translations." He paused to see what effect he was having on her. She still couldn't bring herself to look at him, which gave him great pleasure.

"My security teams did indeed destroy the Church of the Holy Sepulchre, the Dome of the Rock, and the Wailing Wall," he continued. "I put them there for that exact task. But only at a time of my choosing. There have been many attempts over the years to destroy one or more of those sites by various religious fanatics and cults. They thought if they did, they could bring about the End Times. And maybe they could have. But my people were always there to stop them. I had to wait until the time in which I was ready. And I'm ready now."

Through a gargantuan effort, Rachel forced herself to look at him, and tried to speak, but her mouth would not respond to her mental efforts. His spell infused her spirit. She tried to turn away again, but unlike before, when she had trouble looking at him, she now couldn't look away. He held her attention as if he had her under a hypnotic spell. She could only focus on him, hearing Voland's voice and nothing else.

"I know you have felt a deep emptiness for years, Rachel. Most of your life in fact. That is why you threw yourself into your work. Until you had few friends outside of co-workers. Until it consumed you. But I – Lucius Voland – can make you whole again, dear Rachel. Just as I've done with all of the people you saw here in my ballroom the night of the party. Become one of my people. Side with me against my enemy. You can't imagine what awaits you here." He smiled a fatherly smile which warmed her heart.

Rachel's mind flashed back over her years of endlessly struggling to be the best of the best, caught forever in the rat race. Depriving herself of any kind of real life outside her career. Endless nights of loneliness. She looked Voland in the eyes and felt safe and secure. Her past pains diminishing, fading from her mind.

Yes...he's right...maybe I can become one of his people...they seemed so happy and it's so peaceful here in his palace...I would want for nothing...whiling away my days drinking and dancing...not a care or need in the world...

The thought of it gave her a sense of peace she hadn't felt in...well...possibly never.

Yet there was something at the edges of the thought she couldn't quite focus on. It was like a shadow in one's peripheral vision. When one turns to look at it, it slips away from view. It's not really gone though. It's always there. One can just never quite focus on it.

It's Jesus... just at the edge of my vision...Voland is trying to block me from seeing him...that's Voland's enemy Jesus...

She sensed hatred welling up in Voland. He doubled down on trying to control her. "Ignore him, Rachel. You belong with me."

No! This is wrong! Rachel came to her senses through sheer strong will. *This is evil. I need to get out of here while I still can.* Rachel squeezed her eyes shut so hard they hurt. It took a gargantuan effort to push Voland's enticing offer from her mind. But she did. And he knew it.

"Away with her," Lucius Voland bellowed in seething anger and hatred. His voice welled from the pit of hell, breathing fire from the depths where anguished souls reside.

His men grabbed her and as they dragged her away, blackness consumed her again. Merciful blackness.

Rachel was in a cold, hard place. Distant thunder rocked her. Her eyes fluttered open, and she became aware of laying on a stone floor. She was cold and the clothes she wore smelled of perspiration. Her neck ached for lack of a pillow. She sat up and took in her surroundings. She was in a rather large old-fashioned jail cell made of stone bricks. It was downright ancient actually. And big enough to hold at least a dozen people. It looked like something one would see on a visitor's tour of structures from the Middle Ages, right down to the barred door and window. A square of soft moonlight beaming from the window to the floor was the only real light source. There was also a trickle of light from the hallway outside the cell door.

I must still be in the palace, she thought.

Distant thunder again gently rocked the palace. But it wasn't thunder, she realized. It was too sharp and loud without any real rumbling. Rachel slowly climbed to her feet, using the cold wall for assistance. The effects of the drug seemed to be wearing off. Though it wasn't enough to mitigate her bleak circumstances, it was certainly a step in the right direction.

She stepped to the window and looked out. It was the dead of night. Nearly pitch black beyond the window except for the horizon, made jagged by the silhouetted buildings and trees of the Jerusalem cityscape. It must be midnight or after.

Flashes on the horizon told her all she needed to know about the cause of the thunder-like sounds. Those were artillery shells; the city was under siege.

Did Rick get out? Fear and guilt gripped her. She never made it back to the hotel. Maybe he tried calling her. She'll never know though. Her phone was long gone, along with her clutch. Probably still in the passenger foot well of Jason's Mercedes.

"It's begun," Jason said from behind her.

She whirled around and saw him standing beyond the barred door. The light in the corridor illuminated only half his face; the other side was completely shrouded in darkness.

"What has begun?" Her throat hurt a little, possibly a side effect of the drug.

"The war between Israel and Syria and their respective allies. Of course, we caused all of it." He smiled, which took on a particularly creepy appearance in the lighting, being only half a smile with one eye above it. "But now it's taken on a life of its own. Probably go nuclear before it's all over."

She was revulsed by him and didn't bother to hide it.

"I liked you, Rachel, I really did. But there are more important things in life." He smirked.

"Like what?" she asked in disgust.

"Not dying for one thing." He brushed imaginary lint from his jacket lapel.

"We all die." Rachel hoped this was not the time for her to leave this planet, not yet.

"Lucius offers eternal life. He tried to tell you."

She grimaced at him, glad they were separated by bars, hoping he didn't have the keys to enter.

"You have any idea how crazy that sounds?" She immediately regretted asking him that. It was obvious he was deranged – something she didn't need to comment on – and if he *did* have a set of keys, he might enter the cell and harm her. Or kill her. Speaking her mind, sometimes at the wrong time, was second nature to her, and got her into trouble more times than she cared to think about. She realized now that it was due to pride and ego. She remembered the Bible had something to say about that. Rick could give her the exact scripture quote, chapter and verse, without even looking it up. She hoped she would live long enough for him to do that. If he was alive still. Pangs of guilt and worry kicked her again and knotted her stomach.

"You have your god and I have mine," was all he said in a weak and pathetic voice.

She knew then and there he was a miserable, feeble little man. Any attraction she had for him vanished instantly. She turned her back on him and looked out the window at the distant explosions. She wasn't afraid of him anymore.

"Lucius will be stopped," she said.

"By whom? He's respected worldwide. No one's figured out he destroyed the holy sites in Jerusalem, or the missile accident in Ashdod, because all the investigators are in his back pocket. He's also responsible for the destruction of The Great Mosque in Damascus and no one would even suspect him for that anyway. Oh, yeah...and he was also responsible for the death of your friend, Carl."

Rachel wasn't really listening; she didn't care what he had to say. It was all academic, anyway. Lucius Voland was evil and responsible for much pain and suffering. Simply put, he was mankind's main villain. All the particulars and fine details were irrelevant – except for one that just now occurred to her. "Why am I still alive?" she asked, perplexed, still staring out the window.

No answer. She turned around. Jason was gone. Stepping away from the window, Rachel put her forehead against the stone wall. She could feel gentle vibrations through it from the shelling of Jerusalem. She slid down to a kneeling position, clasped her hands in prayer, and did something she hadn't done since junior high school.

At first, she whispered, then her voice grew bolder with her plea. "Please, God, the world needs you. And please look after Rick. Protect him. I got us both into this mess. But we need you to get us out. In Jesus's name, amen."

She remained in that position until her knees hurt. As she came to her feet, male voices from outside drew her to the window. They were coming from below the window, probably at ground level. A sliver of the rising sun peered over the horizon. So it wasn't just after midnight; it was before dawn. The light gave the area just beyond the window more detail. Based on the tree level, Rachel guessed she was four or five stories up. That's why she couldn't make out what the men were saying. All she knew was that it sounded like two men. One was angry, and one was pleading. Then silence, followed by a deep man's voice giving instructions. Several more seconds passed, then she heard the sounds of many vehicle doors opening and closing. A group of automobile engines started, wheels rolled, and the sounds faded out.

Rachel lowered herself to a sitting position and leaned back against the wall. She wept for herself, for Rick, for the world.

CHAPTER SEVENTEEN – SAFE AND SOUND

ALMOST FIFTEEN HOURS EARLIER, around 4:30 p.m., as Rachel was freshening up in her hotel room to meet Jason at the bar, Rick walked out of the elevator into the hotel's parking garage and stepped into Abe's van. Abe had given him the vehicle's spare set of keys a long time ago and told him to use it whenever he needed to, but he never felt right doing that after Abe died. He thought it would be disrespectful. But if there ever was a need, it was now. Rick didn't trust Jason Carter because he worked for Lucius Voland. Yes, he had to admit there was some jealousy involved. Rick had developed quite the crush on Rachel the moment he'd met her. It went unrequited, and probably always would, but it sure made working for News World enjoyable. Spending day after day with Rachel Williams was heaven even when she was demanding. Especially when she was demanding. At least then he knew she really needed him.

Rick drove the van out of the garage and parked it on the street about a block from the hotel's entrance. He didn't know at which bar she was to meet Jason and it wasn't in his nature to ask, but he understood it was close by. He knew Rachel well enough to guess that she'd walk to it.

He had followed her at a discreet distance, rolling slowly in the van, and his heart palpitated at the thought that she might look back and discover him. How would he explain it then? How could he avoid looking like a creepy stalker? All the worry was for naught, however. She never noticed and he successfully followed her straight to the bar.

He found a spot next to the curb under a tree, where he could park facing away from the bar. It was the perfect stakeout location. He could watch the bar through his passenger sideview mirror and the odds of getting caught by her were so slim as to be negligible.

Time passed and there was no sign of her coming out. Rick sat there so long he feared dozing off when he was awakened by a Facetime call from Daniel Murray. He ignored it because Dan might ask him what he was doing, and Rick was a lousy liar. He didn't want to miss Rachel leaving the bar while on a call. The call went to voicemail, and in a few minutes, the front door to the drinking establishment swung open, and Rachel and Jason emerged. Based on their gait, Rick concluded they were tipsy. They also looked a little too friendly with each other for Rick's tastes. Jealousy stabbed at him, taunting him. He pushed it out of his mind and focused on the reason he was there: to keep Rachel safe. Thoughts of Lucius Voland and Armageddon were secondary to Rick's objective.

He watched them get into Jason's car – a classy and expensive Mercedes. Rick followed at a safe distance as they drove in the direction of the hotel. When they passed it, Rick thought they were heading to dinner at some nearby restaurant and jealousy reared its ugly head again. As the Mercedes left the city, Rick dropped way back but continued to follow them. The traffic was virtually non-existent in the countryside which increased the possibility of being discovered a dozen-fold.

It was when he saw Lucius Voland's palace looming in the distance that terror gripped Rick tightly like a vise clamped on his heart. He never guessed that Jason would head that way.

As the Mercedes rolled onto the palace's long driveway, Rick sped the van passed it not caring if he was seen or not. A few hundred feet further down the road, he killed the lights and pulled the van onto the shoulder so quickly he almost lost control. Not caring whether the vehicle was adequately hidden, he got out and sprinted back to the driveway, being thankful for all the times he lugged heavy equipment blocks for Rachel. It built up his stamina in ways he never realized until now. Rick kept to the shadows as he ran across the lawn up to the circular driveway in front of the palace. He hid in the brush and watched Jason park the Mercedes behind a row of other vehicles – SUVs and Humvees – and walk around to the passenger door, where he hoisted Rachel's unconscious body out and carried her into the palace.

Rick was so far out of his realm of experience he felt completely helpless. He tried Facetiming Daniel but couldn't get a signal. Then he tried a regular phone call with the same result, followed by a text, which wouldn't send. He tried to reach the Jerusalem Police. Still no signal. He plopped down on the grass and detested himself for being a useless, cowardly fool.

Hours passed as he tried repeatedly to contact Dan Murray and others at News World, as well as the police. All attempts failed. He toyed with the idea of returning to the van and driving back to Jerusalem, or at least close enough to get a signal to call for help, but he feared that Rachel would be moved from the palace while he was away.

A military strike on Jerusalem lit up the sky like a thunderstorm on the horizon, and he realized any small chance of driving back to the city evaporated. The sound of the distant explosions were sharp and reverberated in his chest. The assault went on for hours, settling down but not quite ceasing in the wee hours of the morning, as the sun peeked over the horizon.

The front doors to the palace swung open and Lucius Voland marched out with Jason Carter at his side. Security guards followed them down the steps to the vehicles. Lucius suddenly whirled around and faced Jason. The security guards stayed a safe distance away from the pair.

"You failed me, Jason," Lucius said in a voice that was more animalistic than human.

"I'm sorry," Jason said fearfully. "I was trying to make up for her escaping the explosion when she was at the café with Carl Thompson. To see if she'd join us."

"You knew she was too strong-willed to turn," Voland seethed, spit spraying from between his teeth. "You only brought her here because you're a weak, sentimental fool. That's why you delayed detonating the bomb at the café until she walked a safe distance away."

Jason babbled in panic. "No! No! I was waiting—"

"You think you can lie to me?!" Lucius shouted, towering over him. "You know I can't personally kill anyone directly unless they've given me their allegiance. In an ironic twist, you knew she wouldn't give herself to me, therefore she'd be safe from the coming Armageddon."

Jason silently cowered in fear as Lucius stepped closer.

"But you belong to me!" Lucius shouted as he produced an ornamental dagger and slashed Jason's throat so swiftly, all Rick saw was a flash of metal and a spurt of crimson before Jason's limp body dropped out of view.

Rick gasped at the sight but was too far away for Lucius or his guards to hear. At least he hoped he was, and based on their lack of response, he was most likely correct.

The dagger vanished from where it came just as quickly as it appeared. Lucius turned to his guards. "Remove him," he barked, his hands thrust into the air like a conductor standing before a symphony.

Several guards picked up Jason's body by the arms and legs and hid him behind some bushes. Then Lucius and his guards all piled into the vehicles, with Lucius climbing into the passenger seat of the Humvee stationed at the front of the line. The convoy moved out swiftly, the tires kicking up dust in their wake.

It took a long time for Rick to get up the courage to enter the palace. It was nearly a half-hour, though it felt much longer to him. He had no choice. From what he gathered from Lucius and Jason's conversation, Rachel was inside and still alive. He threw a rock through a window and climbed in. If any alarms sounded inside, they were silent ones. Retrieving the rock he had just thrown, he clutched it like a weapon and roamed the palace until he found what he took to be the most ancient part of the centuries-old building. He was inside one of the spires that held a winding stone staircase. He climbed up the staircase, two steps at a time, for several stories, his shoes echoing on the stone walls with each step. From there he followed a corridor hoping he wasn't wrong in his guess as to the location of the cell where Lucius had locked up Rachel.

He spied her curled up on the floor just past a shaft of light pouring in through the barred window. She didn't seem to be breathing. On a hook on the outside wall near the cell was a key. He worked it into the lock with some effort, fearing for a moment it was either the wrong key or he wouldn't be able to get it to fit even if it was the right one. He finally got it seated and popped the lock open. The old metal door scraped the floor as it opened. Still, there was no movement from Rachel. His heart pounded with anxiety.

"Rachel," he said, just above a whisper as he moved closer to her, crouching. He didn't want to startle her, or alert anyone who might still be in the palace. It was an enormous place and very likely someone else was guarding the halls.

She moaned, stirred from her position, and sat up. At first, the sight of Rick stunned her; she saw he was pale and shaking with fright.

"Rick!" Tears flowed down her face and she too shook.

"Shhh...we might not be alone. Come on, I'll explain later."

He helped her to her feet and they quietly left the cell, sticking close to the wall as they descended the stone spiral staircase to the first floor.

They were headed for the front door when Rachel stopped them. "I need to check on something first. It's important." She ducked into the side room off the entryway, which led to the ballroom.

Rick was infuriated, tried to grasp her arm but she moved too quickly. He kept his thoughts to himself and followed along, as he always did, quiet on his feet.

Inside the ballroom Rachel stood before the glass case where Lucius displayed his artifacts. The whip and the Spear of Destiny were gone. Rick saw they were missing as well.

She stood with her arms crossed on her chest, trying to stop her shaking. The look in her eyes when she turned to Rick was one of panic. "Lucius and Jesus fight today. Can Lucius possibly win?"

Rick shook his head and shrugged his shoulders. "From everything I've read in the Bible, and many books on the End Times and eschatological studies, the standard answer is no. But there is so much symbolism that must be interpreted, and scholars through the centuries have disagreed on many of those interpretations, so..."

"You're trying to tell me you don't know, right?" She was impatient and scared.

"That's right," he said, embarrassed. "Come on, let's get out of here." He turned to lead the way and Rachel followed this time.

They peered out the front door and saw no sign of Lucius or his men. Why would they? *Lucius had bigger concerns than two insignificant humans to deal with,* Rick thought.

They descended the steps leading to the driveway. Rachel slowed and glared with astonishment at the blood stain on the bottom landing.

"Ignore that," Rick said, trying to shield her eyes with a hand. He knew it was Jason's blood and his corpse was in the bushes just off the steps but there was no reason to tell her that.

Rick quickly led her across the front lawn to where the van was partially hidden and unlocked the passenger door for her.

Rachel noticed all was quiet on the horizon as she got into the vehicle. "Hear that? No more bombing." She closed the van's door. She noticed a few plumes of smoke scattered here and there, furling into the sky, but that was it.

Rick got in behind the driver's seat, turned on the engine, and wheeled the van around, headed toward Jerusalem.

"Shouldn't we be getting further away from the city, not closer?" she asked.

"If the world is coming to an end, I think it would be better to be closer to Jesus, so I'm taking us to St. Joseph's Church. Is that all right?"

She thought it was sweet of him to ask. "Sure," she said with a warm smile.

As Rick drove, he explained how he followed her to the bar, then to the palace, and what he witnessed transpire between Lucius and Jason.

"Jason was a jerk," he said, "but ironically, he saved your life that day at Jonah's Café with Carl."

"What did Lucius mean that he can't kill people directly?" Rachel asked.

"The devil can tempt us, influence us, try to get us to stray, but he can't do it directly. He needs others to do the dirty work. He's limited by human behavior."

"I guess humans even foul up the devil now and then," she chuckled, glad she could find something amusing even as the world might be coming to an end. Rick grinned with her.

"Human intervention might change the outcome of this yet," she said, though Rick doubted that.

The traffic was thick with cars evacuating the city as they approached it. No cars were heading back in, so their side of the highway was clear. Had there not been a deep grassy divide between the highways, they were certain both sides would be full of traffic leaving the destruction.

Warning horns blared from towers throughout Jerusalem signaling all to vacate. As the pair drove, they saw bombed out buildings, turned over cars, and debris littering the roads. Rachel spotted a handful of people and families hurrying into vehicles and speeding off. She sighed in relief at the sight of the survivors and hoped the shelling had completely ended, but if not, silently prayed it wouldn't start again until long after everyone was out.

"Are you sure it's not a bad idea to go to St. Joseph's?" she asked Rick, not really wanting to usurp his decision. Her comment was more one of fear. "Won't it be empty?"

"Let's take our chances," he said as he swung the van around the corner. Ahead of them the historic church sat untouched by the attack, with tens of thousands of people in front of it, still clogging the streets and sidewalks. She was dumbfounded that they had survived the bombings.

"Wow!" she exclaimed.

"I've been closely following the developments here," Rick said as he carefully weaved the van through the crowd, which separated for him to drive through. "The crowd is in the millions, but the core group is 144,000."

Rachel wracked her brains. "Why does that number mean something to me?"

"It's from the Book of Revelation. Twelve thousand from each of the twelve tribes of Israel. They're God's special army. Whether they realize it or not," he laughed. "To use a cliché, God works in mysterious ways."

Rick managed to get the van to the foot of the stairs leading up to the church. They got out and mounted the steps, weaving in and out of those who sat there. Rachel surveyed the crowd below. Besides Christians, there appeared to also be Jews and Muslims, based on their modes of dress, as well as many from non-Abrahamic religious faiths. This was something she had noticed on her first venture to the church but being so focused on her mission at the time, she put it out of her mind. Not now – this time the scene held much more significance.

"They're not all Christians." Her voice sounded almost joyful.

"God is greater than our prejudices." Of that, Rick was sure.

As they neared the top of the staircase, they both noticed Father Marco and Rabbi Noah talking to a large group of people standing on the steps.

"They're preparing for the final conflict with the Antichrist," Rick noted. "Lucius has probably gathered all his followers right now and is on his way."

It dawned on Rachel that she could have been one of Lucius's followers had he successfully seduced her with his power last night. If she'd fallen, she would now be on her way to the church to battle these people. The thought sickened her. And she knew Jason would be among them if he wasn't already dead.

They continued up the steps to where Eric the Deacon waited in front of the church doors. He gave her a wide, welcoming smile. "Good to see you again, Rachel. Jesus awaits you."

She was speechless and glanced several times between Eric and Rick. They grinned at her like two men in on a joke.

"What? You didn't realize you've been serving him this entire time?" Eric laughed lovingly.

"Am I the last to know this?" Rachel asked. *How could that be?*

Eric and Rick both broke into a belly laugh. Rachel just grinned and shook her head at them as if they were ornery children.

Eric opened the heavy church door for Rachel. Rick hung back as she stepped onto the threshold.

"Aren't you coming?" she asked.

He shook his head no. "My place is with the others." He motioned to the massive crowd that stretched as far as she could see.

Rachel nodded understandingly and gave him a parting hug before she entered the church.

The door closed behind her and the silence of the church enveloped her. The church was empty except for Jesus, who was standing a distance away in the Sanctuary. Though he was at the far end of the church, Rachel could feel his radiance as though he were standing next to her. She walked over to him, her soft-soled shoes echoing in the sacred silence within the holy place.

Reaching the foot of the Sanctuary, she looked up into the eyes of the Son of God. He spoke to her in a soft, compassionate voice. It was a voice bursting with an eternity of wisdom, infinite patience, and a love so deep as to be incomprehensible by human standards.

Rachel dared to ask a question and did so reverently. "What was the purpose of keeping my servitude hidden from me?" It wasn't accusatory. She asked him the way a student would ask a teacher.

"Your actions were of your own accord. Your own will. It just so happened that yours and my Father's will were the same."

"You came a few weeks ago. Why have you let things go on? So many people die?" She was confused but sought answers. A journalist at heart – or maybe this time she was simply a woman seeking to deepen her faith.

"For the same reason I have not interfered in mankind's activities over the last 2,000 years," Jesus said with kindness. "My Father bestowed free will upon mankind. We let you all follow your own paths and desires. Everyone is embodied with the right to choose. You can see where that has led. My coming here physically has resonated through the souls of all, whether they have acknowledged it or not. It gives everyone a final chance to choose."

Everything he said now made perfect sense to Rachel. He gave people the extra few weeks to decide with whom their spirit aligned, and the opportunity to change their ways if they desired. It was the merciful thing to do. Something that undoubtedly helped millions of people. It certainly helped her. A mere few weeks ago she didn't really believe in much of anything. But that had all changed, she knew.

"Time to bring it to an end," he said. Jesus descended the short flight of stairs from the altar so gracefully it looked as if he were floating.

"Follow me," he said as he walked passed her.

Rachel obeyed Jesus and walked behind him to the front of the church whereby the doors opened on their own. They were instantly assaulted by crowd noises, but it didn't matter; she felt safe and secure in Jesus's presence.

Alert with the intensity of her feelings, she thought the crowd seemed louder than before and wondered if it was her imagination. A glance to the sky told her it wasn't. Hundreds of dark dots filled the heavens outward toward the horizon. She'd been a foreign correspondent in dangerous spots long enough to know what those were. Fighter jets. And they were flying in the church's direction.

"Are they coming to our aid?" she asked Jesus.

"No," he answered matter-of-factly, not a trace of concern in his voice. He pointed to another part of the sky, to another group of growing dots. "But those are."

The jets engaged each other high above the church, like two clusters of bees battling to the death over territory.

Just then, tanks appeared from all angles and roared into the screaming crowd. Dozens of them screeching grinding metal, chewing up the streets with their treads. They were flanked by hundreds of men who sported machine guns and wore black uniforms with insignias that indicated they were with Lucius's security company.

To Rachel's horror, they began spraying the crowd with bullets.

Rachel whirled around toward Jesus. "What are you going to—?" But Jesus was gone.

Feeling helpless, she stood an open target at the top of the stairs watching the mayhem unfold below her. She scanned for Rick, for Father Marco, Rabbi Noah, and Eric the Deacon. But they were nowhere to be seen, apparently lost in the crowd. She wondered if they'd fled or were fighting Lucius's forces.

A whistling in the air above her drew her attention. It was an incoming artillery shell. For just a moment, she regretted returning to the city and wondered if Jesus would be disappointed in her. After all, she was only an imperfect human, full of doubt and fear. There were those who followed him 2,000 years ago who felt the same way. And those were his disciples. *How could someone without that intense of a connection to him fare any better?* she wondered.

She turned to run from the horror, to scramble into the church. The shell landed in the crowd within a few hundred feet of her. The resulting explosion was deafening. The concussion swept her off her feet and vibrated through her with such violent force she was convinced it had damaged something inside her.

All these thoughts crossed her mind in the smallest fraction of a second, before she was conscious of floating in a quiet and peaceful white void.

Rachel awakened in a lush green field filled with vibrant, colorful flowers. The sweet aroma overwhelmed her senses. The sky was the brightest blue she'd ever seen but there was no sun in sight, no matter which direction she looked.

She stood up effortlessly and pain-free. She examined her body and saw there was no apparent injury from the explosion. She felt alert and energetic and her mind seemed opened to another level of consciousness. She looked around and saw the field went on forever in three directions. The fourth led to a gentle rise that she couldn't see over from where she stood.

Disturbing sounds from beyond the rise drew her attention. She didn't know if they had just begun or if she'd only now become aware of them. Either way, she wasn't afraid. Feelings of peace and contentment flowed through her.

She walked up the gentle slope expecting to crest a hill, but it was a cliff that looked down upon a deep desert valley. Impossibly deep by earthly standards. Off to one side of the desert was another steep cliff that dropped to an ocean made of fire that stretched on into infinity, just like the field behind her.

Two huge forces rushed toward each other on horseback. Even though she seemed too far away to make out any details, she saw with inhuman crystal clarity everything that was happening.

Jesus road a white horse and clutched a sword above his head. He led an army of angels so large Rachel couldn't wrap her mind around its magnitude.

Leading an army of demons toward Jesus and the angels was Lucius Voland, atop a black horse, with the spear in one hand and the whip in the other. He was larger and distinctly more demonic than the human version of himself that Rachel had seen.

The two forces clashed, angels against demons, swords clanging together. A spear thrown, a crack of the whip. Jesus and Lucius circled each other and engaged their weapons. Thunder sounded and lightning flashed all around them. Inhuman screams were mingled with songs of praise from the multitudes.

Rachel's head felt dizzy as she tried to comprehend what she was witnessing. Even with her elevated consciousness, it was too abstract and otherworldly.

The battle worked its way to the edge of the cliff that ended in the shear drop to the infinite fiery ocean below.

Lucius and Jesus leaped from their horses and continued the battle on foot wielding sword, whip and spear.

Rachel watched, transfixed, as Jesus drove Lucius right to the edge of the cliff. With a wide sweep of his sword, Jesus disarmed Lucius of his whip and spear. Then he seized him with God-given strength by the shoulders. And although they seemed miles away, and thousands of feet below from where she stood, she heard Jesus clearly say, "You made your choice eons ago, as did all the fallen angels."

With all his mighty fortitude, Jesus hurled Lucius off the cliff to the depths below. Lucius glared defiantly as he plummeted silently into the flames, not uttering a sound. Lucius's army of demons were sucked into the flames as if bound to him by invisible tendrils, leaving only Jesus and his angels behind, triumphant for all the ages.

Jesus turned and looked up at Rachel. His eyes glowed brightly, consuming her in blinding whiteness.

Rachel blinked and looked up into the faces of three men staring down at her. It was Rick, Father Marco, and Rabbi Noah. She laid sprawled on the top landing of the church stairs just in front of the doors.

They helped her to sit, and she saw thousands of people in the streets. They sang, they danced, they celebrated, all while praising God in loud voices, hands raised in the air. No death or destruction was apparent, as if it never happened. The sky was a bright, clear blue, though not as bright or blue as the place she'd just been, she thought. There was no longer an air battle between fighter jets in the skies above.

"It's over?" Rachel asked, incredulous.

"Yes," Father Marco said. "The Earth suddenly opened and swallowed the Antichrist's forces."

Rachel was perplexed. "But the Antichrist had the whip and the spear. And set up the obelisk."

"All for naught. Driven by ego and pride. His only way out was to turn to God for forgiveness. The easy path. But for eons, it has been the only one he wouldn't consider."

Rick extended a hand; she took it and he helped her stand up.

"You missed it all," Rabbi Noah said to her, putting an arm around her shoulder.

Rachel rubbed her forehead. "I don't know about that. I witnessed...something. It was truly marvelous. Miraculous. Overwhelming. I saw Jesus fighting... He was the conqueror."

"That sounds marvelous, but the human mind has limitations," the Rabbi said. "Your mind probably interpreted things the best it could while you were blacked out. But you are right. Jesus did win!"

Rachel looked out at the celebration. "Did we really stop Armageddon?"

Father Marco grinned and bowed with humility. "Well...not us, exactly. But we played our part. And many nations on both sides didn't show up for the war."

Confused, Rachel looked at each man's face for clarification.

"It's true. It's all over the news," Rabbi Noah said.

Rick stepped up. "It was actually your doing, Rachel."

Rachel shook her head, thoroughly lost. "I don't understand."

"You remember," Rick continued, "I advised you not to take action against the Antichrist, that it was folly to even try?"

"Yes, I remember. Go on."

Rick placed his hands on her upper arms and looked her directly in the eyes. "Well, I was wrong."

"No, you weren't," she said. "Everything I did accomplished nothing." Her expression was one of confusion, still searching for clarity.

"Not true," Rick said as he let go of her. "You set events into motion that led to Lucius getting a head wound from which he recovered, as foretold in the Bible. What wasn't anticipated, however, was that event awakened much of the world from its slumber. Billions of people are familiar with that Biblical story. Half the world ceased hostilities against each other and clearly saw who the real enemy was. You helped make that happen."

Rachel stood in awe of Rick's explanation. She didn't want to accept or believe that she played a key role in a drama that spanned eternity and infinity. She was humbled by the thought. *I'm just a news reporter*, she thought. And yet she remembered the story of Queen Esther from the Bible, one her mother had told her long ago. Perhaps she indeed was born "for such a time as this." Rachel knew everyone born has a purpose. Was this hers?

"What happens now?" she asked. "And where's Jesus?"

Father Marco stood off to the side, gazing in rapture skyward. "He's coming."

They all followed his gaze. A blazingly, bright white spot in the sky grew larger and larger. Within it were white figures filled with joy, riding on horses coming toward them.

It was Jesus and his angels – his second coming was reality.

ABOUT THE AUTHORS

JACK SNYDER

Jack Snyder is a prolific award-winning screenwriter with eight produced feature-length screenplays under his belt, three of which he directed. His films have been distributed by 20th Century Fox, NBCUniversal, Warner Brothers, and Sony. Several have shown theatrically and aired on The Showtime Network, The Movie Channel, the Syfy Channel, and the Lifetime Movie Network.

Jack got his start in filmmaking by writing and directing the indie thriller, Ghost Image, starring Elizabeth Rohm (American Hustle, Joy), and Stacey Dash (Clueless). The film won multiple awards and was distributed on premium cable networks worldwide through 20th Century Fox, which only picks up 20-30 independent films per year out of the thousands submitted.

Following that success, Jack went on to write and direct the crime drama Fatal Call, which is streaming on Amazon Prime and available on DVD and Blu-ray. The third film he wrote and directed, a thriller titled Family of Lies, airs regularly on the Lifetime Movie Network and is available on DVD through Sony Pictures.

In addition to writing his own original scripts, Jack has done many screenplay adaptations of novels. He had the honor of being chosen to adapt the best-selling horror novel, Cold Moon Over Babylon, written by the late Michael McDowell, a novelist and screenwriter most famous for Beetlejuice and The Nightmare Before Christmas. The Academy of Motion Picture Arts and Sciences, the organization that gives out the Oscars, requested a copy of Jack's screenplay for its Core Collection. The screenplays in this collection are used for research and study purposes by producers, academics, and students. The film produced from the screenplay, titled Cold Moon, stars Josh Stewart (The Dark Knight Rises), Candy Clark (American Graffiti, Twin Peaks), Frank Whaley (Pulp Fiction, Ray Donovan), and Christopher Lloyd (Back to The Future). The film was released theatrically and is currently available on DVD, Blu-ray, and many online streaming services.

Though several of Jack's screenplays would fall under the thriller category, he's written in every genre, such as historical dramas, comedies, science fiction, western, and faith-based.

His many other produced screenplays have starred such celebrities as Florence Henderson (The Brady Bunch), Pam Grier (Jackie B rown), Judge Reinhold (Beverly Hills Cop), Kristy Swanson (Buffy the Vampire Slayer), Kevin Sorbo (Hercules: The Legendary Journeys), John Schneider (The Dukes of Hazzard, Smallville), and many others.

When Jack is not writing or directing movies, he and his wife hike the many canyons in the San Fernando Valley or hang out with their son and two Chihuahuas on Zuma Beach in Malibu.

PAMELA COSEL

Pamela Cosel is a freelance writer and editor who was first published as a journalist in 1980. She has written for newspapers, magazines and online in subsequent decades, having also worked in television news at KXRM in Colorado Springs, CO, and KXAN in Austin, TX. Pam covered the Democratic National Convention in Denver in 2008 as a blogger for KXRM, the year Barack Obama won the presidential nomination.

Pam is a multi-faceted project manager in communications, marketing, public relations, and tourism. Her experience also includes communications work in the non-profit sector, such as with United Way and Hospice. Her background includes 14 years of work in city government in communication departments and producing special events, recently retiring from her role as the public information officer for the City of Taylor, TX, in order to focus on expanding her writing and editing business of ATXEditing.

Pam's expertise in planning and managing special events reached a global scope when she worked as the internal communications manager for World Youth Day '93 in Denver, the international gathering of 250,000 youth and young people from around the world for a week of religious activities held at the calling of Pope John Paul II. As part of her job, she coordinated the communication logistics for the initial, outdoor meeting of President Bill Clinton and Pope John Paul II at Denver's old Stapleton International Airport. Later, Pam was hired to produce two special events in one day for television entertainer and musician John Tesh in conjunction with his "Live at Red Rocks" concert in Denver.

She holds a B.A. in Communication from Regis University, Denver, and at commencement received Regis University's Community Service Award. Born and raised in Chicago, she moved to Colorado in 1973, and later spent two years living in the High Desert of California. She relocated to Austin, Texas in 2010 where she loves the warm weather, the music, and the people of Texas. She sings soprano with Chorus Austin, fulfilling her passion for music which spills over into playing the accordion, mandolin and folk harp. She has three adult children and four grandchildren.

SYED NADIM RIZVI

Syed Nadim Rizvi is a researcher/writer and community leader who is best known for his great communication skills. He's multilingual in English, Urdu and Hindi languages. Also an excellent orator within his community, he has devoted his life towards promoting peace and harmony in the world.

Nadim is concerned with the current tensions and misunderstandings amongst the followers of the Abrahamic traditions (Judaism, Christianity, and Islam). He truly thinks that through Jesus and his teachings the world can attain true peace and harmony. He has studied the Holy Bible to learn more about the largest religion in the world. He wanted to investigate for himself the true meaning of the Holy Scriptures and not be influenced by others, particularly those who negatively distort the image of religion.

His detailed study and research about the holy sites in the Middle East led him to be part of the team which undertook the project of writing about the second coming of Christ.

He is currently engaged in producing two faith-based films under development and many more books coming to promote peace and interfaith harmony to unite the world in a unique way.

Made in the USA
Lexington, KY
22 May 2019